The Ways She Makes Me Sin

A Steamy Step-Aunt and Niece, Protector turned Lover Sapphic Mafia Romance!

A. Goswami

Free Sapphic Romance
By A. Goswami

Hello Dear Readers,

Please don't forget to download your **free two book 600-page** Lesbian Romance bundle worth $6.99 by me, A. Goswami, that I would like to present to you as a thank you for reading and enjoying this book.

Download them right now by clicking here

For paperback readers, copy, and paste this link in your browser : mailchi.mp/8f0f411551ce/a-goswami

Chapter One

Sophia

The mirror isn't just a reflection—it's my stage, and I'm the star. I tilt my chin, squinting at the angle of my eyeliner, the subtle shimmer catching the soft light. Perfection. My lip gloss—a sheer berry tint—glides on like silk. A final pout, and yeah, if I were anyone else, I'd kiss me.

"Fifteen minutes, Sophia!" Dad's sharp voice cuts through my ritual from somewhere downstairs. "We're running late!"

I roll my eyes so hard they could sprain. "I'll be down in ten!" I yell back, fully intending to take my sweet time anyway. Rushing? Not my style. Beauty like this doesn't just happen—it's crafted. And if the world can't wait for it, the world can choke.

The final touch is a spritz of vanilla perfume, followed by a few artful flips of my hair, which falls in loose waves down my shoulders. I snatch my phone from the dresser and snap a couple of mirror selfies, angling just right to catch the warm light on my cheekbones.

I wink at myself in the last shot, smirking. *If only that asshole ex of mine could see me now. Eat your heart out, loser.*

The clatter of Emmy's giggles drifts up the stairs, and I know my little tornado of a sister is being her usual hyperactive self. Time to make an entrance. Sliding my heels on, I hurry out, the sound of my steps loud against the wooden floors.

Halfway down the staircase, chaos hits. Emmy darts out of nowhere, barrelling into me like a mini freight train. I yelp, catching her just before we both tumble down.

"Whoa, killer! Where's the fire?" I laugh, hoisting her up in my arms. Her brown curls bounce as she squeals in delight.

"You're late!" she sings, poking my cheek like it's payback for nearly flattening her.

"And you're adorable," I counter, attacking her face with playful kisses until she squirms and giggles. "C'mon, Em. Let's make the olds happy and pretend we care about being on time."

Holding Emmy's hand, I guide us down the rest of the steps. Mom's waiting at the foot of the stairs, looking like she's ready to grace the cover of *Vogue.* Her emerald-green maxi dress hugs her figure perfectly, her red lipstick bold against her fair skin. She flashes me a tight smile, the kind that says she's holding her impatience by a thread.

Dad, on the other hand, isn't bothering to hide his irritation. Dressed sharply in a tailored black suit, his blonde hair slicked back with precision, he checks his watch for the millionth time.

"Sophia, finally," he sighs, his tone a mix of relief and exasperation. "We're going to lose our reservation if we don't leave now."

I shrug, offering a cheeky grin. "Good things take time, Dad."

He doesn't look amused, but Emmy squeezes my hand, giggling. Mom sighs, smoothing her dress, and Dad motions us all toward the door.

As we step out, the night feels crisp, lights from downtown Los Angeles glowing in the distance. We shuffle into the back seat of our trusty old Prado, and Dad steps on the accelerator the second the doors shut. The car hums to life, and the soft glow of the dashboard lights makes everything feel cozy. I lean back, adjusting my dress, trying to ignore the faint scent of Emmy's strawberry lip gloss that she seems to smear everywhere.

"Hey, Emmy, grab my phone," I say, holding it out to her. "Take a picture of me real quick. I need a new post for tonight."

Emmy groans dramatically, crossing her arms. "Why do you always need pictures? You're already pretty!"

"Aw, thanks, Em, but it's not about being pretty—it's about aesthetics. Now, come on, help a girl out," I coo, striking a pose that screams effortless Pinterest queen. I angle my face toward the window so the passing streetlights catch my cheekbones.

"No," she says flatly, smirking.

"What do you mean, *no*?" I narrow my eyes at her, my voice dropping into mock offense.

"No more pictures, Sophia! You're obsessed!" she teases, sticking her tongue out at me.

"Oh, I'm obsessed? That's rich coming from the girl who spends hours making slime videos." I hold the phone closer to her face. "Click the damn picture, Emmy."

She grabs the phone and holds it out, angling it deliberately wrong so it catches nothing but my shoulder and half of my nose.

"Really? You think this is acceptable?" I demand, snatching it back and showing her the blurry mess she just created.

"It's my artistic interpretation," she says with a smug grin.

"You're a menace," I mutter, lunging to tickle her sides. She squeals, thrashing against her seatbelt.

"Girls," Mom's voice cuts in from the front, clipped and warning, "keep it down back there."

"She started it!" Emmy shouts, trying to shield herself from my tickle attack.

"You're the one who refused to capture my beauty!" I counter, pulling away dramatically.

"Do not make me come back there," Mom says, glancing over her shoulder with a raised brow. Her emerald earrings catch the light, and her sharp look is enough to make us both sit up straighter.

Up front, Dad is juggling a phone call and traffic. "Yes, yes, I know we're late. Just hold onto the table for us—ten minutes tops," he says, his voice edging into that charming, businesslike tone he uses when he's trying to smooth things over.

Mom leans toward him, whispering something that's probably advice on how not to sound like we're total flakes.

Meanwhile, Emmy crosses her arms with a victorious grin. "You're not getting any pictures tonight, Sophia."

"Fine," I say, sitting back with a huff. "But when you're older, you're going to regret not helping me document my fabulous youth."

She rolls her eyes, and I can't help but grin. It's impossible to stay mad at Emmy for long—especially when she's the only person who can out-sass me.

The Prado hums along, Dad still sweet-talking the restaurant, Mom issuing warnings like it's her second job, and Emmy smirking like she just won an Oscar for Most Annoying Sibling. It's chaotic, but in its own way, it's home.

I sink into my seat, letting the world outside blur into streaks of light and shadow. Dad's got his usual lead foot on the accelerator, and the Prado glides past most of the cars on the road. My gaze drifts lazily to the highway ahead, the cool glow of streetlights bouncing off the windshield.

And then it happens—a low, rumbling growl from the sky.

It rolls through the air, distant but menacing, pulling me upright. I lean forward, squinting at the horizon. Above the city in the distance, a dark mass of clouds churns ominously, spilling toward us like ink seeping into water.

"Rain's coming," I mutter, just as the first fat droplets splatter against the windshield.

Dad flicks on the wipers, their rhythmic squeak filling the car. "Just a drizzle," he says, brushing it off.

Before I can sit back, a blur of headlights streaks past us on the left. A car—sleek, fast, and reckless—zips by, its horn blaring.

"Son of a—" Dad swerves just enough to make my stomach lurch, his muttered curse drowned out by Emmy's startled squeak.

Her hand clamps onto mine like a vice. "Sophia, I don't like this," she whispers, her wide eyes darting between the window and me.

"It's okay," I say, squeezing her hand. My voice is calm, even though my heart's decided it wants to race.

"Everyone alright?" Mom twists in her seat, her tone sharp with worry.

Another thunderclap booms, loud enough to rattle the air, followed by a flash of lightning that turns the sky white for a heartbeat. Emmy flinches, her fingers digging into my palm.

I glance at my phone, hoping for a distraction. My wallpaper —a black and white photo of Amelia Hart in her Lockhead

Electra 10E—offers zero comfort. I swipe to check the GPS. Fifteen minutes.

"Dad, slow down," I say, leaning forward. "I'd like to get there alive, thanks."

"She's right, James," Mom agrees, her voice leaving no room for argument.

He grumbles but eases off the gas. The rain intensifies, hammering down on us now, drowning the world in gray.

I stare out the window, a pit forming in my stomach. Something about tonight feels... *wrong.*

The rain lashes against the windows, the wipers barely keeping up as visibility drops to a blur of headlights and streaked water. I'm staring out, trying to shake the gnawing unease in my gut, when another car—a massive black Cadillac SUV—roars past us.

But instead of speeding ahead, it slows down, its taillights glowing like eyes in the dark as it drops directly in front of us.

"Son of a...!" Dad mutters, tapping the brakes.

Before we can process, another SUV glides up on the right, its sleek body nearly brushing ours. Then another appears on the left, edging closer until its hulking frame fills the window on Emmy's side. I try to strain my eyes to see who's inside, but the matte black tint offers zero visibility, which only increases my anxiety.

A final one emerges in the rearview, cutting off any escape from behind.

I twist in my seat, heart thudding painfully as I see it—us, boxed in like prey.

"What the hell's happening?" I whisper, my voice shaky despite myself.

The SUV on Dad's side swerves, its bulk nearly grazing the

Prado.

"James!" Mom shouts, panic seeping into her voice.

Dad grips the wheel, his knuckles white. Emmy clings to me, her breath hitching.

The air feels heavier now, thick with fear and dread. Something isn't right.

Something is *very* wrong.

The SUV on Dad's side slows, creeping alongside us, its hulking frame just centimeters away. The passenger window slides down with a mechanical whir, and out of the darkness, a hand shoots out—clutching a semi-automatic gun.

For a split second, my eyes lock onto his forearm, where a tattoo snakes around his skin—a serpent coiled tightly around a skull, its fangs bared, glaring at me like a warning from hell.

Emmy's shriek cuts through the rain-soaked air like glass shattering. I want to scream too, but nothing comes out, my voice locked somewhere deep inside my chest.

"Hold on!" Dad barks, trying to steer through the narrow gap between the SUVs. The car jolts as he clips the one to the right, metal screeching against metal.

"Take cover!" Dad yells, but it's already too late.

The gun roars to life, spitting fire and chaos. The first burst shreds through the front of the Prado, and Dad jerks violently as blood sprays against the windshield.

"James!" Mom screams, her hand flying toward him, but the second volley catches her, silencing her mid-cry.

Everything feels like it's happening in slow motion, yet it's over in seconds.

I fling myself over Emmy, wrapping my arms tightly around her as her small body shakes with sobs.

"It's okay, Emmy," I whisper, my voice trembling, my own tears mixing with the rain streaking down my face. But it's not okay.

Nothing is.

The acrid smell of gunpowder fills the air. My parents' lifeless forms are slumped forward, and I know, somewhere in the back of my mind, that they're gone. But I can't think about that now. All I know is that Emmy needs me.

She cries into my shoulder, clinging to me like I'm her last tether to safety. I stay like that, holding her tightly, trying to block her from the shattered, blood-soaked reality around us.

The Prado rolls to a slow stop, and silence falls, save for Emmy's muffled sobs. The stillness feels like it stretches into eternity, until I feel hands on me—rough, unwelcome hands pulling me away from Emmy.

"No!" I scream, my voice finally breaking free as I claw at the air, struggling to stay with her. "Don't take her! Emmy, hold onto me!"

Her cries grow louder as she grips my arm, but it's not enough. They're prying me away, tearing me from her.

"Let go of her! She's my sister! Please!" I sob, my nails digging into flesh, my words drowned out by the wail of sirens.

I thrash against them, screaming, until my voice is raw. In the blur of blue lights and chaos, all I can focus on is Emmy's terrified face disappearing into the crowd. But in the back of my mind, that tattoo burns itself into my memory—snake and skull, etched like a brand of terror.

Eve

2 weeks later

The winding road to the cemetery is flanked by towering oaks, their skeletal branches silhouetted against the overcast sky. A light mist clings to the ground, weaving between the gravestones like a ghostly veil. The cemetery sits on the outskirts of the city, a quiet stretch of land cradled by low hills and lined with weathered tombstones that seem as old as time itself.

I steer my black G-Wagon through the wrought iron gates, the tires crunching on the gravel drive. The air feels dense, heavy with rain-soaked earth and the quiet hum of grief that lingers over gatherings like this.

Parking a distance from the crowd, I kill the engine and sit for a moment, gripping the steering wheel tighter than I need to. The low rumble of the car fades, leaving only the muffled sounds of movement from the cluster of mourners ahead.

I step out into the chilly air, straightening the lapels of my long black coat, its weight somehow comforting. My boots sink slightly into the damp ground as I scan the area. The crowd is small, intimate—friends, extended family, people from the community.

And then I see *her*.

Sophia rises from her seat near the front, her back straight, her movements deliberate. She walks toward the small podium near the graves, her head held high despite the obvious grief pulling at her.

I freeze, my breath catching in my chest.

She's no longer the gangly teenager I remember. Gone is the awkward girl who used to cling to my arm and beg me to stay. In her place is a woman—stunning and magnetic, with waves of dark brown hair that cascade over her shoulders. Her green eyes, striking against the paleness of her face, glimmer with unshed tears, framed by thick lashes that seem almost unreal. Her lips —God, her lips—full, soft, and heartbreakingly perfect, tremble just slightly before she presses them together in resolve.

She's wearing a fitted black dress, simple but elegant, the fabric clinging to her slender frame and ending just above her knees. A single gold necklace rests at the hollow of her throat, catching the muted light.

Sophia's voice breaks the silence, low and steady despite the raw grief beneath it. "My parents," she begins, pausing to gather herself, her eyes flicking over the crowd, "were everything to me. To Emily." Her voice tightens, and she exhales sharply. "They gave us a home, a family, love. My Dad, who was really my stepdad, never made me feel like I wasn't his blood, and my Mom, what do I even say about her, she was as feisty as she was beautiful, and even more intelligent. She had dreams of flying planes, which she abandoned to raise us. And now... they've left us with a void I don't know how we'll ever fill."

Her words strike like a blade, precise and cutting. I can feel the tension in her voice, the weight of her pain, but also the strength it takes for her to stand there and speak.

I remain at the back, unmoving, unable to tear my eyes from her. There's a quiet grace to her, an unshakable presence that commands attention without demanding it.

She's beautiful, in a way that feels almost otherworldly, and it leaves me breathless. But beneath the admiration is a gnawing ache—guilt, regret, the bitter sting of knowing I've missed the years that shaped her into the woman she is now.

Sophia continues, her voice unwavering despite the tears that finally streak down her cheeks. "I don't know how to move forward without them. But for Emily's sake, for their memory, I'll try."

The crowd murmurs softly, a ripple of agreement and quiet sobs. But I can't hear them. All I can hear is her voice.

And all I can think about is how I left her. How I left *them.*

The rest of the ceremony unfolds in muted reverence, a blend of tearful whispers and the priest's solemn voice. I stay at the back, watching as the coffins are lowered into the earth. A gust of wind carries the scent of damp soil, mingling with the faint perfume of the flowers draped over the caskets. Lilies, white and pristine, like a fragile promise of peace in the middle of all this grief.

Sophia stands with Emily pressed close to her side, her arm wrapped protectively around the girl's trembling shoulders. Emmy is a shadow of her usual self, her face blotchy and pale, eyes red from crying. She clutches a stuffed bear, its once-fluffy fur now matted from her desperate grip. Every so often, her small frame shakes with a silent sob, and Sophia bends slightly, murmuring something meant to soothe her.

As the crowd begins to thin, people stepping forward to pay their respects, I hesitate. I don't belong here. Not after what I've done. But my feet move anyway, carrying me closer until I'm standing at the graves.

Sophia looks up, and our eyes meet.

Her green gaze burns with recognition, widening for a split second before narrowing into something sharper. Her lips part slightly, like she wants to speak, but the words don't come.

Emmy presses her face against Sophia's side, her small hand

gripping her sister's dress. Sophia straightens, her expression hardening.

I deserve her anger. But it still feels like a knife.

"How are you paying for all of this?" I ask, my tone sharper than intended. It's easier to deflect the anger in her gaze than to confront it.

Sophia's lips press into a thin line. "We weren't broke," she replies curtly.

"I know," I say, holding her gaze. "But wills take time to execute. Do you have enough money to take care of yourselves until then?"

She frowns, her green eyes narrowing in curiosity, a flicker of something unreadable crossing her face. "Are you trying to buy our forgiveness, Auntie Eve?"

"No," I say firmly. "I'm doing what James would have wanted. Ensuring you're safe after an event like this." My voice softens slightly, though my words remain pointed. "I hope you realize you can't stay on your own now. The cops will leave in a few days, and even though they'll promise to keep an eye on you…" I shake my head. "The mafia will buy them out. They always do. You need to relocate—somewhere secure—for a few months, at least."

Sophia's expression hardens, her jaw tightening. "And let me guess," she says bitterly, "you've already got a plan."

"I do."

"You're unbelievable," she snaps, her voice rising. "You think you can waltz in here, after abandoning us for five years, and just take over? Make decisions for us like nothing's happened?"

Her anger is palpable, and I let it wash over me, knowing I deserve every word. "I'm not here to take over," I reply evenly. "But I'm not going to stand by while you and Emmy are sitting ducks."

Her lip trembles, but she quickly steels herself. "We've been fine without you, Aunt Evelyn. We don't need your charity."

"It's not charity," I say, taking a step closer. "It's what your parents would have wanted. And it's what I need to do—whether you like it or not."

Her eyes glint with defiance, but for a moment, she says nothing. Emmy shifts closer to her, clutching the hem of her dress, her face still buried in her stuffed bear.

"I'm not leaving this city," Sophia finally says, her voice low but steady. "This is our home. I won't uproot Emmy, not after everything she's already lost."

I exhale, my patience fraying. "And I won't let you stay somewhere unsafe. Whether you hate me or not, I'm not leaving you to fend for yourselves against the mafia."

Her silence stretches between us like a taut wire, ready to snap. Finally, she breaks it. "Where do you expect us to go?" she asks, her voice quieter now, the anger ebbing into something closer to resignation.

"My estate," I answer simply. "It's isolated, secure, and fully staffed. You and Emmy can stay there until things settle."

Sophia glares at me, but I can see the wheels turning in her mind. "You're serious?"

"Dead serious," I say, meeting her gaze without flinching. "You don't have to trust me. But you can't afford not to take my help."

Her defiance falters for just a moment, her eyes darting to Emmy, who clings to her silently. When she looks back at me, I see the weight of responsibility settle over her.

"Fine," she says, the word heavy with reluctance. "But don't think for a second that this makes up for anything."

"I don't," I reply quietly. "I never will."

∞∞∞

The small precinct office smells of stale coffee and damp paper. A bulletin board on the far wall is cluttered with faded mugshots and crime alerts, and the fluorescent lights hum faintly overhead. I stand stiffly in the dim room, facing Detective Caldwell, a middle-aged man with salt-and-pepper hair and a badge that looks like it's weighed him down for decades. He crosses his arms, his expression wary, as though I'm the threat here, not the people who just assassinated my family.

"With all due respect, Ms. Lockhart, we can't authorize you to take them," Caldwell says, his voice measured but firm. "The girls are safest under police watch until we have more leads."

I take a breath, my fingers flexing at my sides. "And what exactly does that look like, Detective? Two squad cars parked outside their house while the mafia picks off your officers one by one? Don't insult my intelligence."

Caldwell's jaw tightens. "We've handled situations like this before. The Carmine family—"

"The Carmine family," I interrupt, my voice dropping to a deadly calm, "just executed my brother and his wife in front of their children. You think I'm going to sit back and let your 'handling' of the situation get Sophia and Emily killed next?"

Caldwell's gaze falters for a moment, but he recovers quickly. "We're investigating every angle. Your brother owned a shipping and logistics company, and it's possible—likely, even—that his business had dealings with the Carmine organization."

The words hit like a punch, and I step closer, my boots heavy on the worn linoleum floor. "Are you suggesting James was involved with them? That he was complicit?" My voice is sharp now, slicing through the room like a blade.

"We're not saying he knew," Caldwell says quickly, his hands raising defensively. "But the Carmine family has their hooks in a lot of businesses in this area. It's a lead we have to follow."

Anger flares hot in my chest, but guilt twists alongside it. If James had gotten tangled in this mess, I wasn't there to help him. I left, and now—

I shake off the thought and focus on the present. "Whether or not that lead pans out doesn't change the fact that Sophia is legally an adult. If she agrees to come with me, there's nothing you can do to stop her."

Caldwell hesitates, his lips pressing into a thin line. "Ms. Lockhart, we're trying to do what's best for them. Taking them out of police protection—"

"They're not protected," I snap. "They're exposed. You can't guarantee their safety, and I won't gamble their lives on your guesswork."

He exhales, clearly frustrated. "If something happens to them under your watch—"

"Then it's on me," I cut in. "I've spent my life handling worse than the Carmine family, and I'll handle this too. Now either help me, or get out of my way."

The room falls silent for a moment, heavy with tension. Finally, Caldwell nods grudgingly. "Fine. But don't come crying to me if this blows up in your face."

I meet his gaze with ice in mine. "It won't. Because I won't let it."

Without another word, I turn and walk out, my fists clenched at my sides. Whatever guilt I carry, whatever debts I owe James and Sophia, I'll pay them. Starting now.

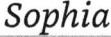

Sophia

The memory plays in my mind like an old film reel, muted colors with sunlit edges. I was eleven, and boredom hung over me like a cloud, the kind that makes the air feel too still. The house had been too quiet that afternoon, the grown-ups wrapped in their conversations or glued to their phones, leaving me to wander the hallways, restless and forgotten.

Then Aunt Eve walked in, her keys jingling in one hand, a half-smile tugging at her lips. "Let's get out of here, kiddo," she said, tossing her leather jacket over her shoulder like she was in a movie herself.

"Where are we going?" I asked, my eyes lighting up despite my best attempt to act unimpressed.

"Somewhere better than here," she replied, holding out her hand.

Cut to the cinema parking lot: the sun was dipping low, painting the sky in soft oranges and purples. Eve had a way of making the mundane feel special, like the way she drummed her fingers on the steering wheel in rhythm with the music or how she sang along off-key just to make me laugh.

Inside, the theater was dim, smelling of butter and nostalgia.

We sat in the back row, our arms weighed down with popcorn and candy she'd insisted we smuggle in. The movie was some animated adventure about a girl and her dragon—something I barely remember now, except for how it felt.

Eve leaned down, whispering in my ear during the trailers, "Don't tell anyone I said this, but these movies are my guilty pleasure." Her breath tickled, and I giggled, feeling like I was in on some secret meant just for us.

The dragon soared across the screen, its wings stretching wide, and I remember looking over at her instead of watching the movie. Her profile was sharp in the glow of the screen, her blonde hair pulled back in a ponytail, her lips quirked in a rare, genuine smile. She wasn't just my aunt then. She was my hero.

Halfway through, I spilled popcorn everywhere, and she laughed so hard the people in front of us shushed her. Instead of apologizing, she grinned and whispered loudly, "Rebel move. We're legends now."

The ride home was quiet but not empty. The windows were cracked just enough to let the cool night air in, and I rested my head on her shoulder, the scent of her leather jacket comforting in a way I couldn't explain.

"You're my favorite," I murmured sleepily.

"Don't let your mom hear that," she teased, but her voice softened. "You're mine too, kiddo."

The headlights carved tunnels in the darkness as we pulled into the driveway, and for that one night, everything felt perfect. Like the world had paused just for us.

The memory of my fifteenth birthday flickers like a fever

dream, vivid and blurred at the edges, soaked in laughter, music, and something I didn't understand at the time. The party had been perfect—friends, family, the warm glow of string lights in the backyard, the air thick with the scent of flowers and freshly baked cake.

But it wasn't the party I remembered most. It was *her*.

Aunt Eve had shown up late, as always, making an entrance that turned every head. She wasn't dressed like the other adults in their sensible slacks and polite smiles. No, she was a force—leather hotpants clinging to her muscular legs, a low-cut black top that hinted at her toned arms and broad shoulders, her blonde hair loose and wild, like something untamed.

I couldn't take my eyes off her.

When the music slowed, she grabbed my hand without hesitation, pulling me into the middle of the makeshift dance floor. "C'mon, birthday girl," she said, her grin infectious. "You're not too old to dance with your aunt."

Her hands found my waist, steady and sure, and she twirled me effortlessly, making me feel like a princess. My laughter mingled with hers, light and free, and for a few moments, it felt like the whole world had shrunk to just the two of us.

"You're getting too tall," she teased, flipping her hair dramatically as I stumbled back into her arms after a spin.

"And you're getting too old," I shot back, but my voice trembled slightly, betraying the way my heart raced.

Her hands tightened briefly on my waist, and for a fleeting second, I thought her eyes softened, lingering on me like I was something more than just a kid. But it passed as quickly as it came, and she hoisted me into the air, spinning me until I squealed, the world blurring around us.

Later that night, long after the last guest had left and the house had gone quiet, I lay in bed replaying every moment. The way her hair had smelled faintly of vanilla. The way her laughter had vibrated against me when I leaned into her chest, clutching her like I never wanted to let go.

I told myself it was admiration, the kind you feel for someone larger than life. But as I lay there, my body warm and restless under the blankets, I knew it was more.

My hand slipped beneath the waistband of my shorts, trembling as I let the memory of her guide me. Her legs—long, strong, commanding—wrapped around my thoughts, her plunging neckline teasing me even now. I imagined what it would feel like to kiss her skin, to press my lips to the curve of her shoulder, the line of her throat.

My breath hitched as I pictured her looking at me the way I looked at her. Wanting me. Her hands on me, pulling me closer, making me hers.

"Eve…" Her name fell from my lips, a whisper at first. Then louder, more desperate, as my mind conjured images I shouldn't have been thinking. Her hands gripping my hips. Her lips at my ear, murmuring something I couldn't quite make out. Biting my earlobe, marking me as hers, even though she shouldn't . Her thighs—God, her thighs—wrapped around me, pulling me closer.

I moved faster, the sensation overwhelming, but I didn't care. My breath came in ragged gasps, and I bit my lip, trying to keep quiet, but her name kept slipping out. "Eve… Eve… Eve…"

It was too much, too fast, but I couldn't stop. My body felt like it was on fire, my mind flooded with thoughts I couldn't control. The way she'd lifted me into the air like I weighed nothing, her muscles flexing against my small frame. The way her hair had fallen in waves, her lips quirking into that half-smile that made me feel like I was the only person in the world.

The girls had told me it would feel like nothing you have felt before, and they weren't lying. But they had also told me they watch porn to do it, to first get themselves ready for their fingers to enter. But I didn't need to watch any porn. Eve. My Eve was enough for me. She was all the aphrodisiac I needed to insert my finger in my virgin pussy.

I imagined those lips on mine, soft but firm, her hands guiding mine, showing me what to do. The thought made me press harder, rougher, until I cried out, muffling the sound into my pillow.

"Eve," I moaned one last time, the word breaking into a sob as my body spasmed, the unfamiliar wave crashing over me. My legs shook, my fingers frozen in place as my heart thundered in my chest.

When it was over, I lay there, staring at the ceiling, guilt swirling with the aftershocks. My body felt spent, but my mind wouldn't stop. I hated myself for what I'd done, for thinking of her like that.

But as much as I wanted to, I couldn't take it back.

The next morning, she was gone, never to be seen again.

No goodbyes. No explanations. Just a void where she used to be.

And I was left with a longing I didn't know how to name.

Chapter Two

Sophia

(2 weeks later)

The low hum of the G-Wagon fills the silence between us, punctuated only by the crinkle of foil as I hold out the sandwich I made for Emmy.

"C'mon, Em. Just take a bite," I plead, trying to keep my voice light. "You're gonna starve by the time we get there."

But she doesn't answer. Her small face is practically glued to the window, her nose pressed against the glass, her brown curls catching the light filtering in through the tinted windows. Her wide eyes are sparkling with wonder, darting around like she's afraid she'll miss something if she blinks.

I sigh, defeated, and wrap the sandwich back in its foil. "Fine. Starve, then. But don't come crying to me later."

Still no response. *Typical.*

I glance out the window as the car slows, turning onto a winding driveway flanked by tall iron gates. As they creak open, the estate comes into view, and even I can't help the tiny hitch in my breath.

It's massive.

Stretching across what feels like acres, Evelyn's estate sits nestled in the heart of Montana's rugged beauty. The property is bordered by endless woods, their edges blurred by the mist that seems to hang permanently in the cool air. The driveway is long and lined with towering Douglas firs, their needles dusted with leftover rain. Patches of autumn leaves litter the gravel, crushed into a mosaic of gold and amber. The air feels colder here, sharper, carrying the faint scent of pine and damp earth.

The house itself rises into view as we round a bend—a stately structure of dark stone and steep gables, with ivy crawling up one side as if nature had tried and failed to reclaim it. The windows are tall and arched, their glass reflecting the gray Montana sky above, and the massive front doors are framed by stone columns that look older than time itself.

Emmy gasps audibly, her breath fogging the window. "It's a castle," she whispers, her voice full of awe.

I roll my eyes, but even I can't deny how... impressive it is. Intimidating, even. "It's not a castle, Em. It's just a house."

"Then why does it look like it belongs in a storybook?" she shoots back, her excitement bubbling over.

She's not entirely wrong. The estate feels like it's been plucked straight from the pages of a Gothic novel—secluded, regal, and eerie all at once. The woods surrounding it seem endless, stretching into the misty horizon, and there's a small, glimmering lake just visible through the trees on the right. A stone wall wraps around the property, broken only by the gates we've just passed through.

As we approach the main house, the gravel crunches beneath the tires, and I feel a strange mix of apprehension and curiosity settle in my chest.

"This is where we're staying?" Emmy asks, her nose still pressed to the glass.

"Looks like it," I reply, more to myself than to her.

Montana always felt vast, untamed, and wild. For the first time since this nightmare began, I wonder if Eve's estate is the safest place—or the most dangerous.

The G-Wagon slows as the manor looms closer, and I lean forward, glancing at the driver—an older man with a neatly trimmed beard and a faded baseball cap. His hands grip the wheel with the kind of steady calm that suggests he's seen it all.

"So," I start, breaking the silence. "What's the story with this place? Did Auntie Evie stumble on it during a treasure hunt, or was there a sale on mansions I didn't know about?"

The driver chuckles, his eyes crinkling in the rearview mirror. "She bought it two years ago. Said it was for privacy."

"Two years?" I arch a brow, glancing at the house again. "Didn't know authors made that kind of money. Guess I should ditch dreams of flying planes, and start cranking out novels."

He laughs softly. "She's done well for herself. And she put a lot into this place—restoring the house, upgrading security. It's... impressive."

"'Impressive' is one word for it." I lean back, crossing my arms. "Cold and pretentious also come to mind."

He doesn't respond, just keeps driving.

"And what about her?" I ask, staring out at the estate's stone façade. "She as 'impressive' as the house?"

He hesitates before answering. "She's... focused. Doesn't say much, but she gets things done."

I snort softly. "Sounds about right." My gaze lingers on the house. "Guess we'll see if her highness still remembers how to have a conversation."

The car rolls to a stop just before the main house, giving me my first real look at the place. It's... massive. Like something out of a fairytale—or a horror movie, depending on your mood. The manor stretches wide and tall, its stone walls weathered but solid, the kind of gray that looks like it's been carved straight out of the mountains.

The façade is intricate, with arched windows framed in wrought iron and a towering central gable flanked by smaller peaks. Ivy crawls up one side, softening the imposing structure with a touch of wild beauty. At each corner of the house, smaller turrets rise, their pointed roofs giving the whole thing an almost castle-like vibe.

In front of the house, a circular driveway loops around a grand stone fountain—dry now, but still stately. Beyond it, the manicured lawn stretches out in neat, verdant perfection, framed by the dense woods that seem to go on forever. To the side, I spot a smaller building, likely an outhouse or guest quarters, with the same stone and slate design, blending seamlessly into the estate.

It's beautiful, sure. But it's also cold, detached—just like her.

Emmy lets out a low whistle beside me. "I still think it's a castle."

"More like a fortress," I mutter, staring up at it. "Fitting."

The driver steps out to open the door for us. As Emmy hops down, I follow, taking in the imposing double doors—carved dark wood with intricate iron accents.

Descending the wide stone steps toward us is a woman who looks like she's stepped out of another century. She's all grace, with a long skirt swishing lightly around her ankles, a pastel blouse tucked neatly at the waist, and a bow perched in her curly jet-black hair. Despite her petite frame, there's a sharpness to her movements, a hidden strength in the way she holds herself. Her beady black eyes twinkle as she smiles.

"You must be Miss Sophia and Miss Emmy!" she says, her voice warm and lilting. "I'm Miriam, the head housekeeper. Welcome to Lockhart Manor."

Before I can respond, she claps her hands together. "Oh, but let's hurry inside. Looks like the rain's not done with us yet."

Emmy runs ahead as Miriam ushers us through the doors, babbling cheerfully. "It's been years since we've had children here. Miss Lockhart doesn't usually take visitors."

Inside, the air shifts—cooler, heavier, and unmistakably Eve. The high ceilings stretch above us, lined with dark wooden beams, while the walls are a deep charcoal gray. Shelves upon shelves of books dominate the sitting room visible to the left, ranging from military strategy to classic literature. Interspersed between them are combat trophies: a gleaming set of daggers, a mounted crossbow, and a display case of antique pistols.

But it's the artwork that catches my eye—bold, sensual pieces depicting sapphic lovers in various states of intimacy. The unapologetic eroticism feels both jarring and fitting, and I wonder if Eve is a straight woman who's just a lover of random lesbian art, or is she gay herself. Because *that* would be a revelation!

Miriam keeps chatting, leading us into a great hall with Gothic chandeliers, a massive stone fireplace, and a long dining table flanked by high-backed chairs. Every inch of the space exudes authority and elegance, with hints of something darker underneath.

"Miss Lockhart will meet you shortly," Miriam says, still smiling. "She's been very particular about making sure you feel at home."

I glance around, skeptical. Home? Not exactly.

Emmy's fingers curl tightly around mine as we step further into the great hall, the sheer size of the space making us feel impossibly small. The wooden dining table stretches nearly the length of the room, its surface polished to a gleaming shine. Each chair surrounding it looks like it belongs to a medieval throne room—high-backed, carved with intricate designs, and so antique-looking I half-wonder if sitting on one might break it.

"We're not sitting there," I say to Emmy, shaking my head as she eyes one of the throne-like chairs. "Feels like we'd need crowns just to pull it off."

She giggles, and I lead her toward a cozier corner. The sitting area looks more inviting, with a deep crimson couch big enough to swallow you whole and a matching armchair arranged around a low coffee table. The table is a heavy slab of dark wood, its surface scattered with books that look old enough to belong in a museum, alongside a tray with crystal glasses and a decanter of amber liquid.

We sink into the couch, Emmy's legs swinging as her eyes dart around the room. "Did you know we were coming to Hogwarts today?" she whispers conspiratorially.

I laugh, a genuine giggle bubbling out before I can stop it. The sound echoes against the high, arched ceilings, bouncing back to us in a way that suddenly makes the room feel much bigger—and much quieter.

"That's the first laugh these walls have heard in a while."

The voice startles us both, low and rich, cutting through the air like a blade. My head whips around toward the massive stone staircase to our left. The steps are wide, carved from smooth, gray stone, with thick handrails and balusters that could've come straight out of a Gothic cathedral.

And descending them, with a presence so commanding it stops me cold, is her.

Auntie Eve.

Her blonde hair is pulled back into a no-nonsense ponytail, her fitted black blazer hugging her athletic frame as she moves with deliberate grace. She reaches the bottom step, her piercing blue eyes locking onto mine with an intensity that makes my stomach flip.

"It's good to see you again, Sophia," she says, her voice steady, unreadable.

And just like that, all my anger, all my rehearsed lines, scatter like leaves in the wind.

Eve

The echo of Sophia's laugh catches me off guard, curling through the great hall like a breath of life in a place that's been silent for far too long. My hand brushes the cool stone railing as I descend the wide staircase, each step deliberate. It's reflexive, this measured control—something to ground myself as my eyes fall on her.

Sophia turns toward me, and for a moment, the air in the room feels sharper.

She's... beautiful. I knew she'd grown up, but this? Her dark hair tumbles over her shoulders in loose waves, framing a face that's all soft curves and sharp eyes. Her lips—full, plush, and glossed with a faint sheen—catch the light, and my gaze lingers half a second too long before I force it upward.

Her dress doesn't help. It's fitted, clinging to her petite frame, the fabric teasing the curve of her small waist and the gentle swell of her chest. A warmth stirs low in my stomach, unwanted and unwelcome. My jaw tightens as I push the thought away. It's nothing. It's been a long time since I've…

No. Not *this*.

"It's good to see you again, Sophia," I say, keeping my voice even as I reach the bottom of the staircase.

Her green eyes flick to mine, calm but distant. "It's… impressive," she replies after a beat, gesturing vaguely to the room. "The estate, I mean. It feels like a castle."

I tilt my head slightly, studying her expression. She's holding something back—I can see it in the way she keeps her arms loosely folded, her posture deliberately casual.

"It's meant to feel secure," I reply.

She lets out a small, dry laugh. "Secure, sure. Let's just hope it doesn't feel like a prison."

The words are light, but there's an edge to them. Not defiance, exactly. More like skepticism. It stings more than I expect.

Emmy, oblivious to the undercurrent between us, bounces up beside her. "Aunt Eve! This place is amazing! Do you have secret passageways?"

I crouch slightly, letting Emmy's excitement pull me from my thoughts. "Not that I've found yet," I say, softening my tone. "But you're welcome to look."

Her giggle is pure, unguarded, and I smile despite myself. The joy on Emmy's face is a balm to my soul. The estate has done for Emmy what a million toys could never—it has given her a brief escape from the pain of losing our parents. Here, she is smiling without a care in the world, her laughter filling the air as if her grief is momentarily forgotten. It's a fleeting reprieve, but one that makes her look like every nine-year-old should—happy, carefree, and untouched by sorrow, even if only for a little while.

"Miriam will show you to your rooms," I say, straightening. "After you're settled, I'll give you both a proper tour."

Sophia tilts her head, her lips quirking into a faint smile that doesn't quite reach her eyes. "Thanks. I guess we'll see how much of a castle it really is."

As I turn to lead them, I feel her gaze on me—a weight that lingers, presses. For the first time in years, I feel unsure of myself, unsteady.

She's not a child anymore. That thought settles deep in my chest, humming with a dangerous energy I don't have the strength to acknowledge. Not now. Not ever.

∞∞∞

The soft click of heels echoes against the stone walls, pulling my attention to the staircase. I look up, expecting... I don't know what. Certainly not *this*.

Sophia is descending, and for a moment, the air feels heavier, thicker.

She moves with a kind of natural grace that shouldn't belong to someone so young—each step precise yet unthinking, her hips swaying with an almost hypnotic rhythm. The gentle roll of her hips draws the eye like a magnetic force, the fabric of her skirt shifting just enough to hint at the curves beneath, teasing, taunting. It's maddening, the way she seems unaware of how provocative she looks—or maybe she's not unaware at all.

My gaze catches on her tank top, the deep neckline clinging to her curves in a way that feels almost obscene. Her breasts press against the fabric, full and taut, the soft swell teasing with every step she takes closer. The tank is snug, framing her in a way that makes it impossible not to notice, impossible to ignore.

The skirt she's wearing is high-waisted, pleated, cinched tight with a leather belt that gleams with a golden buckle. It doesn't give her height—she's petite, impossibly so—but it emphasizes the length of her thighs, smooth and exposed, and the thought that flashes through my mind isn't just wondering what's beneath the fabric. It's imagining what I'd do if I ever found out.

And her hair—it's different. Straightened, sleek, cascading over one shoulder like silk, exposing the pale column of her neck and the sharp, elegant lines of her collarbones. The kind of neck you could press your lips to, run your teeth along, mark as yours.

I tear my eyes away, forcing my jaw to unclench. But then there are her lips. They're painted a deep, sultry red, full and dangerous, the kind of lips that could ruin a man—or a woman.

She looks... older. No, not just older—tempting. Beautiful in a way that feels utterly sinful, the kind of beauty that feels like it shouldn't belong to someone so young, and yet there it is.

My hand tightens around the crystal tumbler in front of me, the coolness of the glass a lifeline against the heat spreading low in my stomach. This isn't right. It's not. I know that.

But as she draws closer, her eyes meeting mine with quiet confidence, I feel it: the slow, insidious crack of restraint. She's a fantasy—one I have no business indulging in, no matter how much my body betrays me.

I force myself to straighten, my voice steady as I speak. "Sophia. I trust your room is to your liking?"

It's a poor attempt to sound normal, and even I can hear it.

Sophia saunters to the chair across from me, sitting with an effortless grace that feels anything but casual. She crosses her legs slowly, deliberately, her skirt shifting just enough to draw attention, and begins playing with a strand of her hair, twisting it between her fingers.

"It will do," she says, her voice nonchalant, almost dismissive, as if she's rating a hotel suite and not one of the finest rooms in the estate.

I lean back in my chair, steeling myself. "And Emmy?"

"She's napping," Sophia replies, brushing a hand along her neckline in an absent gesture that draws my eyes, despite myself. "She's tired. I wish you hadn't tempted her with a room of her own. She needs to be with me."

"You can ask her to move back," I offer evenly.

Sophia shakes her head, a faint smirk tugging at her lips. "She saw what her room looks like. It's everything a little girl brought up on fairytales could ever dream of. I'll try to convince her to let me sleep in her bed, but..." She shrugs, her voice light. "She's too possessive about her space."

I nod, though the image flashes in my mind: Sophia asleep, her hair tousled across a pillow, her clothes riding up her legs, up her soft belly, revealing just a tiny hint of an areola.... I exhale sharply, forcing the thought out. "Are you hungry?"

"Very," she says, her lips curving into something that feels like a challenge.

I glance toward the shadows. Miriam emerges with two men following, each carrying silver trays. They set them on the table with quiet efficiency, removing the lids to reveal roasted salmon glazed in honey and mustard, fresh asparagus, a bowl of creamy garlic potatoes, and a platter of crusty bread.

Sophia's eyes widen, her cool demeanor slipping for just a moment. "Wow," she breathes, leaning forward. "Guess lunch in the 'castle' has its perks."

I almost smile.

Almost.

"I've installed high-grade security cameras throughout the estate," I say, keeping my voice calm, deliberate. "Every entrance, every angle that could be vulnerable is covered. The perimeter is monitored 24/7, and I've doubled the security staff. The local sheriff—Tessa—has agreed to provide additional support. She'll coordinate with the cops back in your hometown while they investigate your parents' murder."

I glance at Sophia, expecting some kind of acknowledgment, but she just sits there, her chin propped on her hand, her gaze distant, wandering. It's like I'm talking to myself, and my patience thins.

"Are you even listening?" I ask, my tone sharper than I intend.

Her head snaps up, and her eyes meet mine, and for a second, I forget how to breathe. Those eyes—intense, blazing, filled with something between fury and despair—pin me in place.

"Do you even realize what's happened to us?" she says, her voice low but vibrating with restrained anger. "Our lives have been ripped apart. All I can think about is that night. Every second of it. How they…" She swallows hard, her voice trembling slightly before she pushes through. "How they died. Over and over, like some sick movie I can't turn off. So forgive me if I don't care about cameras or patrol schedules right now. Talking about it doesn't help, Eve—it makes it worse."

Her words hit like a blow, and I can feel the tension between us, sharp and raw. Before I can respond, her voice softens, catching me off guard.

"But even though I hate you for leaving me…" Her gaze dips briefly before locking onto mine again, softer this time. "I know you were a soldier. A damn good one. I trust you've taken care of everything."

Her honesty cuts deeper than any accusation she could've

thrown at me. I nod slowly, the weight of her words settling in my chest. "I have," I say, my voice quieter now. "I'll make sure nothing happens to you. Or Emmy."

She doesn't respond, her eyes sliding away again, but the sting of her words lingers, sharper than I'm ready to admit.

We eat in silence, the only sounds the faint clink of silverware against plates and the low crackle of the fire. Sophia hasn't said much since her last outburst, her attention focused on her plate. I let her have the quiet, figuring she needs it.

Then, without warning, she looks up, her green eyes catching the light in a way that makes my stomach tighten. "Have you gotten taller?"

The question is so unexpected that I stop mid-bite, staring at her. "What?"

"In the last five years," she says, setting her fork down with a deliberate motion. "Have you grown taller?"

"That's not how it works, Sophia. I'm an adult. Adults don't just keep growing."

She leans back slightly, tilting her head like she's appraising me. "Well, it seems like you have. You're just... all legs, aren't you?"

I chuckle softly, shaking my head. "I'm a lot more than just long legs."

The words slip out before I can think better of them, and the moment they're out, I catch the faintest flicker of something on her face—curiosity? Amusement?

Sophia picks up a grape from the tray, rolling it between her fingers like it's the most interesting thing in the world. She doesn't even look at me as she pops it into her mouth, lips parting just slightly before she pulls it in. My throat tightens as I force my gaze to stay on her eyes—anywhere but her mouth.

"And what is that? Strong muscles and a bit of a 'holier than thou' attitude to go along with those legs?" she asks, her tone airy but laced with challenge.

I glance at her, keeping my face neutral. "No. Integrity, discipline, and a pair of blue eyes that'll take your breath away… along with these legs."

She chuckles softly, picking up another grape, this time letting it linger at her lips before slipping it between them. "Oh, I've noticed the blue eyes already, Evelyn," she says, deliberately rolling my name on her tongue, her tone like silk laced with thorns. "They scan everything, don't they? They check out… everything."

"Everything that could be dangerous," I reply, leaning back in my chair, my grip on the armrest tightening.

"Or tempting?" she counters, her tongue flicking out briefly to catch a drop of juice on her lip.

My jaw tightens, but I keep my voice steady. "The two aren't mutually exclusive."

Sophia smirks, leaning back as well, her movements languid and deliberate. "You're deflecting," she says, picking up another grape and letting it roll across her bottom lip.

"And you're fishing," I counter, though my eyes betray me as they flick down, just for a second, before I force them back up.

"Am I?" She tilts her head, her fingers toying with the stem of the grape. "Maybe I'm just trying to figure out what makes Aunt Evelyn tick. You know, beneath all that integrity and discipline."

"Nothing you need to concern yourself with," I reply, my voice tighter than I'd like.

She pops another grape into her mouth, chewing slowly, deliberately, before speaking. "You know, I wouldn't need to ask if you hadn't disappeared. I think I'm owed a little 'getting to know' of my long-legged protector now."

The words cut deeper than I expect, and I lean forward slightly, meeting her gaze. "You're safe here. That's all you need to know," I say, my tone firm, final.

"For now," she says, her voice soft but pointed. Her lips curve into a faint smile as she reaches for another grape, and this time, I can't stop my eyes from following the movement.

The tension crackles between us, thick and unspoken, and I find myself gripping the edge of the table like it's the only thing keeping me tethered.

This isn't a game I can play. Not with her.

Sophia reaches for the bottle of wine, her movements slow and deliberate, as if she's daring me to say something. The deep red liquid flows into her glass, the light catching on the curve of it as she tilts the bottle back. She doesn't even hesitate.

"Don't you think you're a little young to be drinking?" I say, keeping my tone measured, though the sight of her so at ease, so defiant, gnaws at me.

She glances up at me through her lashes, her lips curving into that infuriatingly subtle smirk. "I'm nineteen," she says, taking a small sip, her eyes not leaving mine.

"The drinking age is twenty-one," I reply, leaning back slightly in my chair, my arms crossing over my chest.

She sets the glass down, her fingers lingering on the stem as she tilts her head. "Since when have you been so into following rules? You weren't exactly 'by the book' when you took me to that R-rated movie a few years ago."

I narrow my eyes. "That's different."

"Different how?" she presses, her smirk widening. "It was full of sex scenes, Evelyn. You didn't seem so motherly protective then."

The memory hits me before I can block it—the flickering lights of the theater, her wide-eyed curiosity as she whispered questions at the screen, and my half-hearted attempts to keep her focused on the plot.

"That wasn't... intentional," I say, though even to me, it sounds weak.

She takes another sip of wine, the glass pausing at her lips as her eyes sparkle with something wicked. "Sure, it wasn't."

"I didn't know how graphic the movie would be, especially for a kid." I mutter, shaking my head as I try to regain control of the conversation.

"And now I'm not...a kid. In fact, I have taken a liking to graphic, explicit stuff as I have grown up," she replies smoothly, setting the glass down with a quiet clink. Her voice is softer now, but there's an edge to it, a challenge beneath the surface.

The way she's looking at me—calm, confident, with that glint in her eye—makes my pulse quicken despite myself. I clench my jaw, willing the tension to dissipate.

"You shouldn't drink," I say finally, though it feels like a losing battle.

"And you shouldn't try to lecture me when you clearly don't believe half of what you're saying," she counters, leaning back with a self-assuredness that leaves me grasping for my usual control. Her lips curve into a slow, deliberate smile, and then she finishes, her voice dripping with teasing defiance.

"Mommy."

The word slams into me like a physical blow.

Mommy.

It echoes, low and sultry, curling around my mind like smoke I can't escape. My chest tightens, heat surging through me so fast it makes my breath catch. I grip the armrest harder, the leather biting into my palm as if the pressure might ground me, might stop this—this—whatever the hell is happening.

Her voice, the way she said it—slow, deliberate, teasing—plays on a loop. My pulse hammers, my body reacting before my brain can catch up. It's wrong. It's so damn wrong.

And yet...

I can't stop the way my eyes flick to her lips, still curved in that infuriating smirk, red and full, tempting in ways I have no business even acknowledging. I feel the blood rush to my ears, my skin, every nerve ending alive, screaming at me to do something. To stop this. To say something. To—

Her tongue darts out, wetting her lower lip, and I feel it like a punch to the gut. Heat pools low in my stomach, sharp and insistent.

No. No, no, no.

I force my gaze away, swallowing hard, but it's still there—the sound of her voice, the look in her eyes. It's burned into me now, a brand I can't erase.

I narrow my eyes at her, my patience unraveling fast. "What are you playing at?"

Sophia shrugs, the movement casual but loaded, like she knows exactly how close she's pushing me to the edge. "Nothing," she says, her voice light as she gathers her hair, pulling it over one shoulder in a slow, deliberate motion. The strands fall in a graceful cascade, catching the light as she flips them effortlessly. "I'm just asking you not to tell me what to do or not do. I make my own decisions. You're here to protect me, not to micromanage my lifestyle habits."

My glare sharpens, and hers doesn't waver. It's the battle of blue eyes versus green: a 39-year-old soldier, forged in war, against a 19-year-old rebel who's just made her pussy wet. The thought hits me like a punch to the gut, and the fury bubbling under my skin feels like the only thing holding me together.

"Make sure Emmy eats after she's up," I say, my voice clipped as I push my chair back and rise. "Call for Miriam if you need anything. She'll handle it."

"What about my tour?" she asks, her lips curving into a slow, wicked smile, her tone as smooth as the wine she shouldn't have been drinking.

I pause, my hands curling into fists at my sides as I look back at her. "Not without Emmy," I say, my voice quieter now but no less firm. "And I have a feeling I shouldn't be alone with you for long periods."

Her smile widens, a glint of triumph sparking in her green eyes. I turn on my heel, forcing myself to walk away, the sound of my boots echoing sharply against the stone floor. But I don't escape her.

Her laughter follows me, low and knowing, wrapping around me like a chain. By the time I reach the end of the hall, her image is burned into my mind—her lips, full and red, daring me. Her voice, seductive and teasing. And worst of all, the thought that refuses to leave: the way those lips would feel against mine, pulling me in, breaking me apart.

It replays over and over, a broken record I can't escape.

Sophia

The hallway is bathed in a low, ambient light, the kind that hums softly, casting long shadows that stretch across the polished floor. Emmy's already waiting for me, her wide eyes practically glowing with excitement, her hands clasped like she's about to unlock some grand mystery.

"This is such a bad idea," I mutter, tugging at the thin strap of my silk nightdress, which keeps slipping off my shoulder. The movement adjusts the hem too, riding higher up my thigh than I'd like. Not that it matters—no one's supposed to see us, right? The fabric is soft against my skin, clinging in all the right places.

I glance down at myself and sigh. "If Eve catches us, she'll probably explode. Or worse, she'll glare at me with that 'I'm disappointed' face. Again."

Emmy grins, her enthusiasm undeterred. "Stop being such a buzzkill, Sophia. It's just a walk. She won't even know."

"Won't know?" I hiss, following her as we sneak down the grand staircase. "She's got sensors everywhere. She's basically a blonde Terminator. But angrier. And taller."

Emmy giggles, clapping a hand over her mouth to muffle the sound as we cross the great hall. The space feels massive, cavernous, with its modern lighting casting sleek beams across the Gothic arches. Shadows move with us, dancing along the edges of the room, making every step feel like we're in some forbidden heist.

When we finally step outside, the estate transforms. The air is cool and crisp, and the moonlight makes the lawn glisten as if it's dusted with silver. The woods beyond the gates seem alive, the trees swaying gently like they're sharing secrets with the night breeze.

I let out a low whistle, tucking a stray strand of hair behind my ear. "Okay," I whisper, glancing at Emmy. "You win. It's gorgeous."

She beams, spinning in place like the night belongs to her. And maybe it does. But as I look back at the house, I can almost feel Eve's gaze burning into me, even if she's not actually there.

Emmy practically drags me down the front steps, her little hand clutching mine with surprising strength. Before I can even protest, she lets go and takes off running, her giggles ringing out like chimes in the quiet night.

"Emmy!" I hiss, my voice a harsh whisper as I follow her. "Get back here! Emmy!"

She's already halfway across the manicured lawn, her pink teddy—Mr. Wonkers, complete with his wonky eye—bouncing in her grip as she runs. The chill in the air bites at my skin, making me shiver as I sprint after her, the hem of my nightdress brushing against my thighs.

I finally catch up, grabbing her by the arm and pulling her close. "Don't run off like that! What if Eve sees us?"

Emmy wriggles in my grasp, her face glowing with excitement. "Look around, Sophia! Who wouldn't want to run like a pony across these beautiful fields?"

I roll my eyes, wrapping my arms around her to keep her from bolting again. "Any other nine-year-old, Emmy. Normal kids would hate stepping out into the dark, especially with a ghostly manor like this behind them. But no, not you. You love it."

"Of course I do," she says, grinning as she wiggles out of my hold. Her gaze shifts suddenly, and she points toward the side of the estate, where the guest house sits in shadow. Smaller than the main manor, but no less grand, its baroque architecture looks like something out of a historical drama.

"Let's explore that!" Emmy exclaims. "Eve didn't give us a tour. I bet there's a game room in there!"

"No way," I say quickly, but she's already running again, Mr. Wonkers flapping in the breeze as she barrels toward the guest house.

"Emmy!" I groan, chasing after her. "You're going to get us

killed!"

The stars above sparkle like a splash of diamonds on an inky canvas, their brilliance almost distracting me from the cool wetness of the grass beneath my feet. Each step sends a shiver up my legs as the dew clings to my skin, and the night air bites sharply, making my nipples strain against the thin satin of my nightdress. The fabric clings, the initials *S.H.* embroidered near the hem, barely visible in the dim light.

As I close in on Emmy, her giggles echoing through the stillness, my eyes catch a movement in the darkness near the guest house. A figure—shadowy, almost indistinct—emerges and starts toward her.

My breath catches, and in an instant, I'm back there—flashes of gunfire, my parents' screams, the weight of Emmy in my arms as I shielded her.

"No," I whisper, panic tightening my chest.

"Emmy!" I scream her name this time, louder, my legs pumping as I run, my bare feet slipping slightly on the damp grass. The shadowy figure moves faster now, closing in on her, and so do I. My pulse is a drumbeat in my ears, every muscle in my body straining as I fight the fear threatening to paralyze me.

Please, please let me get to her in time.

The figure draws closer, just as I do, and then the moon slips free from behind a cloud. The light spills across the lawn, revealing the shape of my pursuer.

Eve.

Her long legs carry her swiftly, her toned body clad in running shorts and a sleek black sports bra, her blonde ponytail swaying behind her like a metronome. She reaches Emmy first, crouching to place a steadying hand on her shoulder.

"Thank God, it's only you," I say, my breath hitching as I slow to a stop a few feet away.

But instead of the calm reassurance I expect, Eve straightens, her blue eyes locking onto me with a glare so sharp it could slice through steel.

"What the hell were you thinking?" she snaps, her voice low but vibrating with restrained anger. "Sneaking out like this? And dragging Emmy with you?"

"I wasn't dragging her—" I start, but she cuts me off with a sharp gesture.

"You think this is a joke?" she continues, stepping closer, her tone clipped and furious. "You don't leave the house unannounced. Not in the middle of the night, not without telling me. Do you have any idea how dangerous this could've been?"

Emmy looks up at her, wide-eyed but silent, clutching Mr. Wonkers tightly to her chest.

"It was just—"

"No," Eve interrupts, her voice colder now as she looks directly at me. "You don't get to justify this. Not after what happened. You know better, Sophia."

Her words hit like a slap, the weight of her anger settling heavily in the air between us. My chest tightens, and for once, I don't have a comeback.

"Follow me, both of you!" Eve barks, her voice sharp enough to make Emmy flinch, her little fingers tightening around Mr. Wonkers. I see the way her lip trembles, her eyes shiny with unshed tears, and it twists something protective deep in my chest.

I take a step toward Eve, narrowing my eyes. "Don't shout in front of Emmy," I say, my voice firm, almost daring her to push back. "She doesn't like it."

Eve spins on her heel, her glare cutting straight through me.

"What do you expect me to do? Laud you for the absolutely stupid thing you just did?"

"No," I admit, biting back a sharp retort. "I agree—it was stupid. But you don't have to shout. Not at Emmy. It was my fault."

Eve's eyes flash, her voice rising. "I'm not shouting at her! I'm shouting at you!"

"Not in front of her!" I growl, stepping closer.

Her breath hitches, her gaze locking with mine, and for a moment, the air between us crackles. Her chest rises and falls quickly, and I catch her eyes flicker down—to the thin satin of my dress, to where my nipples strain against the fabric—before snapping back to my face.

"Just follow me back to the house," she says, her voice lower now, almost strangled. She turns on her heel, striding toward the manor without looking back.

I grab Emmy's hand, squeezing it gently. "It's okay," I whisper. But as I follow Eve, my pulse is hammering, and I know this isn't over.

Eve

I storm inside the manor, the cold air from outside still clinging to my skin as I pull my phone out, cursing under my breath. The sharp sound of my boots echoes in the quiet, each step as clipped as my mood. The call connects on the second ring, and a groggy voice answers.

"Yeah, Boss?"

"Don't 'Boss' me," I snap, my tone razor-sharp. "Where the hell were you? Who's monitoring the cameras? Do you have any idea what just happened?"

There's a pause, followed by a nervous cough. "I checked them earlier. Nothing seemed—"

"Earlier isn't good enough!" My voice cuts through the line like a whip. "Two kids wandered across the estate. Unchallenged. Do you understand how dangerous that is? If it wasn't me out there, it could've been someone else. Someone deadly."

"Yes, ma'am," he stammers, his tone now fully alert.

"Good," I growl, cutting the call with a swipe.

When I turn around, I see them—Sophia and Emmy, standing close together. Emmy's clutching that ridiculous stuffed toy like it's her lifeline, her wide eyes shimmering. The anger in my chest ebbs slightly, guilt taking its place.

I crouch to Emmy's level, softening my tone. "I'm sorry I was loud, sweetheart. But you can't do that again, okay? It's too dangerous, and I need to know you're safe."

She nods, looking up at Sophia, who gives her a reassuring smile. "Okay, Aunt Eve," Emmy whispers, her voice small.

"Good girl," I say, patting her shoulder. "Now go back to bed."

As Emmy shuffles off, I straighten, expecting Sophia to follow. But something stops me. "Sophia. Stay."

She turns, her arms crossing over her chest. The casual movement sends the soft swell of her breasts upward, her cleavage deepening. The satin clings to her body in all the wrong ways—no, the right ways—and her nipples are unmistakable beneath the thin fabric, inviting a nibble of teeth or a desperate lick of a tongue.

My teeth.

My tongue.

I swallow hard, my throat dry as images I have no right conjuring flash through my mind. My hands on her waist, sliding that dress up, my mouth on her neck, her breasts, pulling those pert peaks into my mouth until—

Stop. Fucking stop.

But my body doesn't listen. My chest tightens, my pulse quickens, and I can feel the heat pooling low, sharp and unbearable.

Her green eyes flicker with something—defiance, maybe amusement—and when her lips part, just slightly, I'm done for. My gaze betrays me, lingering on her mouth, her body, every sinful inch.

"We need to talk," I say, my voice rougher than I intend, like I'm choking on the words. But it's the only thing keeping me from stepping closer, from reaching out, from losing everything.

I take a step closer, crossing my arms to keep myself grounded. "Do you even understand how serious this is?" I say, my voice low and sharp, the frustration bubbling too close to the surface. "Your parents' killers are still out there. The cartel that took them down is ruthless. This isn't some game, Sophia. This is life and death, and you—"

"We were bored!" Sophia snaps, cutting me off, her voice rising like a wave, crashing against every word I've carefully prepared.

I blink, stunned for a moment, as she presses forward, her green eyes blazing. "Emmy can't just sit with her thoughts right now, okay? Neither can I. You've trapped me in these stone walls like I'm some Disney princess! What the hell were we supposed to do?"

My jaw tightens, but she doesn't give me a chance to respond.

"There's no TV here, I have no phone—no way to even distract myself. I didn't even get the chance to buy a new one after my old one broke that... that night," she says, her voice cracking slightly before her anger surges back. "So what do we do? Count the number of paintings showing girl-on-girl action? Is that how you pass your time here, Eve? Looking at them and fingering yourself?"

"I'll make sure you get what you need," I say, my voice firm, trying to pull the conversation back under control.

Sophia scoffs, her laugh sharp and cutting. "And you know exactly what I need, don't you? You always know exactly what other people need!"

"Mostly, I do," I reply, keeping my tone even. "We were trained to be alert. Perceptive."

Her green eyes flash with something dangerous, something that sends a chill and heat racing through me at once. "Well then, is your training telling you how I want to run away from here? How I want to live my life like a normal nineteen-year-old? Go out on dates? Have fun? Get *laid*?"

The last words hit like a slap, and I feel my composure slip for a moment. My pulse spikes, and I try to cover it, clearing my throat. "It's a matter of a few months. Your college will start, and by then, I'll make sure all of this is handled. Then you can go on dates."

"And get laid?" she presses, one eyebrow arching, her voice laced with teasing venom.

I hesitate, my throat dry. "What you do after that is none of my business."

"Oh, so your protectiveness has an expiration date?" she fires back, stepping closer. "You'll care until a bloodthirsty cartel isn't after me anymore? Before that and after that, you don't give a fuck, right?"

"I do," I snap, but the words come out too fast, too sharp.

Her voice drops, soft and cruel, her gaze locking onto mine. "Then don't you care who takes my virginity in college?"

The air leaves my lungs in a rush. My mind freezes, the words circling like a siren in the dark. She's a virgin. *Fuck.*

Heat surges low in my stomach, sharp and unforgiving, as a thought—dark, sinful, and entirely unwelcome—snakes through my brain. *Sliding my strap inside her, stretching her, making her scream as I take her... making her mine.*

I clench my fists at my sides, forcing my breath to even out, but she's watching me, her lips curving in a way that feels like she knows exactly what she's doing. My sinful mind tells me she's doing this on purpose, that she knows how I think about her sometimes.

The sinful part of my brain wants me to end my misery, and hoist her up in my arms, and kiss her until her pretty little mouth can't come up with any more comeback.

"Cat got your tongue, Auntie Eve?" she whispers, her voice a dangerous mix of challenge and seduction.

I glare, forcing myself to stand tall, to regain control, even as my body betrays me. "This conversation is over."

"Is it?" she murmurs, tilting her head. "Because you look like you've got a lot on your mind."

And God help me, she's right.

Chapter Three

Sophia

The first thing I notice is the sunlight streaming through the sheer curtains, painting golden patterns across the walls. I rub my eyes, groaning softly as I push the blanket off me. My room—well, my borrowed room—comes into focus.

It's massive. The kind of room that could belong to a Gothic princess, with dark wood paneling and deep burgundy drapes framing the tall windows. The bed, a monstrous four-poster with intricate carvings, swallows me whole, the softest sheets I've ever felt tangled around my legs. A chaise lounge sits in the corner, next to a bookshelf stocked with leather-bound books I'm certain have never been opened. The air smells faintly of lavender, a delicate touch against the cold austerity of the space.

I sit up, running a hand through my messy hair, and last night's heated conversation slams into me like a freight train.

God, Eve.

Her sharp voice. Her piercing blue eyes locking on mine. The way they lingered—too long, too hungry—on my chest. I can still see the faint flush on her pale cheeks when I'd thrown my words like knives. *Virgin.* The word echoed in the space between us, and I swear her breath had hitched.

My pulse quickens at the memory. I wanted her then. In that moment, my arrogant, dismissive protector. I wanted her lips on my skin, her hands gripping me, pulling me into her lap. Or maybe it was the other way around—I didn't care. All I know is I was angry, turned on, and desperate to see her break.

A knock on the door jolts me from lingering sleep and wandering thoughts.

"Come in," I call, quickly adjusting the strap of my tank top.

Miriam steps inside, her warm smile as disarming as ever. Behind her is the man who served us dinner last night, his hands full with brown shopping bags.

"Good morning, Sophia," Miriam says brightly. "How was your night? Did you sleep well?"

"Well enough," I mumble, watching as the man sets the bags down on the chaise.

"Miss Lockhart sent some things up for you," Miriam continues, clasping her hands. "She said to go through them and let her know if they're to your liking."

I blink, confused. "Stuff?"

Miriam, sensing my hesitation, winks. "The kind of stuff that keeps you from getting bored."

I laugh softly despite myself. "Of course. Thank you."

"Breakfast will be ready in about an hour," Miriam adds. "Take your time."

I nod, watching as she leaves, closing the door behind her. My gaze drifts to the bags, curiosity bubbling as I reach for them.

What is Eve up to now?

I kneel beside the chaise, pulling the first bag closer, my curiosity flaring. Inside, sleek and silver, is a brand-new MacBook Pro, carefully wrapped in a discreet black box. My eyebrows shoot up as I lift it out, running my fingers over the packaging. *So she didn't want Miriam or anyone else seeing this. Interesting.*

Setting it aside, I reach into the next bag and pull out an iPhone. The latest model, still sealed in its box, similarly tucked away in plain black wrapping. I let out a low whistle. "Well, Eve, you've certainly got a flair for overcompensation," I murmur, smirking to myself.

The third item stops me dead.

It's an erotic artwork, vivid and bold, encased in a sleek leather portfolio. I open it, and my breath catches. The image depicts two warrior princesses entangled on a battlefield. Their weapons lie discarded beside them, their bodies pressed together, curves melding perfectly as their skin glows with sweat and battle dust. Their lips are barely apart, breaths mingling, but it's their lower halves that make my breath hitch —hips aligned, thighs spread, their pussies pressed together in a way that's as raw as it is beautiful.

"Damn," I whisper, running a finger along the edge of the frame. *She hid this one for a reason.*

The final item is a hardcover book. Eve's debut novel, *Arrows Through the Heart,* with a strikingly similar cover: the same two women, though less explicit, leaning into each other as chaos rages behind them.

Opening the book, a note slips out.

"I not only enjoy looking at erotic girl-on-girl art in my pastime, I also enjoy writing about them."

I laugh softly, shaking my head as I pick up the note, lingering on her bold handwriting. *Oh, Auntie Eve, you are so much more fun than I gave you credit for.*

∞∞∞

The clink of silverware against plates fills the otherwise quiet dining hall. Emmy is already lost in her new iPad, scrolling through TikTok with a look of pure contentment, Mr. Wonkers balanced precariously on the edge of the table.

Across from me, Eve eats her omelette in silence, her movements precise, calculated, just like everything else about her. But it's her outfit that's caught my attention this morning—a full-sleeved black Adidas crop top, hugging every line of her toned arms and shoulders, paired with sleek Nike leggings that seem painted on. She looks like one of the warrior princesses from her artwork come to life—if Candice Swanepoel had more abs and less of a friendly demeanor.

I lean back in my chair, letting my eyes linger a moment longer before breaking the silence. "So, are you heading for a workout after breakfast?"

Eve glances up at me, chewing slowly before nodding. "After your shooting lesson."

"Shooting lesson?" I ask, raising an eyebrow.

Eve sets her fork down and leans back slightly. "Yes. Every morning, starting today. You'll learn how to handle a firearm. Safety, precision, technique. And once you're competent, I'll get you your own."

My lips part in surprise, but no words come out at first. A flurry of questions hits me all at once.

"You're buying me a gun?" I finally manage, my voice a mix of curiosity and disbelief.

Eve's gaze sharpens, her blue eyes locking onto mine. "If you're going to survive in a world where people want you dead, yes. You'll need one."

The way she says it sends a shiver down my spine. I glance at Emmy, who's blissfully unaware of the weight of this conversation, and then back at Eve.

"Well," I say slowly, a smirk tugging at my lips, "should I be flattered that you trust me with a deadly weapon?"

Eve doesn't smile. "Trust has nothing to do with it, Sophia. This is about necessity."

Her words land heavy, and for once, I don't have a witty comeback. But that doesn't stop the flicker of excitement deep in my chest.

The quiet hum of breakfast is shattered by a burst of wild laughter echoing through the great hall. It's loud, carefree, and utterly out of place amidst the solemn silence that had settled over the dining table. Emmy looks up from her iPad, intrigued, while my fork pauses mid-air. Eve's eyes narrow, her head turning toward the commotion with the precision of a hawk locking onto its prey.

The source of the chaos makes her entrance a second later: a young woman, red hair tumbling down her back in fiery waves, her freckled face glowing with the kind of unrestrained joy that feels almost jarring in a place like this. She's dressed in a loose, flowy skirt with mismatched patterns, a cropped, off-the-shoulder top, and an armful of jangling bracelets that announce her arrival even louder than her laugh.

"Iggy Maxwell!" comes a sharp but warm voice from behind her. Miriam.

She strides into the room, shooting Iggy an exasperated look.

"I've told you to keep your volume down," she scolds, though there's an edge of amusement in her tone.

Iggy halts in the doorway, clearly realizing she's walked into a much quieter atmosphere than expected. She looks around, her eyes landing on the three of us at the table. For a moment, she freezes, then schools her expression into a sheepish smile, though the energy buzzing around her is impossible to ignore.

"Sorry about that," she says, her grin widening. "Didn't mean to, uh, disturb the... vibes."

I glance at Emmy, who's trying not to giggle, and then at Eve, who looks like she's weighing whether to reprimand or dismiss the whole situation. My own lips twitch into a smirk.

Miriam steps forward, placing a hand on Iggy's shoulder and gently guiding her toward the table, her bohemian skirts swishing softly with her movements. "Come on now, let's introduce you properly before you cause more chaos," she says, her tone warm despite the exasperation.

Eve leans back in her chair, watching with a faint smile as Miriam stops near Emmy and Sophia. "This," she says with a flourish, "is my daughter, Ignatius. But everyone calls her Iggy."

"Hi," Iggy says, her grin as wide as ever, her energy practically bouncing off the walls. "I come here after school sometimes—senior year perks. Had no idea today was gonna be this exciting, though."

Her gaze lands on me, and she whistles, loud and unapologetic. "Whoa. I've only seen beauty like yours on my Insta Explore page. Damn, Eve, you didn't mention your niece was an actual fairy."

Eve nods slightly, her expression unreadable, but I'm quick to respond with a smirk. "Thanks! You're pretty gorgeous yourself. Are you naturally a redhead?"

Iggy beams. "Oh, honey, one hundred percent. Wouldn't trade it for anything." She winks, flipping her fiery waves over her shoulder before turning to Emmy, who's watching her with wide-eyed curiosity.

"And who's this cutie?" Iggy exclaims, leaning down to Emmy's level and pulling her into a warm hug. Emmy giggles softly, clutching Mr. Wonkers tighter.

Iggy pulls back, her gaze falling on the stuffed bear, and her eyes light up. "Wait, why hasn't anyone introduced me to the teddy bear? This is unacceptable."

Emmy bursts into laughter, her shyness melting away. "This is Mr. Wonkers," she says proudly, holding him up.

"Well, Mr. Wonkers," Iggy says with mock seriousness, shaking the bear's little paw, "it's an honor to meet you. You and I are gonna be best friends."

The whole exchange earns a chuckle from Emmy, a soft smile from Miriam, and a rare flicker of amusement in Eve's eyes. As for me, I can't help but grin.

This place might actually be fun with Iggy around.

∞∞∞

The air grows colder as I descend the stone steps, trailing behind Eve, who moves with her usual commanding stride. My eyes flick down—*damn it.* Her leggings cling like a second skin, the muscles in her thighs and glutes flexing with every step. For a moment, I lose track of where I'm going, but I catch myself before I stumble. I roll my eyes at myself and focus forward.

The shooting range feels like something out of a spy thriller. The exposed stone walls and vaulted ceiling scream dungeon, but the modern lighting strips and polished floors tell another story. Targets line the far wall—human silhouettes, bullseyes, even a few shaped like wolves. Tables to the side display an arsenal of neatly arranged weapons, from handguns to rifles, and boxes of ammunition stacked like deadly building blocks.

But it's the paintings that make me stop.

The first, large and commanding, is of a blonde man in a U.S. military uniform. He holds a sniper rifle at his side, smiling confidently, his blue eyes warm and proud. The resemblance to Eve is striking.

"That's Richard Lockhart," Eve says, her voice quiet but steady.

Her father.

My gaze shifts to a smaller painting beside it. This one feels more intimate. A younger Eve and James are standing with their arms slung around each other, grinning wide. A beautiful woman with soft brown curls and a twinkle in her eye stands just behind them, her hand on their shoulders.

"That's my mother," Eve says, almost reverently.

But my eyes linger on James—my stepfather who raised me like I was his own flesh and blood. He looks so young here, so full of life, and the sight of him smiling hits me like a punch to the chest.

I miss him.

The ache is sharp and sudden, an overwhelming wave of grief I wasn't ready for. I realize, with a clarity that almost hurts, that losing him cuts just as deeply as losing my mom. The two people who made me who I am are gone, and the weight of that feels unbearable.

I swallow hard, blinking away the sting in my eyes, and let my gaze shift back to Eve. She's staring at the paintings too, her expression unreadable but heavy with the past.

I take a deep breath, the weight of the moment settling on my shoulders. "I'm ready to begin."

Eve raises an eyebrow, clearly unimpressed. "We'll see about that." She steps to the table, picks up a sleek black handgun, and inspects it with the kind of precision that makes it clear she could do this blindfolded. She hands it to me, grip-first, her movements sharp and deliberate.

"This is a Glock 19. Lightweight, reliable, good for beginners," she says. "But remember, a weapon's only as dangerous as the idiot holding it."

I smirk, taking the gun. "Thanks for the vote of confidence, Auntie Eve."

"Rule one," she continues, ignoring my jab, "never point this at anything you're not ready to destroy. Rule two: finger off the trigger until you're ready to fire."

"Got it. No accidental shootings."

"Exactly. Feet shoulder-width apart," she says, circling me like a drill sergeant. "Bend your knees slightly. You're not posing for a magazine."

"Shame. I'd make this look good," I mutter, adjusting my stance.

She steps closer, her hands on my waist to shift my position. "This isn't about looking good. It's about survival."

Her hands linger a moment too long, and I can't help but grin. "Are you sure you're not just using this as an excuse to manhandle me?"

Her lips twitch, almost smiling. "I don't need excuses, Sophia."

Oh.

She steps back, folding her arms. "Grip the gun firmly. Your dominant hand here, support with the other. Don't hold it like you're sipping tea."

"Noted."

"Now align the sights," she instructs, leaning slightly to the side, her voice dropping lower. "Front sight centered between the rear sights. And for the love of God, stop holding your breath. Breathe steady—don't want you passing out on me."

"Wouldn't you enjoy that? More peaceful," I quip, lining up the shot.

"Focus, smartass."

I smirk but obey, adjusting my grip. "Was your Dad this intense when he taught you?"

She blinks, the question catching her off guard, but she recovers quickly. "Worse. He didn't tolerate backtalk."

"Good thing I'm cute then."

She exhales sharply, and for the first time, there's a hint of warmth in her smirk. "Take the shot before I regret this."

The trigger clicks, and the room erupts with sound. The recoil jolts through me, adrenaline surging.

"Not bad," she says, stepping closer, her voice softer now. "Let's try again. This time, stop thinking you're charming."

"But I am," I tease, already lining up for the next shot.

∞∞∞

"Breathe," Eve commands, her voice low, steady, cutting through the haze of my frustration. I exhale sharply, my grip tightening on the gun. It doesn't help; my shot misses again, and I lower the weapon, my jaw clenching.

"This is pointless," I mutter, glaring at the target. "It's not working."

"You're trying too hard," she replies, her tone calm but unyielding. "Shooting isn't about brute force. It's about control. Balance."

Before I can bite back with some sarcastic retort, she moves behind me, her presence suddenly overwhelming. Her hands settle on my shoulders, firm and steady, and the warmth of her touch sends a jolt straight to my core.

She grabs me tight, and her fingers sizzle on my body. They dig in, and I feel like a doll being played with by its owner. A chiseled, blue-eyed, owner who's making me question my moralities.

"Raise the gun," she murmurs, her breath brushing against the shell of my ear. I swallow hard, lifting the weapon, but my body isn't cooperating. Not when I can feel every inch of her so close.

Just bite my damn ear!

Just mark me as yours and be done with it!

Her hands slide from my shoulders to my arms, guiding me, her fingers firm yet careful. "Relax. You're holding too much tension," she says, her voice softer now, almost coaxing.

My breath catches as her palms shift lower, resting lightly on my hips. She adjusts my stance, her fingers pressing into the curve of my waist. "There," she says, her grip tightening just slightly. "Feel that? That's stability."

What I feel is anything but stable. My knees threaten to buckle as she lingers, her chest brushing lightly against my back. Her lips are close enough that I can almost feel them graze my skin.

"Focus," she whispers, her voice lower, rougher. "You're distracted."

Distracted? Yeah, I am distracted, wondering how the cold

floor of this dungeon will feel on my back when you push me down, and straddle my face with your gorgeous thighs, Auntie Eve!

I force my eyes to the target, but all I can think about is how her hands would feel gripping me tighter, her lips marking my neck, her voice rougher still. My fingers tremble on the gun, and I bite my lip to stop a whimper from escaping.

"Take the shot," she commands, her tone dropping as her hands flex against my waist, grounding me.

I fire, the recoil jolting through me, and the bullet strikes the target. Barely.

Eve steps back, her hands lingering for a fraction longer than necessary before falling away entirely.

"Better," she says, her expression unreadable.

I turn to face her, my chest heaving, my voice trembling with equal parts adrenaline and frustration. "I think I need more… hands-on training."

Her lips twitch, just barely, before she nods. "You'll get plenty. Now again, from the top."

And just like that, I'm hers to command all over again.

∞∞∞

Eve hands me another magazine, her movements precise and practiced, her sharp blue eyes locked on mine. "Faster this time," she says, her tone clipped. "Slide it in, release the catch, and rack the slide. Don't think—just do."

I groan, my arms feeling like jelly. "My hands are tired. My brain is tired." I pause, biting back the thought that nearly slips out. *And my pussy is tired of wanting you.*

Instead, I smirk, leaning the gun down on the table with a sigh. "I need a water break. Or better yet, a Starbucks break. Is there a secret drive-thru in the woods outside?"

Eve doesn't roll her eyes, but I can see the temptation flicker across her face. "No Starbucks in the woods," she says, her lips twitching ever so slightly. "But I can ask the chef to whip up a cold coffee, my style. We'll rest here, and someone will bring it down."

"Cold coffee made by you?" I ask, raising an eyebrow.

"My recipe," she corrects, stepping back and leaning against the stone wall, her arms folding across her chest. The pose somehow makes her look even more commanding.

"Well, now I'm curious," I tease, wiping my brow.

"You'll like it," she says simply, glancing at the nearby intercom. She presses a button, speaking into it with the same precision she seems to apply to everything. A low, professional request for cold coffee follows, and then she turns her attention back to me.

As I slump onto the bench, I can't help but admire the way her shoulders relax, just slightly, the tiniest crack in her armor. The air between us feels lighter now, less charged, but the tension lingers like a distant hum.

"Rest up," she says, her voice softer. "Because when we're done, you'll be reloading in your sleep."

"Great," I mutter, grinning despite myself. "Just what every girl dreams of."

"Not every girl," Eve replies, her lips curving into the faintest smirk. "But I sure did when I was your age."

I blink, caught off guard. "You dreamt of reloading guns as a hot, young teenager? Why? Every jock in school must've been falling over themselves for you. Weren't you into being the popular girl?"

"No," she says simply, leaning back against the cold stone wall, her arms crossing over her chest. Her voice dips slightly, laced with dry humor. "I was more interested in running faster than them, wrestling better than them..." She pauses, letting her words hang heavy in the air before her smirk deepens. "...and fucking girls better than them."

My jaw drops, and I clutch my chest dramatically, eyes wide. "Auntie Eve! You naughty, naughty girl! So, you've been into girls since school?"

She shrugs, completely unfazed by my theatrics, her confidence rolling off her like a well-worn coat. "Since I knew what lust was," she says, her voice unapologetically steady. "All my lust was reserved for women, right from the start. Men never had a chance."

"Well, damn," I mutter, still trying to process this new side of her. "Here I was, thinking you were some straight-laced soldier who never broke a rule. Turns out you were a certified heartbreaker in combat boots."

"Not combat boots back then," she says, the hint of a laugh in her tone. "Running shoes, mostly. But you're not wrong about the heartbreaker part."

I lean forward, tilting my head with curiosity. "So, who was your first?"

Her smirk fades slightly, her gaze growing distant for a moment. "My brother's ex," she says quietly.

"What? Did I hear that right?" I ask, leaning forward, my curiosity threatening to spill over.

"Unfortunately, yes," Eve replies with a chuckle, the faintest hint of nostalgia tugging at her lips. "James was a heartbreaker in his own right. Carol's heart was shattered into a million pieces the night she rang our doorbell in the middle of a storm. She came to return some of James' stuff. Little did she know, she'd be going back with some of mine."

My eyes widen. "What did you send her back with?"

Eve smirks, her gaze flickering as if replaying the memory. "A new sexual identity and my wet panties."

I gasp, clutching my imaginary pearls. "Auntie Eve! You didn't!"

Her laugh is low and throaty, shaking her head as if she can't believe herself. "Oh, I did. And fuck, I can't believe I'm sharing all of this with you. I used to watch my language around you, you know. When you were a kid."

"Well, I'm not a kid anymore," I shoot back, grinning. "I've grown up. I'm at that perfect age where I deserve some wet panties as well."

Eve freezes, her lips parting slightly as her eyes lock onto mine. The air between us shifts, thickening. "Are you…?"

"I'm bi. I think," I admit, shrugging. "Although I've always preferred masturbating to lesbian porn. But then again, even straight girls like that, right? Honestly, I never understood how that worked."

Eve chuckles, the sound low and intoxicating. "It's simple. Women know how to make love. We know the power of a tongue over a penis."

"Wow," I say, tilting my head. "So your expertise isn't just in guns, huh? It's tongues too?"

Eve leans back, her smirk turning devilish. "Tongues. Torture. Temptation. I'm well-versed in all three."

My breath catches, her words wrapping around me like a spell. But the sound of footsteps on the stairs shatters the moment. I snap my head around to see Miriam descending, carrying two frosted glasses of iced coffee on a tray.

"Saved by the coffee," Eve murmurs, her voice soft and tinged with something unreadable.

Saved? Or interrupted? I'm not sure which.

Eve

The door to my study closes behind me with a soft click, sealing me in the one space where I can let my guard slip—just a little. I stalk toward my desk, the weight of the mahogany grounding me as I drop into the leather chair with a low sigh. My hand instinctively goes to the corner of the desk, brushing over the worn edge where my fingers often linger.

The room feels oppressive tonight. The towering shelves filled with books on strategy, war, and survival surround me, mocking me with their calm order. My computer hums softly on the desk, the glow of the screen illuminating the chaos in my mind.

Sophia. *Goddamn Sophia.*

I rest my elbows on the desk, pressing my palms to my temples as the memory of her voice, her laughter, her *body* refuses to fade. The way her skin felt under my hands during training—warm, soft, and maddeningly close. The way her waist had fit perfectly in my grip, like it belonged there.

My fingers twitch, and I grit my teeth. *Too tight. I held her too tight. And God help me, it wasn't enough.*

The thought of my hands sliding lower, gripping her small,

perfect ass, spins into my mind unbidden. Of spinning her around, pinning her to the cold wall of that damn shooting range, and growling into her ear: *Why do you want me to sin? Why do you want me to go to hell for you?*

I slam my eyes shut, leaning back in my chair, the leather creaking under the motion. *Get it together, Lockhart. She's nineteen. She's James's stepdaughter. She's your responsibility—not your downfall.*

My jaw tightens as I open my computer, the keys cool against my fingertips. A blank Word document stares back at me, daring me to focus on something productive.

But I can't. Instead, I type: *All the Ways She Makes Me Sin.*

The title sits there, glaring at me in stark black and white.

Art imitates life, doesn't it?

I shake my head, closing the laptop with more force than necessary. Standing abruptly, I walk to the window, staring out at the moonlit grounds. The shadows seem to whisper accusations.

"You're losing it," I mutter, running a hand through my hair. "You're supposed to protect her, not want her."

But the worst part? I know this is only the beginning.

My gaze sharpens, searching for anything—a flicker of movement, a glint of something unnatural—but all I see is the quiet expanse of woods and manicured lawns. I close my eyes, and James' voice echoes in my head, as clear as if he's standing next to me.

"If something happens to me, you have to take care of my girls as your own," he'd said, his tone unusually solemn. It was Sophia's 15th birthday. The room had been full of laughter, the glow of candles lighting up her face as she grinned at me. I'd laughed it off. "Why would anything happen to you, James?" I'd teased, punching his shoulder lightly. But he hadn't smiled.

"I'm serious," he'd said, gripping my hand. "I can only trust you. Sophia worships you, and I know you have a soft spot for her in your heart. You're the only one who can protect them. You will, won't you?"

I'd clasped his hand tightly, forcing a smile. "Like my own."

Opening my eyes, the present rushes back, and with it, the shame. I *am* trying to fulfill James' promise. I've uprooted my life to protect his girls, to keep them safe. But Sophia... *God, Sophia.* The way she looks at me, challenges me. The way I think about her—desire her—is far from what James would've wanted. Not like my own. *But maybe, just maybe, like mine.*

I shut the thought down with a sharp breath, turning from the window to my desk, the motion almost mechanical. Sitting down, I open my laptop again, switching to my email. There's a message from my publisher—another pushy nudge to start my next book—but my attention snags on something else. An email sits in my inbox, its sender's address scrambled and nonsensical, the subject line reading: *This concerns you.*

Every nerve in my body goes on high alert. Clicking the email, the screen fills with black text on a stark white background, no frills, no signatures. Just a short, chilling message:

The girl still has something of ours. We know where you are, and how to get there. Return what is ours, and we won't pay a visit.

I stare at the screen, the words taunting me in stark black and white. My soldier instincts flare, adrenaline sharpening my focus as I force myself to breathe steadily. *Think. Process. Act.*

Leaning forward, I open another tab and begin checking the email's metadata. It's second nature—the tech skills drilled into me during missions where a rogue message could mean life or death. I mutter under my breath as I sift through lines of code. "God, I could use an IT backup right now."

The sender's address is scrambled—nonsense characters

running through what should be a traceable origin point. My fingers move quickly, trying to uncover any hidden IP or location markers. Nothing. It's a dead end. Whoever sent this knows what they're doing.

I lean back in my chair, fingers drumming against the armrest, my mind racing. *This could be a prank. An old enemy trying to toy with me, leveraging the situation because, God knows, I've made plenty of enemies on the field.* Or worse, *this could actually be the mafia.*

My eyes narrow as I reread the message. *The girl.* It has to mean Sophia. Emmy's too young. But what could Sophia possibly have? And do they really know where I am?

My gaze flicks to the window, scanning the moonlit grounds again. If they can breach my personal email, they could reach me. Maybe they're already close.

The thought sparks something feral inside me, and I sit up straighter. "Let them come," I mutter, my jaw tightening. "I'll skin them alive if they set foot here."

Grabbing my phone, I dial a number, my voice low but firm when the line connects. "Tessa," I say. "I need to see you as soon as possible."

Chapter Four

Sophia

The early morning breeze kisses my face as I stand on the balcony, a steaming cup of coffee warming my hands. My hair flows freely, catching in the wind, and I inhale deeply, letting the crisp air fill my lungs. My eyes scan the woods stretching out in the distance, their green hues now tinged with the golden yellows and burnt oranges of early fall. The leaves are changing, nature signaling the inevitable march of time. Fall in Montana, I think. It's as beautiful as it is fleeting.

Movement below catches my eye, pulling my gaze to the front of the manor. There's commotion—a lot of it. Eve is there, front and center, dressed in camouflage booty shorts that cling to her toned hips, and a dark green Nike sports bra that perfectly matches the aviators perched on her nose. She's gesturing animatedly at a group of men in black suits, their earpieces glowing faintly in the morning light. Her body is all taut muscle and authority, and the way the men nod at her every command is hypnotic.

I bite my lip, heat creeping into my cheeks as my eyes trace the line of her long, powerful legs. *That's a woman who could take me however she wants, and I wouldn't mind one bit.* My fingers tighten around the coffee cup as I let the fantasy swirl—her legs around me, suffocating me, holding me in place. A sigh escapes my lips, and I force myself to snap out of it.

At the far end of the grounds, near the estate's main gates, three battered pickup trucks are parked. A few burly men in sleeveless plaid shirts, their biceps bulging with each swing of their tools, are digging into the ground. What the hell is going on? Eve's taking charge of all these massive guys like it's second nature. It's infuriatingly attractive.

Shaking my head, I turn back into my room, closing the glass door behind me. Emmy is sitting cross-legged on the bed, her pink teddy, Mr. Wonkers, clutched against her chest. Her expression is downcast, her usual energy noticeably absent.

"What's up, Emmy?" I ask, setting my coffee on the nightstand.

"Today would've been the first day of the fall session," she says softly. "I miss school. I miss my friends. I even miss math, and I *hate* math."

I smile gently, walking over to sit beside her. "I get it," I say. "But not going to school doesn't mean you get to escape studying."

Her brow furrows. "What do you mean?"

I grab her floral backpack—bright pink with glittery butterflies—and unzip it, pulling out her books. "You're going to be back in school soon, and when that day comes, you need to be ready. So, guess what? I'm your teacher now. Isn't that exciting?"

She groans, flopping back onto the bed dramatically. "Nooo!"

I smirk, flipping through her notebook. "Trust me, kid. I hate this as much as you do. Never thought I'd be a teacher, but here we are. Life has officially peaked."

I tap the pencil against Emmy's workbook, trying to explain fractions in a way that doesn't make my own brain want to melt. "Okay, so if you divide the pie into four parts and you eat two of them, how much of the pie have you eaten?"

"Half," Emmy mutters distractedly, doodling in the margins of her notebook.

"Exactly," I say, circling the answer. "See? You're a genius when you stop pretending to be bad at math."

She grins at me before suddenly putting down her pencil and tilting her head, a mischievous glint in her eye. "Sophie, what do you think of Auntie Eve?"

The question catches me off guard, and my face heats up. "What do you mean, what do I think of her?" I ask, trying to keep my voice steady, wondering if my *very dirty* thoughts about Eve are somehow plastered across my face.

"She's cool, isn't she?" Emmy says, her eyes wide with admiration. "Like cooler than anyone else in our boring neighbourhood. I haven't seen anyone like her."

I lean back, fiddling with the pencil. "I haven't either," I admit softly.

"Where was she all this time?" Emmy asks, her tone turning wistful. "I would've *loved* to take her to school and show her off to my friends. Imagine her driving us in that G-Wagon, with her cool shades and those abs!"

Before I can respond, Emmy jumps off the bed, grabs a marker, and starts drawing little squares on her belly. "Look at me! I'm Auntie Eve," she declares, tying her hair into a messy ponytail and striding around the room stiffly.

"Those don't look like abs, idiot!" I laugh, clutching my stomach.

"They do too! Look how strong I am!" Emmy retorts, flexing dramatically and puffing out her chest.

I wipe a tear from my eye, still giggling. "If Eve saw this, she'd probably make you do push-ups until you cried."

Emmy stops, her expression turning curious. "Do you think she was always like this? All serious and tough?"

I shrug. "I don't know. I mean, she had to be a kid once, right? Maybe she even smiled more back then."

"Do you think she's ever been in love?" Emmy asks innocently, sitting back down and twirling Mr. Wonkers in her lap.

The question makes me pause, my laughter fading. "I don't know, Emmy," I say softly, brushing a strand of hair from her face. "Maybe. But I don't think she's the kind of person who talks about it."

"Maybe one day we'll get her to," Emmy whispers conspiratorially.

"Maybe," I reply, my thoughts lingering far longer on the possibility than they should.

I watch as Emmy grows quiet, her little fingers fiddling with the ear of Mr. Wonkers. The silence stretches, her earlier playfulness fading into something far heavier. Finally, her small voice cuts through the quiet.

"I was very afraid after Mom and Dad died," she says softly, not looking up at me. "I was afraid that one day, the bad guys would come and take you away from me too. And then... then they'd hurt me too."

Her words hit me like a punch to the gut, and I feel my chest tighten. Before I can say anything, she looks up, her wide, innocent eyes locking onto mine. "But now," she continues, her voice gaining a little strength, "being near Auntie Eve, I know she'll protect us. I'm not so scared anymore."

I blink rapidly, trying to keep the tears at bay as I scoot closer and pull her into my arms. Her small frame fits perfectly against mine, and I squeeze her tightly, brushing my fingers through her hair.

"Oh, baby, you don't need to be scared," I murmur, my voice thick with emotion. "She'll protect us. You saw those abs, didn't you?" I force a laugh, trying to lighten the mood. "She'll protect both of us!"

Emmy giggles against my shoulder, her grip on Mr. Wonkers tightening. "Yeah," she whispers. "Her abs are really strong."

"They are," I say, holding her a little tighter. "And so are we. No one's going to take us away from each other. Not ever."

For a moment, we just sit there, wrapped in each other's arms, the weight of the past few weeks hanging in the air. But for the first time since everything happened, I feel a small flicker of hope. *We're going to be okay.* Eve will protect us, and so will I.

∞∞∞

The G-Wagon zips smoothly down the winding road, the towering trees on either side giving way to occasional glimpses of the hills surrounding Dew's Point. The low hum of the engine mixes with the chatter in the backseat, where I'm sandwiched between Emmy and Iggy.

Iggy is unusually close, her thigh brushing mine, and her hand casually rests on my leg, like it's the most natural thing in the world. She's buzzing with excitement, her curls bouncing as she leans forward to share her plans.

"So, here's what we're doing for the sleepover," she begins, her words spilling out faster than the car is moving. "We'll make friendship bracelets with real crystals—I have these amazing ones I found at a flea market. Then, we'll make mood boards from old magazines, do tarot readings, and play truth or dare. Oh, and don't worry, Sophia—I already have vegan marshmallows for s'mores."

Miriam turns in her seat, her eyebrow arched. "And while you're doing all that, don't forget what a *task* it was convincing Miss Lockhart to let you two stay the night. So, no sneaking out, no mischief, and no drama, understood?"

The man in the black suit, stoic and silent until now, chimes in without looking back. "Don't worry, ma'am. I won't let that happen."

I roll my eyes, earning a smirk from Iggy, who leans in close and whispers, "He's hot, isn't he?"

I nod absently, though my thoughts betray me. *Is he though? Would I let him touch me the way Eve did in the gun room? Not a chance. Would he make me as wet? Absolutely not.*

Before I can spiral further, Iggy's hand slides higher on my thigh, her lips curving mischievously. "We'll talk about all the boys we've fucked... or, you know, the ones who made us want girls instead."

I freeze, glancing at her wide-eyed. *So, she's not just chirpy and weird. She's bold. Very bold.*

Dinner was a hearty spread of rustic comfort food—roasted chicken seasoned to perfection, buttery mashed potatoes, a crisp salad, and soft, golden rolls. Miriam's apple crumble, paired with vanilla ice cream, had left me so full, I felt like I'd never move again.

Now, I sit nestled in an armchair near the window, holding my mug of peppermint tea, gazing out at the quiet street outside. The black G-Wagon is parked at the curb, its sleek, modern lines looking almost alien against the humble charm of Dew's Point. Inside, the man in the suit sits rigid, his profile faintly visible in the glow of the dashboard as his eyes scan the house and surroundings.

The street is simple yet picturesque in its own way. A single main road winds through the town, paved but bordered by wooden sidewalks. A few lampposts dot the street, casting a warm glow over the small buildings on either side. Most are old-fashioned, with wooden storefronts, hand-painted signs, and flower boxes. There's a cozy diner with flickering neon, a general store with a wooden bench out front, and a tiny bookstore still lit from within, its display full of leather-bound novels and handmade crafts. The crisp evening air and faint scent of pine seem to belong to a place frozen in time.

I smile faintly, but a pang of nostalgia hits me—unexpected and sharp. *Why does this place feel like a memory I never had?*

Inside, warmth fills the room. Iggy is sprawled on the floor with Emmy, their heads bent together over a Lego castle that's starting to resemble the manor. Emmy's giggles mix with Iggy's chatter, the jingling of her bracelets adding a playful melody.

Miriam hums softly as she cleans dishes in the kitchen, the sound of water running blending with the clinking of plates. For a moment, it feels peaceful. Whole. But the thought is fleeting, wiped away by a memory of similar nights back home—Mom laughing, Dad joking, the world intact.

"Hey," Iggy's voice cuts through, bringing me back. She's smiling at me, her freckles glowing in the warm light. "This little one's sleepy. Mind if I tuck her in?"

I nod, watching as Emmy hugs Iggy, who gently lifts her up. Something about Iggy feels comforting—her vibrant skirts, red hair, bracelets, and that infectious smile. She's like a walking kaleidoscope of color and warmth.

As she carries Emmy toward the hallway, her hips sway slightly under the fabric of her skirt. I catch myself wondering: *Was her hand on my thigh earlier just friendly? Or... something more?*

A soft sigh escapes me. *Maybe yes, maybe no. Maybe coming to a town full of beautiful women wasn't the best idea.*

∞∞∞

The room is bathed in faint moonlight streaming through the half-drawn curtains. Emmy sleeps soundly next to me, clutching Mr. Wonkers to her chest. Her soft, rhythmic breaths fill the silence. At the edge of the bed, Iggy sits cross-legged, her vibrant red hair spilling over her shoulders as she leans slightly toward me, her voice low and conspiratorial.

"Dew's Point is… fine," she whispers, shrugging. "School's a forty-five-minute bus ride, which sucks, but whatever. The people are nice. Like, too nice. Not a kinky bone in their collective bodies."

I stifle a laugh, glancing down at Emmy to make sure she's still asleep. "Not kinky? That's your issue with the town?" I tease, keeping my voice just as quiet.

Iggy grins, her bracelets jingling softly as she adjusts her position. "I'm serious! It's like everyone here is content with baking pies and wearing the same damn sweaters every fall. No one here dreams big or… wants big."

"So what do you want, then?" I ask, genuinely curious.

She pauses, her green eyes gleaming in the dim light. "I want to be wild," she says, her tone suddenly serious. "Wild like the winds. I want to escape to a beach town, or some hippie paradise where you can be anything you want. Do anything you want. Touch who you want, without people judging you or whispering behind your back."

Her words hang in the air, heavy with longing.

I smirk, trying to lighten the mood. "Sounds like you're not just interested in boys."

Iggy laughs, her shoulders shaking slightly. "You're right. I'm not. I want them all—men, women, trans... anyone with a golden heart." She tilts her head, her voice dropping to a near-whisper. "You seem to have a golden heart, Sophia."

Her words catch me off guard, and I feel my cheeks heat up. "Me? A golden heart? You barely know me."

"Maybe. But sometimes you just... know," she says, her gaze steady on mine. "You carry this warmth. Like you'd do anything to protect Emmy. That kind of love—it's rare. And beautiful."

I don't know what to say, so I look down at Emmy, brushing a strand of hair from her face. "She's all I have," I say softly.

"And she's lucky to have you," Iggy replies, her voice just as gentle.

There's a long pause, comfortable but charged, as if the air between us has thickened. Iggy shifts closer, leaning back on her hands. "So, what about you?" she asks. "What do you want to be?"

I let out a soft laugh, shaking my head. "That's a loaded question."

"I've got time," she says with a grin, gesturing to the sleeping Emmy. "She's not going anywhere, and neither am I."

I sigh, letting my guard down just a little. "I don't know. I used to want a normal life, you know? Go to a flying school, become a pilot, meet someone, settle down. But now..." I trail off, staring out the window. "Now, I just want to feel safe. To stop looking over my shoulder. To stop feeling like my world could fall apart at any second."

Iggy nods, her expression softening. "That's fair. But you're not alone anymore, Sophia. You've got Emmy. And... well, you've got me now, too."

Her words warm something inside me, and I give her a small smile. "Thanks, Iggy. That means a lot."

She grins, her playful energy returning. "Of course. And for the record, I think you're already pretty wild. You just don't know it yet."

I raise an eyebrow. "Wild? Me? Have you met me?"

"I have," she says, her grin turning mischievous. "And I can tell there's a rebel hiding under all that 'big sister' energy. You just need the right person to bring it out."

"Oh, and let me guess," I say, rolling my eyes with a smirk. "That person is you?"

"Maybe," Iggy says, winking, her lips curving into that mischievous grin she wears so effortlessly.

"And how do you plan on bringing it out?" I tease, raising an eyebrow.

"I don't know," she says, leaning closer, her bracelets jingling softly. "By making sure I do whatever you ask me to. Show you I can be that confidant of yours in that huge estate—someone who's always there for you."

"That might just make me fall for you instead of bringing out my wilder side," I quip, feeling the corners of my lips twitch with amusement.

"Fall for me?" she echoes, her grin widening.

"Yeah," I say, shrugging. "Like...like you, in a very non-friendly way, because here's a newsflash for you—I like touching whoever I want as well, especially hot girls."

Iggy's smile softens, her eyes glinting with something deeper. "I sort of knew."

"How?"

"The way your breath caught in your chest when I slid my hand up your thigh," she replies matter-of-factly, her gaze steady.

"You noticed that?" I ask, feeling the heat rise to my face.

"Yeah. And other things," she adds, her voice lowering slightly.

"What other things?" I say, trying to sound nonchalant, but the curiosity burns through.

"Like the way you bite your lips when Eve's around."

Fuck. Did she see that?

I burst into a soft giggle, careful not to wake Emmy. "She's my aunt, Iggy!"

"Step-aunt," she corrects, her grin turning wicked. "And she's hot. So fucking hot. Come on, tell me you haven't checked her out. Hell, *I* check her out. If she wasn't so scary and serious and John Rambo-like, I would've tried to sleep with her. A hundo percent."

"A hundo percent?" I laugh, clutching my chest dramatically. "No. I have no plans to sleep with the only woman who can save my ass out there in the wild."

"But isn't that hotter?"

"No! That's a recipe for disaster!"

"Then you better stop biting your lips when she's around," Iggy says, tilting her head knowingly. "She'll catch on to it, and let me tell you—the way you look? I'm pretty sure she wants a piece of you, too."

My mouth falls open. "What?! No way."

"Oh, absolutely," Iggy says, giggling. "She's got it bad. And honestly, why wouldn't she? You're young, beautiful in that whole *French-girl-who-just-stepped-out-of-a-black-and-*

white-movie way, and probably ready to be deflowered. Then there's her—all tall, muscular, ab-riddled, and drowning in all that pent-up sexual frustration from writing those steamy lesbian romance novels without fucking anyone in years. She's your protector, your step-aunt. I can't compete with that!"

I blink, my head spinning. "Wait. You…wanted to compete? For me?"

Iggy shrugs, her grin faltering just a bit. "Yeah. Look around you—I don't usually hang out with literal goddesses. I was hoping I'd finally get to…have a bestie who I can, I don't know… taste."

"You want just a taste?" I ask, my voice low as I lean forward. The space between us evaporates until we're face to face, only inches apart.

Iggy's eyes flicker down to my lips before meeting my gaze again, a teasing smirk playing on hers. "Just a taste…for now."

My heart thuds, the air thickening between us. Her words, her tone, her presence—it all makes me question everything. My lips twitch into a sly smile. "For now, huh?"

She leans closer, her whisper brushing against my skin. "Unless you'd like more."

I don't reply, but my body does, my pulse racing as our breaths mingle in the quiet, electric space between us.

What the hell do I want? My heart pounds in my chest, my mind spinning as Iggy's words linger in the air between us. *She wants a taste. A taste of me.*

My thoughts betray me instantly, jumping to where they've been since the moment I stepped foot into that estate. Eve. Her legs, her abs, the way her hands gripped me too tightly in the gun room. She's been the star of every filthy, forbidden thought I've had since arriving. And no one can compare. Not her abs. Not her lips. Not the way she flushes pale pink whenever I say something outrageous.

But Eve's a dream—a filthy, naughty, completely off-limits dream I'll never live out.

And then there's Iggy. This spicy little Montana redhead, with her bohemian skirts and a laugh that jingles as much as her bracelets. She's the opposite of Eve in every way, but damn if she doesn't make my pulse quicken. *How does she taste? Does she taste like cherries, like those lips?*

I can feel my cheeks heat up as my eyes flick to her skirt, noticing how it rides higher when she leans forward. *Has she been doing that on purpose? Flicking it just enough to make me notice her thighs?*

A taste wouldn't be bad, would it? Just *one* taste.

I've been trapped for days now, locked in a manor that's suffocating me with its stone walls and its haunted shadows of my parents. Tortured by Eve's unapologetic perfection, her gym-honed body taunting me every single time she moves. Is it so wrong to take a break from dreaming about something I can't have, to enjoy what's right in front of me?

I deserve this. I deserve *her*.

One good, mind-blowing makeout session before I go back to my gilded prison to suffer in silence under Eve's gaze. That's all I'm asking for.

And maybe, Iggy deserves this too.

I feel the weight of the moment, her breath warm against my cheek as she leans closer, her green eyes searching mine. I can smell her faint citrusy perfume, the lingering sweetness of the lemonade we had earlier.

I don't think. I don't hesitate.

I close the gap between us, my lips pressing against hers in a soft, tentative kiss. Her lips are as sweet as I imagined, soft and inviting, and when I feel her exhale against me, it's like a spark igniting something deep in my chest.

Finally, I think, leaning in further. *Finally.*

The kiss starts soft, tentative. My lips brush against Iggy's, testing the waters, but the second they meet, something ignites. She presses back, her lips moving with mine, warm and intoxicating. My fingers curl around her wrist, and without thinking, I tug her with me, slipping quietly out of the room and into the washroom down the hall. The door clicks shut, and the moment we're alone, Iggy moves like she's been unleashed.

Her hands grip my waist, spinning me around and pressing my back firmly against the cold tiles. The contrast between the chill of the wall and the fire of her touch sends a shiver racing down my spine.

Her lips slam into mine, desperate and demanding, like she's been starving for this moment. Her kiss is raw, all teeth and tongue, her hunger spilling into me, taking over every thought. Her fingers dig into my hips, holding me in place as if daring me to move away—daring me to try and resist her. I couldn't even if I wanted to.

"You have no idea what you do to me," she growls against my lips before biting down on my bottom lip, tugging it just enough to make me gasp. Her voice is low, gravelly, dripping with lust. "I've been dreaming about this, Sophia—about you."

Her words send a rush of heat straight between my thighs. She feels it, too, her thigh slipping between mine, pressing firmly, forcing me to grind against her. The friction is maddening, pulling a shameless moan from my lips. She grins wickedly at the sound, her lips tracing a path along my jaw, down my neck.

"Fuck, you taste as good as I imagined," she murmurs, her teeth grazing the sensitive skin just below my ear. The bite is sharp, enough to make me gasp again, but her tongue quickly soothes the sting. My hands clutch at her shoulders, my nails digging into her as I try to anchor myself against the overwhelming sensation.

The second Iggy's thigh presses between mine, everything shifts. The sweetness, the hesitation—it's gone. She grabs my hips and forces me down onto her leg, her strength catching me off guard. The friction is instant, electric, and utterly devastating. My breath hitches, and I cling to her shoulders, my nails biting into her skin.

"Grind on me," she growls, her voice low and rough, completely unrecognizable from the Iggy I thought I knew. "I want to feel how bad you need this."

My body obeys without question, rocking against her firm thigh. The sensation is overwhelming—every nerve ignited, every inch of me screaming for more. Her hands guide my hips, pressing me harder against her, making me lose any semblance of control.

And then she leans in, her lips brushing my ear as she whispers, "You still wish it was Eve instead of me, don't you?"

The words hit me like a lightning bolt. My head snaps back, and a long, primal moan escapes my lips before I can stop it. It's raw, animalistic, and so loud it echoes off the tiled walls. But I can't answer. I can't form words. My body trembles as I keep moving, grinding harder against her, the heat between us unbearable.

Iggy's laugh is dark, dripping with satisfaction. "You do, don't you? You wish it was your Eve. I'm just a substitute," she hisses, her hands gripping me tighter, her nails digging into my skin. "But fuck, I love being your substitute, Sophia. You *filthy* girl."

"Eve..." I whisper, and it's like her name is a lifeline and a sin all at once. My breath comes in short gasps as I move faster, grinding harder against Iggy's thigh. The friction drives me insane, but it's not enough. Not even close.

Iggy freezes for a moment, her grip tightening as she lets out a sharp breath. "You're saying her name?" she hisses, her voice a mix of shock and something darker. "Fuck, Sophia. You're a mess. Is that all I am to you—a stand-in for your precious Eve?"

But I can't even hear her anymore. My mind is lost in a haze of desire, of heat, of need. Her words spark something wild and uncontrollable inside me, and suddenly, I'm the one taking control. My hands shoot to her shoulders, shoving her back against the wall, and I climb onto her leg, wrapping my arms around her neck for balance. I start riding her thigh with reckless abandon, chasing every ounce of friction I can get.

My skirt hikes up around my hips, and I don't care. Iggy's eyes widen as she watches me, her lips parted, her breath coming faster. "Sophia," she groans, her voice breaking. "God, look at you…"

I growl in frustration, grabbing the hem of my plaid skirt and yanking it higher. The stockings I'm wearing are in the way, and without a second thought, I hook my fingers into them and tear them apart with a satisfying rip. The fabric falls in shreds around my thighs, and I slam myself back onto her leg, the rough friction of her thighs against my bare pussy igniting every nerve in my body.

"Auntie Eve…" I moan again, louder this time, my voice trembling as I ride her harder. My hips move on their own, grinding desperately against her, my nails raking down her shoulders. Iggy watches me, her jaw slack, her pupils blown wide as she tries to catch up with what's happening.

"You're—fuck—you're insane," she mutters, her hands clamping onto my hips to steady me. "This isn't about me at all, is it? You're thinking about her, aren't you?"

"Eve…" The name falls from my lips over and over, like a prayer, like an incantation, each time sending a fresh wave of heat coursing through me. Iggy's hands tighten, her nails digging into my skin as she helps me move, her own breath ragged.

"Jesus Christ," she growls, her voice thick with lust. "You're fucking yourself on my leg, and all you can think about is her? That's so fucked up, Sophia. But fuck, it's hot. Keep going. Show me how bad you want her."

My head falls back, my body completely out of control as I grind against her with wild, reckless desperation. My thighs tremble, my skin slick with sweat, and I can't stop. I won't stop. My hands tangle in her hair, pulling her closer as I press my lips to hers, swallowing her groans as I ride her harder.

"Say it again," Iggy demands, her voice rough and commanding. "Say her name, Sophia. Scream it if you have to."

"Fuck! Evvveee!!!!" I cry out, my voice breaking as my body reaches the edge, teetering dangerously close to release. "Eve… Eve… Evelyn!"

Iggy groans, her hands guiding my movements as I lose myself completely, my hips grinding in a frantic rhythm, my moans echoing through the room. "Fuck, you're insane," she mutters, her lips brushing against my neck as I collapse against her, trembling and gasping for breath.

But even as the wave crashes over me, the only name on my lips is hers. "Eve…" I whisper, my voice barely audible as I shatter in her arms, my body trembling with the force of it.

And in that moment, nothing else exists. Not Iggy, not the room, not even myself. Just Eve.

∞∞∞

Morning sunlight streams through the lace curtains of Miriam's cozy home, casting a warm glow on the wooden floors.

I sit on the edge of the couch, sipping a cup of steaming coffee, trying to make sense of how utterly normal Iggy seems today. She's crouched on the floor with Emmy, holding up a tiny purple suit with and matching shoes, chattering about how "Mr. Wonkers deserves the absolute best wardrobe."

Last night feels like a fever dream—a delicious, twisted fever dream. Watching Iggy now, with her bright-eyed Montana charm and wholesome giggles, I can't reconcile her with the same girl who was growling my name in the dark, whispering things that made my pulse race and my knees weak.

How is she so unshaken by it all? And how am I supposed to function around her, knowing she saw through me completely and leaned into the chaos without hesitation? She even made me say *Eve's* name—God, my cheeks burn just thinking about it.

Miriam bustles around the kitchen, expertly packing a neat little lunch for us. "I packed extra sandwiches, just in case. Sophia, you seemed to like them last night," she says, smiling warmly.

"They were incredible, Miriam," I reply, genuinely touched by her thoughtfulness. Emmy bounces over to her with Mr. Wonkers, now dressed to the nines, beaming with excitement.

"Miriam, you're the best!" Emmy chirps.

I glance back at Iggy, who's grinning at Emmy as if nothing is out of the ordinary. I shake my head, still baffled. The girl's a paradox—a bohemian small-town sweetheart with a mouth and confidence that could ruin me.

"Emmy, we need to get going!" I call out, standing and adjusting my jacket. But just as we're about to leave, the low growl of a motorbike cuts through the morning air.

Everyone freezes.

We step outside, and there she is—Eve, astride a Harley Davidson, looking like a damn goddess of sin. She's dressed head to toe in black leather—tight pants, a fitted jacket, and aviators perched on her nose, her hair tied back in a loose ponytail. The bike gleams in the sunlight, but it's nothing compared to her.

"Holy fuck," Iggy and I exclaim simultaneously, our voices blending in disbelief. We look at each other, then burst into laughter.

Eve swings off the bike, her movements calculated, almost predatory. She puts the kickstand down, murmurs something to the man in the suit waiting by the G-Wagon, and then starts walking toward us, slow and deliberate.

Iggy leans in close to me, her voice a low whisper. "I get it, Soph. I *get it*. And you know what? I'll help you get her."

"What?" I hiss, trying to keep my expression neutral as Eve approaches.

Iggy's grin turns wicked. "Because you need a little push. The kind I gave you last night. Only this time…" Her voice drops lower. "…I want you grinding on her while you moan her name."

My eyes widen, my cheeks blazing. "How are you this kinky, Montana girl?" I whisper back.

"I was born this way," she says with a wink. "And I'll die this way—probably after joining a cult or starring in some indie porn flick." Then, she leans even closer, her lips brushing against my ear. "But promise me this: if I help you get her, one day, you and Eve invite me for a threesome. I'll deserve it, won't I?"

I can't believe what I'm hearing, but I nod, unable to form words. "Done," I manage, just as Eve stops in front of us.

Iggy straightens immediately, all sweet, small-town girl vibes again. "Miss Lockhart! What a badass entrance!" she says, pulling Eve into a hug as if last night's conversation never happened. "You need to teach me how to ride one of those."

Eve raises an eyebrow, clearly unaccustomed to Iggy's level of enthusiasm. "You can start by not sneaking off into the woods at night, like you did last month." she quips dryly.

Miriam joins us, carrying the packed lunches. "Emmy, did you have fun?" she asks, patting her daughter's shoulder.

"Yes, Miriam! I love it here!" Emmy beams.

"Glad to hear it," Miriam replies, then turns to Eve. "I'll head back to the manor with you and the girls."

Eve nods. "Iggy, will you be okay staying here alone? I might need your mother to stay at the manor for a few nights," she asks, her tone softening slightly.

Iggy glances at me, her mischievous smile barely hidden. "You know what, Miss Lockhart? My services are probably needed at the manor, too. I think I'll come with."

I meet her eyes, and despite myself, I smile. This girl is trouble. Pure, unadulterated trouble.

Chapter Five

Eve

The low rumble of the Harley fades as I pull into the gravel lot of the Dew Point Sheriff's Office. The building is unassuming, a block of weathered brick and glass nestled on the edge of the quiet town. The porch light casts a warm halo over the sheriff's star on the door, the faint chatter of voices inside drifting into the cool evening air.

I step in, boots clicking on the polished floor as I take in the small, orderly space. A few deputies glance my way but don't linger. The hum of activity is constant: dispatch radios crackle, phones ring, and papers shuffle.

I make my way past the main area toward Tessa's office. Her nameplate gleams on the frosted glass door, and through it, I see her sitting at her desk.

When I step inside, the first thing I notice is her uniform. The tailored navy-blue shirt fits snugly against her slim, athletic frame, the silver badge on her chest gleaming. Her breasts, almost too full for her build, press against the fabric just enough to be distracting if you let it. The dark utility belt at her hips adds a stark contrast, emphasizing her lithe figure.

Her raven-black hair is pulled into a sleek high ponytail, not a strand out of place. Her face is as sharp as I remember: a chiseled jawline, deep-set black eyes that seem to read you like a file, and thin lips that curl into a subtle, knowing smirk when she spots me. Her chin is pointed, adding to her severe, commanding appearance, though I know the sharpness fades in certain situations—situations I once knew too well.

She's reclined in her leather chair, flipping through papers with an air of authority. Tessa always had a way of wearing power like it was stitched into her skin. She's not just in the room; she owns it.

"Evelyn Lockhart," she says, her voice steady, though her eyes glint with amusement as they sweep over me. "I heard the Harley. You sure know how to make an entrance."

I lean against the doorframe, arms crossed. "And you sure know how to keep me waiting."

Her lips twitch upward in a half-smile as she leans forward, resting her elbows on the desk. "For me, I think it's worth it."

I settle into the chair across from Tessa, the leather creaking under me. She looks up, dark eyes sharp as always, and leans back in her chair, arms crossing over her chest in a way that's both dismissive and inviting.

"How are you holding up?" I ask, keeping my voice neutral, probing.

She tilts her head, a faint smile tugging at her lips. "Oh, you know. Living the dream—if the dream involves leading a pack of testosterone-fueled deputies who hate taking orders from a woman."

I let out a low chuckle. "Sounds familiar. You and I could write the book on that."

Her smirk widens, but her gaze doesn't soften. "How are Sophia and Emmy? When do I get to meet them?"

"Whenever you want. You just have to drop by."

Tessa leans forward now, resting her elbows on the desk. "I think I lost those privileges a long time ago."

My eyes meet hers without hesitation. "You only lost the privilege of seeing me naked. You still have an open invitation to my house."

That gets a laugh out of her, low and throaty. "What's the point of coming over if I can't see you naked?"

I narrow my eyes at her, my voice dropping. "You really think that's all our friendship was about?"

Her smile turns wicked, black eyes glinting. "Let's not kid ourselves, Evelyn. 'That'"—she gestures loosely with her hand—"included the most mind-blowing sex of our lives. Without it, we'd have burned out fast. You're too stubborn, and I'm too damn proud."

My lips curve into a half-smile. "So, now that 'that' is off the table, how long before we explode?"

Tessa leans back, her grin smug. "Oh, I wouldn't say it's off the table. Let's just call it…paused. I haven't given up on seeing you naked again."

I roll my eyes, though my lips twitch in amusement. "You still have my nudes. Isn't that enough?"

She snorts, shaking her head. "A picture? That's crumbs, Eve. I want the whole meal."

I shake my head, leaning forward. "Anyway, I didn't come here to trade innuendos with you."

Tessa's smirk fades slightly, but the glint in her eye lingers. "Then what are you here for, Lockhart?"

"I need to talk about my nieces' security. And the Carmine case. Did you get any leads on that email?"

Her expression sharpens in an instant, all traces of teasing gone. "Not yet. Whoever sent it knew what they were doing—clean as hell. But we're digging. I'll let you know the second we have anything."

"Good," I say, my tone clipped, though a part of me itches at the uncertainty. "I don't like not knowing who's watching."

Tessa leans closer, her voice soft but laced with steel. "Neither do I. And for what it's worth? If someone's messing with you, I'll make sure they regret it."

I meet her gaze, my lips curving faintly. "You're still good at the promises, Sheriff."

"And you're still good at making me want to keep them," she replies, her tone low and charged.

I lean back in the chair, crossing one leg over the other, trying to shake the heat from Tessa's last comment. I sideline the flirting with a clearing of my throat and focus on what I came here for.

"Have you received anything new about the investigations in Los Angeles?" I ask, my voice steady but probing. "What the hell was my brother involved in with the Carmines? They don't just shoot families for fun. It's messy, and the mafia rarely resorts to something so public."

Tessa leans back, the teasing light in her eyes dimming as her expression grows serious. She takes a slow, deep breath, her fingers drumming on the desk. "The LAPD isn't exactly forthcoming, but through my contacts, I've pieced together a few things. Turns out, James helped the Carmines smuggle drugs through his shipping company about three years ago."

My stomach tightens at her words, but I don't interrupt. Tessa continues.

"Maybe they came back to him, wanted him to do it again, and he refused. Or maybe he decided to work for someone else—the Morenos, for instance, who've been making moves in Carmine territory. Either way, he pissed off someone powerful. This wasn't random. This was calculated."

My jaw tightens, and I nod slowly, processing the weight of her words. "And the police out there?"

"Corrupt," she says bluntly, leaning forward as her voice drops into a hushed whisper. "The Carmines have deep roots in the LAPD. That's why it was good you brought the girls here, Eve. My department may be small, but we're loyal. I can promise you that."

I let out a slow exhale, my gaze fixed on hers. "Thank you, Tessa."

She nods but doesn't let the moment linger. "I've increased patrols on the freeway connecting Dew Point to the city, just in case. There's an officer stationed at every major junction now. I've also added more patrols on the road leading to the manor. We've installed new CCTV cameras along the route and at the town's entrance."

"That's a start," I say, my tone measured.

"I've also put in a request for additional officers for the department," she adds. "Hopefully, they'll approve it soon."

Her dedication is clear, but the pit in my stomach remains. "The Carmines aren't amateurs, Tessa. This will only buy us time."

Tessa tilts her head, her voice steady. "And time is exactly what you need to figure out what the hell they want. They'll make a move, but when they do, we'll be ready."

I nod again, her confidence grounding me. But in the back of my mind, I know—time only works if I use it wisely.

Tessa leans back in her chair, crossing her arms as she studies me with that piercing, unreadable gaze of hers. "Have you talked to Sophia? About the email—the part where it said, 'the girl still has something of ours?'"

I shake my head, keeping my voice calm. "I don't want to scare her. She and Emmy are finally settling in. Sophia's even made a friend—Miriam's daughter, Iggy. Although..." I pause, a smirk playing on my lips. "I think Iggy has a crush on her."

Tessa raises an eyebrow, a slow, knowing grin spreading across her face. "Oh, Iggy? Miriam's wild child?" She chuckles, tapping her fingers on the desk. "That tracks. She's got that free-spirited vibe. Didn't she try to get in bed with you too?"

I laugh, shaking my head. "Iggy's harmless. Plus, she's not Sophia's type."

Tessa narrows her eyes, leaning forward with an amused look. "And how exactly do you know your niece's type?"

I shrug nonchalantly, trying to downplay the question. "We were close once, when she was just a kid. Before I had to leave for that undercover assignment. After that, we grew distant, but I'm trying to reconnect. So yeah, we talk."

Tessa picks up the phone on her desk, pressing a button on the intercom. "Two coffees," she says, her voice steady. Then she hangs up and looks at me curiously. "You hate to talk, Eve. You hate getting close. That's why you pushed me away."

The air feels heavier, and I let out a sigh. "This is different, Tess. She's family. And she's all alone. I need to get out of my comfort zone for her."

Tessa tilts her head, her lips pressing into a thin line. "Yeah, well, I wasn't family. Guess I wasn't close enough for you to make that kind of effort."

My eyes flick to hers, sharp and warning. "Don't do this again, Tess. We were great at sex, but we would've sucked at a relationship."

She lets out a bitter laugh, shaking her head. "We could've tried, you know."

I raise an eyebrow, a faint smirk tugging at my lips. "The police and the military don't mix well. Too much discipline on both sides."

"That's bullshit, and you know it," she counters, her voice quiet but firm. "Two people in love can make it work—doesn't matter the age, gender, or profession."

I lean back, my eyes locking with hers. "Maybe that was the problem. We weren't in love."

Her smile falters slightly, but she doesn't look away. For a moment, silence stretches between us, heavy with words unspoken. Then, the door opens, and a deputy steps in, carrying two steaming cups of coffee. Tessa takes hers without breaking our gaze, and I sip mine, letting the bitterness bite against my tongue.

"Fair enough," she finally says, leaning back. "But for what it's worth, Eve, I'm glad you're here. And I'll make sure your nieces are safe."

I nod, my voice quiet. "Thank you, Tess."

∞∞∞

The woods are quiet except for the faint rustling of leaves in the breeze and the occasional snap of a twig beneath our boots. My eyes sweep the dense treeline, cataloging every shadow, every flicker of movement. The guard trails behind us, silent but alert, his steady presence giving me room to scan the surroundings.

Then I see her.

Sophia and Iggy walk ahead, descending the gentle slope with an ease I can't seem to muster. Miriam hums softly up front, Emmy skips a few paces ahead, but my gaze is locked on the two of them. On Sophia.

She walks ahead, descending the gentle slope with Iggy at her side, and every inch of my body tenses. I shouldn't be looking, shouldn't be letting my gaze linger the way it does, but it's impossible to stop. Those denim shorts—tiny, frayed, clinging to her desperately, knowing how well they wrap around her delicious ass—are a sin all their own. They ride high, leaving the golden expanse of her thighs bare, and when she steps, I catch glimpses of the curve beneath, teasing me, mocking me with what I can't have. Her legs are strong, toned from the hours she's spent moving around the estate, but soft in all the ways that make me ache.

She shouldn't be wearing that bikini top, either. The knot at her back is a single pull away from unraveling, from giving me everything I've spent the last few nights imagining. Her shoulders are bare, smooth, and sun-kissed, catching the dappled sunlight that filters through the trees. Her hips sway with an unintentional rhythm that pulls my eyes lower, and lower still, until I'm biting down on the inside of my cheek just to steady myself.

And that ass—God, that ass. It's the kind that haunts a man. Perfectly rounded, the kind you want to grab with both hands, to squeeze and spread and bury yourself in until you lose your damn mind. My fingers flex involuntarily, aching to feel the heat of her skin, the weight of her in my hands. I wonder if it's as soft as it looks or if it's firm enough to leave bruises—if she'd arch into my touch, gasping my name, or if she'd bite her lip to keep from crying out.

I know I shouldn't be thinking about her like this. She's James's stepdaughter. She's here to feel safe, not to be devoured. But fuck, the thoughts won't stop. They never do.

Iggy's hand is on her waist, and it makes my teeth grind. She leans into Sophia, laughing at something she's said, and my fists curl at my sides. I imagine how easy it would be to close the distance, to replace Iggy's hand with mine. To slide it lower, cupping her ass, feeling the way she'd tense under my touch. Would she gasp, startled? Or would she lean back into me, letting me know exactly how much she wants this—wants me?

The memories of other women flood my mind. The way I've gripped hips so tightly they bruised, pinned bodies beneath me, made them beg with every thrust of my tongue or bite of my teeth. I remember the marks I've left—the faint purples and reds, the crescent shapes from my nails, the soft whimpers and sharp gasps. They've begged for more, for less, for everything. And I gave it to them. Every. Single. Time.

But this? With Sophia? It wouldn't just be claiming—it would be devouring. Worshiping. Destroying. I'd ruin her in the most beautiful way, dragging cries and moans from her throat that no one else could ever match. I'd push her to the edge of sanity, make her body tremble and quake under mine, leave her soaked and shattered, her voice hoarse from screaming my name.

She bends slightly, adjusting her sandal, and the sight of her ass tilting higher nearly makes me groan out loud. My thoughts spiral further, darker, filthier. I imagine peeling those shorts off her slowly, my fingers tracing the delicate lines of her hips. Sliding the bikini top down her arms until her chest is bare, her nipples hardening under the cool air—and under my mouth, my tongue, my teeth.

She shouldn't look like this. She shouldn't move like this. And I shouldn't be standing here, wondering if she's ever touched herself while thinking about me—if those delicate fingers of hers have slid between her thighs at night, her breath hitching as she whispers my name in the dark.

The sound of Emmy squealing breaks my reverie. She dashes toward the lake, Mr. Wonkers bouncing in her hand, completely oblivious to the storm raging inside me. I force myself to look away, to focus on the shimmering water ahead, its surface reflecting the golds and greens of the surrounding forest. But it doesn't work. The lake is stunning, sure, but it's nothing compared to her.

Sophia laughs, the sound light and airy, and it pulls my gaze right back to her. She leans into Iggy again, their closeness sparking a heat in my chest that feels dangerously close to jealousy. I hate it—hate the way Iggy gets to be near her, touch her, make her laugh.

My fingers curl into fists as my mind betrays me again, imagining sliding those shorts down her legs, feeling the heat of her pussy against my tongue, pressing her against a tree, and taking her until she's crying out, begging for more. The thought is maddening, and I hate myself for wanting it. For wanting her.

But none of that matters. Not when she's everything I know I shouldn't want.

And everything I can't stop craving.

∞∞∞

Miriam fusses with the picnic. Iggy's laughter rings out as she dives into the lake. Emmy yelps, still clutching Mr. Wonkers, until Miriam promises she'll guard him like a treasure. But all of it is background noise.

Sophia's thumbs hook into the waistband of her shorts. A shimmy, slow and deliberate, as the fabric slides down her thighs. Bare skin, golden and smooth, flashes in the sunlight.

She steps out, kicks the shorts aside, and turns her head—those green eyes, sharp as glass, lock onto me.

"Get to stripping, Eve."

The corner of my mouth twitches. Her gaze is heavy, burning. I pull off my shirt, one motion, and toss it. Her eyes roam over me, deliberate and slow. My fingers move to the button of my shorts.

She flicks her tongue over her lips. A quick, teasing dart. Her smile—soft, sharp, gone. Then back again. She tilts her head.

"Do you even know what fat is?" Her voice is low, daring. "Ever heard of it?"

"Not since 17."

A quick laugh, short, wicked. Her lips curve wider. "Bet you were such a hottie at 17."

"Am I not now?" The words slip, unfiltered.

Her toes graze mine as she steps closer. Heat rolls off her skin.

"Oh, you are," she murmurs, her gaze dragging up, slow, from my stomach to my chest to my eyes. Her voice drops lower. "You make a girl wonder… how far she's willing to sin."

"Sin?" It's barely a word, caught in my throat.

She leans in, so close I can feel her breath. "You make her want to be bad, Auntie," she whispers. A pause. "Very bad."

She pulls back just as quickly. A wink. Then she's walking away, her hips swaying, the curve of her ass peeking out from her bikini bottom. Her laughter mixes with Emmy's as she wades into the water, her body glistening in the sun.

I don't move. Can't. My nails dig into my palms as my heart slams against my ribs. My head? Wrecked. My body? A live wire.

Sophia's laughter floats back to me, bright and carefree. But the heat she's left behind isn't.

It's *burning*.

The water feels cool against my skin, a soothing contrast to the heat burning beneath it. I move effortlessly through the lake, each stroke powerful and sure. The sound of Sophia's laughter fades as I push forward, my focus sharp, my body cutting through the water with practiced ease.

I reach the opposite bank in no time, standing and smoothing my hair back with both hands. The sunlight dances on the surface of the lake, glinting like shards of glass. The woods around me are alive with the sound of rustling leaves and distant birdsong, but it all feels far away.

Then I hear it—Sophia's splash, her determined strokes breaking the water as she swims toward me. She's slower, her movements less polished, but there's something about the way she's coming toward me that makes my chest tighten.

I wait, watching her approach, until she's just a few feet away. Sophia gasps, her breath coming in heavy pants, and I move instinctively, stepping into the water to meet her.

"You okay?" I ask, a chuckle slipping out before I can stop it. "You look like you're about to drown."

Her cheeks flush, and she glares up at me, water dripping from her chin. "You shouldn't laugh," she says between gulps of air, her voice low and teasing. "Not at a girl who risked her life to come to you."

The words hit me square in the chest, and for a moment, the world seems to tilt. There's something about the way she says it —so soft, so vulnerable—that makes my throat tighten. My heart beats faster, louder.

"Come on," I say, my voice gentler now. "Let's sit in the shade."

I guide her toward the large oak tree near the edge of the bank, its sprawling branches casting a cool shadow over the grass. Sophia collapses onto the ground, her legs stretched out, her chest heaving as she tries to catch her breath. I sit beside her, the damp earth cool beneath us, and instinctively place my hand on her back, rubbing slow, soothing circles.

"You didn't have to swim all the way over here if you're out of practice," I say, my voice low.

She turns her head, her green eyes locking onto mine, her cheeks still pink from the exertion. "I wanted to come to you," she murmurs, her words broken by shallow breaths.

Something shifts inside me. Her voice, the way her body leans just slightly toward mine, the vulnerability in her gaze—it's almost too much. For a brief, reckless moment, I imagine pulling her into my arms, holding her close, feeling her heartbeat against mine.

Instead, I force myself to look away, focusing on the rippling water instead of the temptation sitting so close I can feel the warmth of her skin.

"You're crazy," I mutter, shaking my head, but there's no bite in my words.

Sophia laughs softly, the sound light and airy, like she doesn't regret a thing.

And damn it, neither do I.

"I know what you're doing, Sophia," I say, my voice low, cracking under the weight of restraint. Her breathing finally steadies, but my eyes betray me. They're locked on the droplets of water sliding down her chest, disappearing beneath the thin triangle of her bikini top. My throat tightens. I should look away.

I don't.

She smirks, leaning back on her hands, her wet hair clinging to her neck and shoulders. "What am I doing, Eve?" she purrs, her green eyes glinting like she knows exactly how far she's pushing me. A drop of water rolls down her collarbone, over the curve of her breast, and my pulse hammers in my ears.

"You're teasing," I mutter, my gaze flickering up to meet hers, but it's a losing battle. "That thing you said before running into the water. What did it mean?"

She tilts her head, a strand of hair slipping over her cheek. Her lips part just slightly, soft, wet, and utterly maddening. "It meant exactly what you think it meant," she says, her voice dipping lower, huskier. Her leg shifts, brushing mine, her skin warm and slick from the water.

"Sophia, you keep—" My voice falters as her knee presses against my thigh. "You keep flirting with me, and it's dangerous."

"Dangerous?" she echoes, her smirk deepening. "Or exciting?"

"Stop," I growl, but even I can hear the weakness in my tone.

"Why should I?" she challenges, sitting up straighter, her body inching closer. "What's so dangerous about wanting you, Eve? What's so dangerous about imagining your hands on me, your mouth…" She trails off, her gaze dropping to my lips before flicking back up. "…everywhere?"

I swallow hard, my nails biting into my palms. "Because it's wrong."

"Cliché," she interrupts, rolling her eyes, her voice full of mockery. "You're going to pull the *forbidden card* on me? Really? We're not even blood-related."

"That doesn't matter," I snap, but the words feel hollow. "We shared a bond that felt like we were. You were a kid—"

"No!" she snaps back, her voice sharp, trembling. "Whatever I felt for you then wasn't innocent, and you know it."

"Don't say it," I hiss, stepping back, but her words hang in the air like a live wire.

"Don't tell me what to do… *Mommy*," she murmurs, her voice dripping with provocation as the word slips from her lips. Her leg presses harder against mine, the heat of her skin burning into me, daring me to respond. My chest tightens, my breath catches, and my resolve starts to crack.

"Sophia…" My voice is a warning, but it sounds weak even to my own ears.

"I'm nineteen, Eve," she says, leaning in, her lips hovering dangerously close to my ear. "I'm not a kid anymore. I'm not your blood. But I am someone who's so fucking ruined by you I can't think straight." Her fingers graze my wrist, soft, teasing, deliberate. "You think I'm flirting? No, Auntie, I'm begging. Begging for you to notice me. Begging for you to take me apart."

"Stop," I murmur, but there's no conviction in my voice. Her words cut deeper than they should.

"I can't stop," she says, her voice breaking. "Because I adored you, Eve. I worshiped you as a kid, and now, as an adult, I still do—but it's not the same anymore. It's not innocent. It's raw and messy and…" She pauses, drawing in a shaky breath. "I'm terrified you'll abandon me again. That you'll leave me and Emmy like you did before and completely shatter me all over again. But I'm so shameless, so ruined by you, that I don't even care anymore."

"Stop," I whisper again, my heart pounding as I meet her gaze.

"I can't," she breathes, her voice trembling but resolute. "Because no matter how wrong you think it is… I've never wanted anyone the way I want you."

The tension between us is suffocating, as if the weight of her words has sucked all the air out of the world. I push her leg away—not hard, but firm enough to put space between us—and stand, glaring at her. My jaw clenches as I struggle to keep my voice even.

"James wouldn't have wanted this," I say, my words clipped and deliberate. Her expression falters, but I keep going. "Right now, the only thing on my mind is protecting you and Emmy. Keeping you both alive. Making sure that Mafia scum leaves you alone for good. So you can start fresh in college. So you can have a life, Sophia. A real one."

Sophia stands too, defiance sparking in her green eyes. "And what if that life includes you? What if that's all I want?"

I exhale sharply, running a hand through my damp hair. "You don't know what you're saying. I understand teenage crushes, Soph. These... hormones—they don't see age, gender, or the relationship you have with the person you're lusting after. But all of this? It'll go away the moment you're in college. There'll be other girls. Younger, happier, more flamboyant. Girls who are your type. Ones you can talk about makeup and shopping with."

"I don't want girls!" she snaps, her voice trembling with emotion. "I want a woman. You."

I freeze. She steps closer, her hands clenched at her sides, her voice steady now. "What if those girls are too immature? Too soft? I want your hard body, Eve. I want your arms around me, grounding me, telling me I'm safe. That I'm with someone different—someone they don't make anymore. You are above and beyond any girl I'll ever meet in college."

Her words pierce through me, and I can't breathe. She continues, relentless. "And James—my stepfather, my father—would have wanted his daughter to end up with someone strong. Someone like you. Just as long as you don't abandon me."

I shake my head, retreating a step. "Never happening, Soph. This world won't accept us. I won't accept myself."

Sophia doesn't flinch. Instead, she lifts her chin, her eyes blazing. "Let's see about that."

Her words linger, hanging in the humid air. The wind rustles the oak leaves above us, filling the heavy silence. Across the lake, I hear the faint squeals of Emmy and Iggy, their laughter carrying in the breeze.

Then the sky shifts. Clouds roll in, blanketing the sun, casting a shadow over the lake. Instinctively, my eyes scan the treeline, my soldier's instincts prickling.

"It's time to head back," I say, my voice firmer than before. Without waiting for her reply, I turn, leading the way.

Behind me, I feel her gaze burning into my back, as if her defiance could unravel the walls I've spent years building around myself.

The tension lingers between us as I step into the lake, the cool water biting at my calves. I don't look back at Sophia. I can't. Her words are still ringing in my head, too sharp, too raw, cutting me open in places I've kept sealed for years.

I push forward, diving in. The cold envelops me, shocking my senses into focus. Stroke after stroke, I force myself to concentrate. This is muscle memory—breathe, push, glide. I tell myself it's the same as every other swim, but my chest is tight, my mind slipping back to her voice, her words, her... everything.

A scream splits the air.

My head jerks up, and my heart stops. Sophia. She's clutching her neck, her face twisted in pain, the water rippling around her.

I don't think. I move.

Wading back toward her feels like swimming through cement. My pulse is a roar in my ears. Gunfire flashes in my mind—blood, chaos. No. Not her. Not now. By the time I reach her, my hands are trembling.

"What's wrong?" I demand, grabbing her shoulders. "Are you hit? Show me."

She pulls her hand away, revealing the red mark on her neck. For a second, I can't breathe, and then relief floods me so hard it's dizzying.

"It's just a horsefly," I say, my voice shaking more than I want to admit. "A bite. That's all."

Her laugh is shaky, her shoulders still trembling. "You're sure?"

I nod, my thumb brushing gently over the swollen area. "Positive. Nasty little bastards, but nothing deadly. Hold still." Before I can think twice, I lean in, my lips pressing lightly against her skin. It's instinctive, a move I can't even justify to myself, but it feels right. Too right.

The warmth of her skin, the taste of lake water and salt—it lingers longer than it should. I pull back sharply, clearing my throat. "That should help."

Her eyes meet mine, wide and searching, and I have to look away. My hands are still on her arms, steadying her, grounding her, but I'm the one who feels like I'm going to collapse.

I take a steadying breath, trying to recalibrate my heart rate as Sophia looks at me, her fingers gingerly brushing the red mark on her neck. "The bite will sting if you try to swim back," I say, my voice calm, though I feel anything but. "The water's too deep for you to wade through. Let me carry you."

Sophia freezes for a second before letting out a soft, disbelieving laugh. "You're going to carry me? Like a damsel in distress?"

I hold her gaze, unflinching. "Don't get any ideas, Sophia."

"Oh, I have *plenty* of ideas, Auntie," she purrs, her voice dripping with amusement and something darker. The way she says it—*Auntie*—makes my pulse spike.

Ignoring the way her words curl inside me, I step forward, my arms slipping around her thighs and back. I lift her easily, her body fitting against mine as if it belongs there. And then it happens—she wraps her arms around my neck, her chest pressing flush against mine, her skin warm and slick from the water. A soft sound escapes her lips—a moan. Low, quiet, but deliberate.

My breath hitches, my grip faltering for a split second as her lips brush against my neck.

"Are you enjoying this?" I growl, my voice low, rough, edged with something I can't control.

"Immensely," she murmurs, her voice barely above a whisper, her lips ghosting over the shell of my ear. "You're strong, Auntie. I like how you feel." Her nails scrape lightly along the back of my neck, sending a shiver down my spine.

My chest tightens, my skin burning wherever she touches me. Her body shifts in my hold, her thigh brushing against my hip, and the friction is maddening. I can feel the heat of her skin, the way her breath fans against my collarbone. It's unbearable.

"This is what heroes do, right?" she whispers, her voice low and teasing. "Save the girl? Carry her to safety?"

I grit my teeth, focusing on the water rising around my legs as I move. Each step feels heavier, the storm inside me threatening to break loose. "Stop," I manage, my tone sharp but cracking.

She doesn't. Instead, her lips curve into a wicked smile, and she shifts again, pressing herself tighter against me. "Why, Auntie? Afraid you might like it? Afraid you might want to hold me longer than you should?"

Her words hit like a blow, stealing the air from my lungs. My hands tighten on her thighs, and I can't stop the way my body reacts—the way every muscle tenses, every nerve ignites.

"Stop talking," I snap, but it sounds more like a plea, and her laugh—low, sultry, dangerous—sinks into my skin like poison.

Her laugh, low and wicked, seeps into my skin, and then she moves—leaning in, her teeth catching my earlobe, biting down just hard enough to make my entire body jolt. A sharp inhale escapes me as her voice follows, low and rough. "Please stop walking back to the shore," she growls, the words dripping with something dangerous.

My steps falter, the water rising around us as her legs tighten around my waist, pulling herself flush against me. Her body presses harder, her warmth seeping through the thin fabric between us. A soft moan slips from her lips, deliberate and devastating.

The friction is soft at first, just enough to ignite something I've been trying so damn hard to bury. But she knows exactly what she's doing.

"Sophia," I growl, trying to sound authoritative, but it comes out wrecked. Broken. She hears it. She feels it. And she pushes harder.

"God, I can't stop," she whispers, her voice trembling as her lips trail down my neck. "You feel too good, Auntie. You're strong and hard and—fuck—exactly what I need."

Her hips roll again, dragging her pussy, barely covered by her bikini bottom, against my stomach, and I swear I feel the heat of her through the wet fabric. My hands tighten on her thighs, trying to steady her, to stop her, but it's no use. She's relentless. Her nails dig into my shoulders, and her moan—low, breathless, filthy—slides down my spine and takes root deep in my gut.

"You can't control this," she says, her voice both taunting and pleading. "You're carrying me, protecting me. You're not responsible for me grinding my pussy against you, are you? That's on me. I'm the bad one here. I'm the one who's not listening to you. I'm the one...aaaah...fuck, those abs feel so good on my aching pussy."

Her words hit like a sledgehammer, tearing apart the thin threads of control I'm desperately clinging to. I grit my teeth, my body trembling as she grinds harder, her movements slow, deliberate, and so precise it's like she knows exactly how to destroy me.

"Sophia, stop—" I choke out, but it's weak, pathetic.

"I can't, I fucking can't..." she whispers, her voice cracking with need. "Don't you get it? I've wanted this for so long.

Her lips brush against my jawline, and my knees nearly give out as she moves again, grinding herself harder against me. My bikini shorts are soaked, and the thin barrier between us feels like nothing. Every roll of her hips sends a fresh wave of heat straight to my core, and I hate myself for the way my body responds.

"God, you're so perfect," she murmurs, her breath hot and uneven. "Strong and steady and so fucking good at pretending you don't want this." Her teeth scrape against my neck, and I let out a low, guttural sound that I can't contain.

Her hips grind harder, her body arching against me, and then her tongue glides up the side of my neck in one slow, deliberate lick. The heat of her mouth is unbearable, punctuated by a filthy, breathless moan that makes my entire body lock up. My hands, already gripping her thighs, twitch as her words slide through me like a dagger.

"Pull my panties to the side," she whispers, her voice low, dark, and utterly wrecked. Her lips hover at my ear, her breath hot and heavy as her nails dig into my shoulders. "Please, Auntie. I need you."

"No," I growl, my voice rough and uneven, my chest heaving with the effort of holding on. "I won't. You won't have your way anymore."

Sophia moans, her breath hitching in the middle of a soft, mocking laugh. "Then I'll do it myself," she purrs, her voice dripping with triumph. Her hands slide down, and for a moment, I'm frozen, watching in stunned disbelief as her fingers hook into the waistband of her bikini. She tilts her hips, brushing herself harder against me, and my grip tightens, my nails digging into her skin.

Her green eyes lock onto mine, dark and glittering. "I forgot," she breathes, her lips curling into a wicked smile. "You can't take action, can you? You can't act on your desires for me." She pauses, shifting her weight to grind against me again, her voice dropping lower. "Even though you wish I wasn't your step-niece."

"Stop," I rasp, but my hands betray me, holding her tighter as if letting go would kill me.

Sophia's smirk widens, her nails raking lightly down my back as she whispers, "Or maybe that's why your nails are biting into my ass right now. Because I *am* your step-niece. Because it makes this wrong. Because it makes this filthy."

Her words cut through me, devastating and undeniable. My breath is ragged, my heart pounding so hard I can hear it echoing in my ears. My hands twitch against her skin, trembling with restraint I know won't hold much longer.

Sophia's eyes glint with something feral, unrestrained, as her fingers trail down between our bodies. "Then I'll do it myself," she whispers, her voice drenched in both desperation and triumph.

I freeze, my chest heaving, my grip tightening on her thighs, but I can't stop her. I don't move. My breath catches as her hand slips between us, hooking the thin, soaked fabric of her bikini bottom and dragging it to the side. My stomach flips as the warmth of her hits me—nothing between us now but the slickness of her skin against mine.

Heat radiates from her, molten and unbearable, and it's like my body forgets how to function. My muscles lock, my mind spins, and for a second, the world narrows to that one point of contact. The softness of her against me. The damp, searing heat of her swollen pussy pressing into my skin. It's too much. It's everything.

Sophia lets out a soft, breathless moan as she adjusts her hips, grinding herself harder against my bare stomach. My throat tightens, a low, guttural sound clawing its way out of me as my hands twitch against her thighs.

"God, Auntie," she murmurs, her voice trembling, her nails scraping down my shoulders. "You feel so good. So warm. So… strong." Her hips roll, the slickness of her pussy gliding against me, and my legs almost give out.

I can't think. I can't breathe. Every nerve in my body is screaming, every muscle trembling as she moves against me, unrelenting.

And then something inside me snaps.

With a growl, I shift my grip on her thighs, my body moving before my mind can catch up. My thigh jerks upward, sliding between her legs, and the sound she makes—the half-scream, half-moan that rips from her throat—tears through me like a live wire. She slides down onto my thigh, her warmth flush against me, and her whole body shudders as she grips my shoulders harder, clinging to me like I'm the only thing keeping her upright.

Sophia's breath comes in shallow gasps as she rocks against me, her head falling forward, her lips brushing my ear. "See?" she gasps, her voice wild and uneven. "I knew you'd make things easier for me."

Her hips move faster, grinding harder, her slickness smearing against my skin with every roll of her body. She moans again, louder this time, and it's raw, shameless, desperate.

My gaze is on the opposite bank in a flash. Enemy and Iggy's back is to us, and Miriam is busy setting up lunch on the blanket.

"But don't worry," she continues, her voice breaking into a filthy laugh. "You still didn't do anything, Auntie. You were just… tired of holding me." She grinds down harder, her fingers tangling in my hair as her nails rake against my scalp. "You just let my aching, wet pussy slide onto your thigh to... catch a break."

Her words are a wrecking ball, smashing through the last fragments of my restraint. My breath comes in ragged gasps as her movements grow wilder, her body trembling with every desperate grind. The heat between us is unbearable, and my hands—God help me—tighten on her thighs, pulling her down, holding her in place as she moves.

Her moans grow louder, sharper, every sound tearing through me like fire. And I can't stop it. I don't want to stop it. She's completely unhinged, and I'm drowning in her, sinking deeper into something I can't control and don't want to escape.

Sophia's movements grow frantic, her nails digging into my shoulders as her pussy grinds harder against my thigh. The slickness between us is undeniable now, every roll of her body leaving her wetter, hotter, more desperate. Her breath is coming in sharp gasps, each one hitting my neck like fire.

"Oh God, oh God, oh my fucking...fuck! " she moans, her voice breaking into something high-pitched and raw. "You feel so fucking good. So strong. So perfect."

Her thighs tremble around me, her grip tightening as her movements become erratic. She's completely lost now, her head falling back, exposing the curve of her throat as her lips part in a breathless gasp. Her hips buck against me, faster, harder, dragging herself against my skin with an intensity that makes my chest tighten, my body burn.

I see her tongue, and a relentless urge to stick my tongue down her open mouth, down her elegant throat overtakes me.

Fuck you, Sophia! You're making me burn with lust for you!

"Auntie," she breathes, her voice trembling, her nails raking down my back as she grips me like I'm her lifeline. "I can't—fuck

—I'm so close. Don't stop. Don't fucking stop."

I'm not moving. I'm frozen in place, but her body keeps going, grinding harder, faster, her slickness gliding against my thigh with every frantic roll of her hips. My hands are locked on her thighs, trembling as I try to keep some semblance of control, but it's slipping—God, it's slipping.

"Look at me," she gasps, her voice cracking as she drags her lips across my neck, her breath hot and uneven. "Look at me while I cum on you."

Her words hit me like a blow, and my eyes snap to hers. They're wild, glazed with need, her pupils blown wide as her mouth falls open in a moan that's so filthy, so wrecked, it sets every nerve in my body on fire.

Her hips stutter, her movements losing their rhythm as her entire body tenses. Her nails bite into my skin, and then she lets out a scream—a broken, desperate sound that I muffle with my hand.

She whimpers, moans through my hand, her lust glazed green eyes staring me down with a plea, to let her scream out her orgasm, to let her tell the woods she's come undone for her Eve. For her protector. For her *Aunt*.

Her head falls forward, her breath hitching in sharp, uneven gasps as her body shudders, grinding down against me one last time, harder, slower, dragging out every second of her release.

"Oh fuck," she whispers, her voice trembling, her lips brushing against my ear. "Fuck, Auntie, that was—" She cuts off with a moan, her body still trembling as her thighs loosen around me.

The air is thick, charged, heavy with the scent of her. Her head rests against my shoulder, her breath hot against my neck as she comes down, her body still pressed tightly against mine. My hands are trembling, my heart pounding, every inch of me screaming with the weight of what just happened.

And Sophia?

She smirks, her lips curving into something wicked as she lifts her head, her green eyes meeting mine. "See?" she murmurs, her voice soft, smug, and devastating. "You didn't do anything, Auntie. I took care of myself."

Her words hit like a dagger, and I swallow hard, my body still trembling under her weight.

∞∞∞

The walk back is quieter than it should be, at least in my head. Emmy skips ahead with Miriam and Iggy, her laughter carrying through the trees, but I can't focus. My arms feel heavier, even though I'm no longer carrying her.

Her.

Sophia. Grinding against me. Whispering filth into my ear, stealing my breath, my sanity, and whatever sliver of control I had left.

What the hell is wrong with me? How could I let her? Stand there, frozen, while she… *used* me?

I bite the inside of my cheek, hard, and it's not enough to snap me out of the whirlwind in my head. My soldier's instincts, so honed, so disciplined, had dissolved the second her pussy descended on my thigh in the water. I had been nothing but raw nerves and longing. I had *wanted* it. Wanted her to keep going, to keep saying those dirty little words, to cross every line there was.

Worse, I had wanted to *act*. Just being a silent, dripping spectator had been a victory, because what I had wanted to do —what I *could* have done to her—would have left no room for apologies.

Can you *really* apologize after shoving two fingers deep in your step-niece's pussy, feeling it tighten around you?
Are there words that could justify ripping her bra off with trembling hands and stuffing her perfect, soft breast into your mouth, your teeth leaving marks on her skin?
No. There aren't.

But I wanted to do all of that and more. So much more. And the weight of that want—the aching, unrelenting need—makes me want to shoot myself in the head.

She's grieving. She's lost her parents, her entire sense of stability. This isn't love, no matter how desperately I want to believe it. This is her clinging to whatever makes her feel alive. Whatever makes her forget. I don't even think she realizes how dangerous it is—what we are, what we *could* become.

And me? I'm supposed to protect her. Not give in to her whims, no matter how tempting. I need to be stronger. For her. For Emmy. For myself.

The towering walls of the estate come into view, and the wrought-iron gate stands ajar. Miriam leads the group through, one by one, the small door at the side allowing passage for those on foot. Sophia hesitates at the threshold, her green eyes locking with mine. There's something there—pleading, regret, even shame. Her lips part, as if she wants to say something, but I shake my head imperceptibly. I can't let her crack me again.

I look away and scan the clearing. That's when I see them. Tire marks. Fresh, clear grooves pressed into the dirt. They weren't there when we left. My gut tightens.

"Miriam," I call out, forcing my tone to stay calm. "Take the girls inside. I'll join you in a moment."

She hesitates, looking at me with concern. I give her a small nod, reassuring her, though my hand instinctively brushes the grip of the small pistol strapped to my thigh.

Sophia lingers, her gaze flickering between me and the tracks. I see the questions in her eyes, the apologies too, but I steel myself and wave her on.

"Go," I say, firmer than I intend. Her face falls for a moment before she slips through the gate without another word. I watch her disappear into the estate, my chest aching in a way that makes no sense.

Turning back to the tracks, I crouch to study them. Wide, deep treads. A truck or SUV. They veer off into the woods, toward a service road that's supposed to be locked at all times.

Someone was here. Watching? Scouting?

The grooves are deep and wide, unmistakably fresh. I crouch closer, running my fingers over the disturbed dirt. The pattern of the treads is familiar. My chest tightens.

A Cadillac.

Not just any car—this is the make of the SUV that blocked James's car before his life was stolen. I don't know if it's the same one, but it's enough to set my instincts ablaze.

I rise, pulling my pistol from its holster. My entire body is on high alert, every muscle tensed as I scan the area. The tracks lead further down the service road, snaking into the shadows where the trees grow thicker.

They were *here*.

The thought sends a fresh wave of anger coursing through me, but I temper it with focus. Moving swiftly, I follow the tracks. My boots crunch against the gravel, my pistol aimed downward but ready.

I follow the tracks, my steps measured but quick, my ears attuned to every rustle, every shift in the wind.

The tracks lead to the service road—a private route leading to the lake. It should be locked. Always.

As I round a bend in the service road, my worst fear materializes. The gate—a heavy metal door meant to remain locked—is ajar. The chain and padlock lie broken in the dirt, discarded like an afterthought.

I step closer, my fingers brushing the mangled lock.

How long were they here? What did they see?

The thought ignites a deep-seated panic I haven't felt in years. Without hesitating, I step through the gate and follow the tracks beyond it. They lead toward the main road that connects Dew Point to the estate. My breaths are measured, my eyes darting to every shadow, every hint of movement.

Then, I break into a sprint.

My feet pound against the ground as I tear up the service road, the wind biting against my face. The trees rush past, blurred streaks of green and brown. The pistol in my hand feels heavier with every step, but I don't stop. I can't stop.

My lungs burn, my legs scream at me to slow down, but I push harder. The thought of danger creeping this close to Sophia and Emmy is enough to drown out every physical protest.

Finally, I reach the main road. My chest heaves as I halt abruptly, scanning the area. The asphalt stretches endlessly in both directions, flanked by dense woods. My eyes strain against the distance, searching for movement, for any sign of a black Cadillac.

Nothing.

The silence is deafening. No cars. No cameras—there are none here yet. We weren't expecting this. I wasn't expecting this.

I turn back toward the gate, studying the tracks and the direction they came from. The air feels heavy with warning, and my pulse won't slow.

They're testing us. Watching.

I grip the pistol tighter, swallowing hard. They think they're sending a message.

Let them come.

Chapter Six

Sophia

One Week Later

She has abandoned me again.

This time, her body is still around me, but her emotions aren't. She's a ghost that haunts the estate in camo shorts and tank tops, barking orders to the security team, sharpening her knives, and teaching me how to shoot like I'm some lost cause she regrets signing up for. She barely speaks to me unless it's to criticize how my form is "still all wrong" or to mock me for being unable to hit a stationary target, or, sometimes when we are alone in the shooting range, she reminds me how what I did at the lake a week before was immature.

I meet her barbs with some of my own, not to be outdone. I remind her how her nails had dug into my thighs that day at the lake, leaving marks that I make sure she sees every morning when I come down for breakfast in the shortest skirts I can find.

I *love* teasing her.

It's the only power I have in this giant stone prison, and I wield it like a weapon. That, and teaching Emmy, which I've surprisingly gotten pretty good at. Maybe I should consider becoming a teacher when I leave the estate—if the Mafia doesn't get to me first.

Maybe I should always surround myself with kids, because kids don't roll their eyes at me when I try to joke. Kids don't think I suck at shooting guns or that it was too immature of me to lose control on my step-aunt's thighs.

Late at night, sitting on the balcony outside my room, I let my thoughts wander. The estate is quiet, the woods surrounding it still, save for the faint rustling of leaves. The sky above is endless, sprinkled with stars, a canvas I'll miss when I leave this place.

But what will I do once I'm gone?

I always wanted a college degree, but in what? My interests are scattered. I love fashion, and I love working out. Maybe I should start my own athleisure line—design clothes that scream "power" and "style." I could even have Auntie Eve model them, flaunting her abs in campaigns that would turn heads and twist hearts.

The thought makes me laugh bitterly. No, I should honor my parents instead. Start my own shipping and logistics company and learn from James' mistakes—or maybe just make my own, bigger ones.

Or... I could fulfill Mom's dream. One she handed down to me, and one that's slowly crept up on me as the days have gone by. The dream she never got to chase. Become a pilot.

The idea hits me with unexpected force each time I think about it. I lean back in my chair, staring at the stars as the cold night air brushes against my skin. A pilot. Soaring through the sky, away from the chaos, the ghosts, and the people I can't have.

Maybe I should do that. Maybe I'll finally feel free.

But as the stars wink at me, I can't help but wonder—will I ever be free of her?

In the week that has passed, the security inside and around the estate has grown to near Pentagon levels. Cameras peek at me from behind pillars, their unblinking red lights silently judging. Men in black suits follow me and Emmy as we explore the woods, their presence hovering like shadows, always just out of reach but close enough to unsettle me.

I know I'm being watched. Every moment, every step, every breath. But the question that lingers in my mind, the one I can't shake, is—does *she* watch me as well?

Does she stay up at night, alone in her study, her piercing blue eyes glued to a monitor as I sleep? Does she lean forward, her jaw tightening, her lips parting as the camera captures me shifting under the sheets, lost in dreams of her?

Sometimes, my imagination goes further. Too far, maybe. I wonder if she's installed cameras in my bedroom—secret ones, hidden in the corners or nestled behind the ornate decor. I wonder if she watches me undress, her breathing uneven as she takes in the curve of my hips, the swell of my chest, the way my fingers linger on my skin.

And in the privacy of her secret room—because of course, she'd have one—does she touch herself to the thought of me?

In my dreams, I wish she does. In my dreams, I am already hers.

But reality is harsher. Her silence is suffocating me.

I miss her. Not just the way she looks at me, though God knows I miss that hunger in her eyes—the way it sets me aflame, the way it makes me feel like the only thing that matters in her world. I miss the banter, the sharpness of her tongue that always left me craving more, even when it stung. I miss her smirks, those barely-there curves of her lips that make me want to drop to my knees and worship her strength, her beauty, her very existence.

And now, there's nothing. No banter, no smirks, no stolen moments that leave my heart racing. Just walls, cameras, shadows, and a growing void that's tearing me apart.

She's pulling away, and I don't know how to stop her.

I can feel her frustration, her anger—not just at me, but at herself. She's fighting this, fighting us, and every time she steps back, it feels like a knife twisting in my chest.

In her silence, I'm left with nothing but my thoughts, my fantasies. They're dangerous, all-consuming, but they're all I have.

I close my eyes and lean back against the balcony railing, the cold night air biting at my skin. I imagine her stepping out of the shadows, her strong arms wrapping around me, pulling me in, grounding me. I imagine her voice, low and rough, telling me to stop being so reckless, stop tempting her.

But she doesn't come.

And so, I remain here, trapped between reality and dreams, wondering if she's watching me now. Wondering if she wants me as much as I want her. Wondering if I'll ever be enough to make her stop fighting.

∞∞∞

The hum of the engine fills the air as Eve's black G-Wagon pulls up to the modest airfield. A small collection of hangars sits against a backdrop of rolling hills and a crisp Montana sky streaked with wispy clouds. My heart races—not from fear, but from excitement. I can't believe we're actually here.

I glance at Eve. Her jaw is tight, and she's gripping the steering wheel like she wants to rip it off. Her aviators shield her eyes, but I can feel the weight of her disapproval radiating from her in waves. She parks near a small office building, and for a moment, neither of us moves.

"You're still mad, aren't you?" I ask, unbuckling my seatbelt.

"I don't think you fully grasp what this entails, Sophia." Her voice is sharp, clipped.

I roll my eyes, even as a small grin tugs at my lips. "I think I grasp it just fine. You're just mad I won the argument."

Eve exhales through her nose, her hand tightening into a fist on her thigh.

It had been a battle to get here, no doubt. Eve had shot down the idea the moment I mentioned it a week ago, citing reasons that ranged from safety concerns to time constraints. But I wasn't having it. I told her—loudly, I might add—that I felt like my life was in limbo at the estate, with nothing to do but twiddle my thumbs while the world moved on without me.

"I don't even know what I'm going to study in college!" I'd shouted at her. "What if I have no real skills? This is my chance to try something I had always wanted, something challenging. Or do you want me to waste away at the estate, memorizing the number of erotic paintings on your walls?"

Eve had been unmoved until Emmy chimed in, clutching Eve's arm like she was her lifeline. "Please, Auntie Eve? Sophia's really good at math. She used to help me with my homework all the time, and I got A's because of her. She could be the best pilot ever!"

Eve had groaned, muttered something under her breath, and stalked out of the room. I thought she'd won until she announced at breakfast the next day that she'd made arrangements for me to have lessons.

And now, here we are.

I step out of the car and stretch, looking around. The air smells like jet fuel and freshly cut grass, and my nerves buzz with anticipation. A tall, lanky man in a worn leather jacket and faded jeans strides toward us. He has a weathered face, his skin kissed by years under the sun, and a baseball cap perched on his head.

"Miss Lockhart," he greets Eve with a nod, then turns to me. "And you must be Sophia. I'm Dan Carter, owner of this fine airfield and your instructor for the day."

"Nice to meet you," I say, shaking his hand. His grip is firm but warm.

Eve crosses her arms, her lips pressing into a thin line as she watches him like a hawk.

"Don't worry," Dan says with a grin. "I'll take good care of her."

"You better," Eve mutters, her voice low enough that only I catch it.

Dan leads us toward a small plane parked on the tarmac, its white body gleaming under the Montana sun. The engine cowling bears the name *Cessna 172 Skyhawk*, and I recognize it immediately from my late-night Google sprees.

"This is your starting point," Dan says, patting the fuselage affectionately. "The Cessna 172, one of the most popular training aircraft in the world. Sturdy, reliable, and forgiving for new pilots."

I beam, walking up to the plane like it's a gift waiting to be unwrapped. "Cruise speed of about 122 knots, right? And a ceiling of...what, 13,000 feet?"

Dan's eyebrows lift in surprise. "Someone's done her homework."

"Of course," I say, running my fingers along the smooth metal. "I wasn't going to walk in clueless."

Eve trails behind, her arms crossed, but I catch the slight twitch of her lips. A smile, maybe? I shake off the thought as Dan opens the pilot-side door.

"This is the cockpit," he says, motioning for me to step closer. "Dual controls, so you'll have me guiding you the whole time. That's your yoke—steering wheel, if you will. And this," he taps a dial, "is the altimeter. Tells you how high you are. Over here's the airspeed indicator, and the artificial horizon helps you keep the wings level."

I nod eagerly, leaning in to examine everything. "Throttle lever. Mixture control. Magnetic compass..." I glance at Dan for approval.

"Not bad," he says, chuckling. "Looks like you've got the basics down."

Eve finally speaks. "And the safety features?"

Dan smirks, clearly used to worried family members. "Two-way radio, transponder for air traffic control, and a reliable engine that's as easy to restart as a car."

I shoot Eve a grin. "See? I'm in good hands."

Her expression softens just a touch, but she remains silent. Inside, I'm practically bouncing with excitement.

Dan leans against the side of the plane, his grin easy and warm, the kind of grin that makes you trust him instantly. His weathered face is lined with laugh wrinkles, and his thick salt-and-pepper hair curls out from under a battered baseball cap. His flight jacket, covered in patches from different airfields and aviation clubs, screams *been there, done that*.

"You know," he starts, crossing his arms. "I wasn't always this charming. Back in the day, I was the guy who accidentally rolled a plane during a practice flight. My instructor nearly had a heart attack."

I laugh, the mental image of a younger, bumbling Dan oddly comforting. "How does someone accidentally roll a plane?"

Dan waves his hand dismissively. "Too much rudder, too little common sense. But hey, I landed us safely, so it wasn't all bad. Got me a nickname, though—'Barrel Roll Dan.'"

Eve snorts, and I whip my head around, shocked to see her cracking a smile. "You left out the part where you threw up after the landing," she says, a rare glint of humor in her voice.

"You promised to never bring that up," Dan groans, pointing at her accusingly. "See what I get for helping a friend?"

I glance between them, curious. "Wait, you two go way back?"

Dan nods, leaning closer like he's about to share a secret. "Oh, yeah. Your Auntie Eve here once saved my butt during a mission. It was my first year flying supply runs for the military, and let's just say I wasn't exactly following protocol. Got myself stuck in a tight spot overseas. Guess who swooped in, guns blazing, to haul my sorry ass out?"

Eve rolls her eyes, but there's a faint blush creeping up her neck. "You're exaggerating. You weren't *that* stuck."

"Oh, I was stuck," Dan insists. "Thought I was a goner. So, naturally, I've been her loyal minion ever since."

I grin. "Does that mean I get minion privileges too?"

Dan claps me on the shoulder, his grip firm but kind. "Kid, if you stick with flying, you'll get all the privileges. Just promise me one thing—don't pull a 'Barrel Roll Dan.' We've got a reputation to maintain."

His warmth is infectious, and I find myself relaxing even more. The anxiety I'd felt earlier melts away, replaced by genuine excitement. Eve doesn't say much, but the softness in her eyes as she watches Dan makes me think she's glad I'm in good hands.

∞∞∞

The air in the cell is damp and reeks of mildew and despair. My wrists burn against the coarse rope binding them to the chair, and my mouth tastes of metal from the gag cutting into my lips. Every inch of me aches, bruised and battered, dried blood caking my skin. The dim, flickering bulb overhead casts long shadows, making the walls close in like a suffocating tomb.

In front of me, a man sits. He's masked, but I know him. The tattoo curling around his forearm—the snake coiled around a skull—burns itself into my mind. His laugh is low and guttural at first, then grows louder, filling the room like a chorus of demons. In his hand is Mr. Wonkers, Emmy's beloved pink teddy bear, his wonky eye glaring at me like it knows what's coming.

"No," I try to scream, but the gag muffles my voice. My heart pounds as the man holds up a knife, the blade catching the dim light. His laughter crescendos, drilling into my skull until I think I'll go insane. Then, without warning, he plunges the knife into Mr. Wonkers' neck, sawing back and forth with barbaric glee.

Cotton spills out like a cloudburst, scattering across the filthy floor. But then, the cotton changes. It's not cotton—it's blood. Deep, crimson jets of blood spray everywhere, pooling and dripping.

I blink, horrified, as the teddy bear morphs into Emmy. Her lifeless eyes stare at me, her tiny body slumped, her head hanging grotesquely by threads of sinew and muscle.

"No! Emmy!" My screams tear through my throat, but the man only laughs louder. The knife glints again as he turns his soulless gaze to me.

I wake with a violent gasp, drenched in sweat, my heart

hammering against my ribs. The darkness of my room feels too thick, too silent. I clutch my chest, struggling to breathe, the phantom laughter still ringing in my ears.

The door bursts open with a thunderous bang, and I nearly scream again. A guard rushes in, his handgun drawn, eyes scanning the room like a predator ready to pounce. His sharp, angular face is stern, his movements efficient and calculated as he searches for an intruder.

"Miss Harlow, are you alright?" His voice is deep, controlled, but laced with urgency.

I clutch the blanket to my chest, trying to calm the tremors racking my body. "I'm fine," I whisper hoarsely. My throat feels raw, the words scraping out like shards of glass. "It was... just a nightmare."

The guard lowers his weapon slightly, his shoulders relaxing a fraction. "Are you sure? Should I check the perimeter?"

I shake my head quickly. "No, no need. There's no one here." My pulse is still racing, the horrific images from my dream seared into my mind.

He hesitates, watching me closely, before nodding. "If there's anything you need..."

I swallow hard, my gaze darting around the dimly lit room. The darkness feels oppressive, too much like the cell in my nightmare. My chest tightens, and I blurt out, "Actually... could you take me to Miss Lockhart's room?"

His brow furrows briefly, but he nods. "Of course, Miss Harlow. It's no trouble."

I toss the blanket aside and stand on shaky legs. The cool floor under my feet grounds me slightly, though my head still spins with the remnants of terror. I grab my robe, wrapping it tightly around me as the guard holds the door open, his presence a strange comfort.

"Thank you," I murmur, my voice barely above a whisper.

"Stay close," he says, his tone calm yet firm as he steps into the hallway, leading me through the shadowed corridors toward the only person who might make me feel safe again.

Eve

I'm already awake when I hear the footsteps. Light, tentative, but enough to rouse my instincts. My eyes snap open, and I lie still, listening. It's not one of the staff on their rounds. There's hesitation in the rhythm. Uncertainty.

The knock comes next. Soft, non-urgent, yet enough to tug me out of bed. I don't bother with a robe—what's the point? The estate is locked down, and I've lived through far worse scenarios than someone catching me in a crop top and panties.

The carpeted floor muffles my steps as I cross the room, pulling the door open with my usual precision. Standing in the dim hallway is one of the guards, his posture straight but his eyes carefully cast downward. A professional to the core.

And then there's her.

Sophia.

Her hair is wild and disheveled, strands curling in different directions like she's just wrestled a storm. Her wide green eyes are fixed on me, scanning from head to toe, drinking in every inch of my body like she's forgotten why she's here. She's not smirking now. No teasing curve to her lips. Instead, there's something raw in her gaze, something achingly soft and vulnerable.

For a moment, I can't reconcile this version of her—the one standing barefoot in the hallway, looking like she's barely holding it together—with the confident, infuriating girl I've sparred with for weeks. She's younger somehow, stripped of all her armor. And in that instant, all I can see is the child I left behind, the one I promised James I'd protect.

"Miss Harlow had a nightmare," the guard says, his voice cutting through the tension. "She asked to come here."

Sophia shifts, breaking eye contact as her fingers clutch the edges of her robe tightly. "I... I didn't want to stay alone."

Her words hit me harder than I expect. I nod, stepping aside. "Come in."

I thank the guard with a nod, closing the door softly behind him. When I turn, Sophia is standing in the middle of my room, her bare feet pressing into the thick carpet, her expression torn between defiance and something that looks alarmingly like guilt. She's clutching her arms, her silk nightdress shimmering in the faint light streaming through the gothic windows. For a moment, she looks like she's just confessed to murder.

"How are you feeling?" I ask, keeping my tone even.

Sophia doesn't answer. Instead, she turns away, the moonlight catching her profile, sharp and ethereal. The satin hem of her dress flutters against her thighs as she points at the massive painting hanging above my bed. It's a striking piece: two Renaissance women entangled on a sprawling bed, one with her face buried in the other's chest, lips parted in pleasure, hands gripping soft, yielding flesh. The folds of their flowing gowns cling to their bodies as if painted with sinful intention, every curve and shadow a celebration of indulgence.

"This is the hottest one yet," Sophia says, her voice low and teasing, but it doesn't hide the tremor beneath.

I frown, trying again. "How are you feeling?"

She finally turns to me, a wry smile creeping across her lips. "Better. Now that I'm here with you."

Her words twist something in my chest, but I push it aside. "Did you really have a nightmare, or is this another one of your games?"

The shift is immediate. Her eyes flash, her posture stiffens. "Games? You think I'm making this up?"

"I'm just saying—"

"You're saying I'd pretend to be terrified, to be completely wrecked, just to get your attention? What kind of person do you think I am, Eve?" Her voice rises, sharp and cutting.

I sigh, running a hand through my hair. "Sophia, I didn't mean—"

"No, I get it," she snaps, her cheeks flushed with anger. "You think I'm some spoiled brat who can't tell the difference between real fear and wanting to be close to you. Thanks for that."

Her words sting, more than I care to admit. "I just don't want to see you hurt—"

"Then maybe don't make me feel like I'm a burden every time I come to you," she bites back, her voice trembling. "I thought you were supposed to protect me, not push me away."

"Yeah, but sometimes you leave me no choice but to push you away, when you..." I stop myself, clenching my fists. I can't say it—not out loud.

"When I what?" Sophia challenges, stepping closer, her anger blazing through her voice. "When I show you how much you mean to me? When I try to make you laugh because I see how being a soldier has stripped you of all your humor? When I try to add some color to your boring, dreary life?"

"Add color?" I bark out a laugh, sharp and bitter. "No, you're not adding color—you're adding chaos. Sin and temptation to something that shouldn't be touched."

"Fuck all that!" she snaps, her voice rising. She jerks her hands down, her entire body trembling. "Fuck what's right and wrong for once, Evelyn! You're not my aunt. Okay? Whatever bond you're talking about… that snapped the day James and Anastasia died. You have that bond with Emmy, not me. I'm just a girl who fucking wants you now. A girl who looked up to you years ago, and now feels something so much more than just admiration—hell, so much more than just admiration!"

"What do you admire me for, Sophia?" I shake my head, exasperated. I circle her, then drop into the armchair by the Gothic window, rubbing my temples. "Is it my abs? The way I'm different from other girls you might have kissed? Or is it because I'm just here, convenient, a placeholder for James and Anastasia? Let's call it what it is—you're projecting. That's not admiration, Sophia. It's grief, and it's twisted."

She glares at me, her chest heaving with emotion. "You think I'm projecting? That this is about grief? Do you even hear yourself?"

"Tell me I'm wrong," I say flatly, my voice steady but icy. "Tell me it's not grief fueling whatever this is."

Sophia's voice lowers, taut and trembling. "It's not grief. It's love. And maybe it's twisted to you, but it's real to me."

She takes a shaky breath, her green eyes piercing mine. "You're the one who can't let go of the past, Eve. Not me. You're the one who's terrified of living."

Her words hit harder than they should, leaving me speechless. The room feels heavy, suffocating, as I stare back at her, unable to say anything that won't shatter us both.

"All I wanted was for you to hold me when I sleep tonight

because my mind goes to places it shouldn't at night," Sophia says, her voice trembling with a dangerous mix of longing and defiance. Her green eyes glisten with unshed tears, but there's fire behind them, unyielding. "But I guess my body sleeping next to you would make you burn in hell, so I think I should leave."

She turns, and I lose control.

Before I can stop myself, I'm on her. My hand grips her wrist, yanking her back and spinning her around, slamming her gently but firmly against the wall. Her body collides with mine, her breath hitching sharply. Her wrists are pinned above her head, held in one of my hands. My chest presses against hers, and I feel everything—soft curves molding into the firmness of my frame. Her breasts squish against mine, the thin, flimsy fabric separating us only amplifying the unbearable heat radiating between us.

She gasps, her green eyes wide, her lips parting as if to protest, but no words come. Her chest heaves against mine, her nipples brushing through the fabric of her nightdress, and I hate it. I hate that there's anything between us at all, even as I feel the dampness already spreading beneath my clothes. My breath comes in sharp bursts, and I see it in her eyes: she knows. She *knows*.

I lean in, my voice a growl, trembling with restraint I can't hold onto much longer. "The thoughts I've had about this body of yours have already booked me a place in hell."

Her lips part further, her breath hot and uneven, her eyes locked onto mine. "Then go," she whispers, her voice a broken plea wrapped in a challenge. "Take me with you."

Her words strike me like lightning, and I push harder against her, my body trembling as her softness molds against my hardness. My grip on her wrists tightens as I press my forehead to hers, and I feel her everywhere. Her thighs brush mine, her body heat scorching through the thin fabric, her scent sweet and intoxicating.

I hate how much I want her. I hate that I can't stop. I hate that the curve of her hips is burned into my hands, that I'm already imagining tearing that satin nightdress from her body. I want to taste her skin, her mouth, her cries. I want to take everything she's daring me to touch.

"You want to sleep with me?" I hiss, my voice low, rough, barely holding onto control. "Fine. Let's sleep."

I release her wrists, but the second I let go, my hand finds hers, yanking her to the bed. My head is screaming at me to stop, but my body doesn't listen. My heart thunders, my hands tremble, and when I push her onto the bed, her body bounces slightly, the nightdress riding higher to reveal more of her smooth, golden thighs.

I follow her down, straddling her with a desperation I can't contain. My thighs frame her hips, but I freeze for a moment as the sight of her steals my breath. Her hair fans out against the pillow, her green eyes staring up at me, wide and unblinking, her chest rising and falling as her breath catches. The satin clings to her every curve, leaving nothing to the imagination, her nipples taut beneath the flimsy fabric.

Her thighs shift beneath me, brushing against my center, and I bite back a groan as heat floods my body. I try to stop—God, I try—but I can't help the way my hips press down, the slickness between my legs dampening the barrier of my shorts. I move without meaning to, rubbing against the softness of her thighs, and I see her lips part, her breath catching as she watches me unravel.

Her eyes are so wide, I wonder if they'll go even wider when I thrust two fingers into her, when I hear her cry out for me for the first time. Will they glaze over when I claim her? When I take her virginity with my strap, when her body tightens around me, breaking, trembling, coming apart in my hands?

The thought makes my body tremble, my breath hitch, and I feel madness clawing at my resolve. I'm standing on the edge of something dark, something unstoppable, and the way she looks at me—unguarded, teasing, wanting—is pushing me over.

"You're insane," I growl, my voice rough and uneven, my lips hovering inches from hers.

"No," she whispers, her voice soft but certain. "I'm yours."

Her words tear through me, and I can't think anymore. My body moves, my restraint shatters, and the world narrows to her—her warmth, her softness, her scent, her *everything*.

Her lips are trembling, parted in anticipation, her green eyes half-lidded as they fixate on mine. I'm so close I can feel the warmth of her breath mingling with my own. Her soft, thick lips glisten, a silent plea, and my resolve crumbles further with every heartbeat.

I want to. God, I want to take her mouth, to taste her, to lose myself in her. My hand trembles as I brush a strand of hair from her face, and she leans into the touch, her body arching ever so slightly. My eyes dart to her lips again, so full, so perfect, so completely hers. My head dips lower, and her breath hitches.

But then, clarity strikes like a hammer to my chest. *Not yet.*

Not until I know this isn't just her grief pulling me into her orbit. Not until she's safe, out of the shadows of the mafia, and free from the chaos surrounding us. Not while she's under my protection, depending on me to be her anchor.

Not yet.

I pull back suddenly, like the air between us has turned to fire. Her eyes snap open, wide with shock, the faint smile on her lips disappearing as she watches me retreat. I sit up, sliding off her and the bed, putting distance between us, though it feels like ripping myself apart.

Her voice is small, unsure, as she whispers, "Eve?"

"I'll take the couch," I say, my tone rough, detached, though every inch of me aches to stay where I was. My hands, steady in contrast to the storm inside me, grab the edge of the blanket. I tuck it around her, careful not to meet her gaze. She doesn't resist, doesn't say a word, but I can feel the weight of her shock, the confusion radiating from her as I straighten the sheets around her.

For a moment, the room is silent except for the sound of my ragged breathing. She watches me, her green eyes searching for something—an answer, a sign, an explanation I can't give her.

Not yet.

I stand, turning toward the small couch in the corner. It's a pitiful excuse for a bed, but it'll have to do. Just as I take a step, I pause, unable to stop myself. I lean down, close to her ear, my breath brushing against her skin. She shivers, and for a split second, I hate myself for what I say next.

"You almost had me," I whisper, my voice low, heavy with truth and regret.

I straighten, turning away before I can see her reaction. My footsteps are slow, deliberate, as I make my way to the couch, forcing myself to put space between us. My chest is tight, my body screaming at me to go back to her, but I stay where I am. Because I know—if I cross that line now, there's no going back.

And she deserves better than my weakness.

∞∞∞

Tessa's office smells like strong coffee and a faint trace of vanilla. The blinds are partially drawn, allowing shards of late morning light to streak across her desk, cluttered with case files and a half-eaten bagel. She's leaning back in her chair when I walk in, her black boots propped up on the desk, her uniform shirt unbuttoned at the collar.

"Evelyn Lockhart," she greets, her lips curving into a slow smile. "Always a pleasure to see you darken my doorway."

I don't sit. Instead, I toss a photo of the tire tracks onto her desk. Tessa glances at it, her eyebrows lifting slightly as she picks it up.

"Morning to you too," she says, inspecting the photo. "Looks like someone's been trespassing. What do you need?"

"I need officers stationed at the estate," I reply, my voice clipped. "At least two, round the clock. And I need the area near the service road patrolled more frequently. Whoever it was broke the gate lock. Could've been kids, but—"

"You don't believe that," she cuts in, her dark eyes narrowing as she studies me. "You think it's the same people who—"

"Yes," I interrupt sharply. I don't want to say it aloud. Don't want to give it more weight than it already carries. "I think it's them."

Tessa exhales slowly, setting the photo down and swinging her feet off the desk. "Alright. I can spare a couple of deputies. But it'll cost you."

I frown. "How much?"

"Oh, not money, sweetheart." She leans forward, resting her elbows on the desk, her grin widening. "Dinner."

"Tessa..." I warn, my patience thinning.

"Not negotiable," she says, tilting her head. "I'll get your boys on the estate. Hell, I'll even throw in an extra patrol car for the freeway. But only if you have dinner with me. Sunday."

I cross my arms, narrowing my eyes at her. "You're impossible."

"I've been called worse," she quips, leaning back again and stretching. Her ponytail swings behind her, and the way her uniform pulls across her chest tells me she knows exactly what she's doing.

"Fine," I bite out. "Dinner. But nothing fancy."

"Don't worry," she says, her smile smug. "I'll keep it casual. Just you, me, and some mutual reminiscing. Maybe a bottle of wine."

"No wine," I snap. "I need a clear head."

I glare at her, but she only chuckles, leaning forward. "Seriously, though. What's the deal with your guards? The ones in black suits? Why not hire more?"

"They're not exactly on my payroll," I admit. "They're former colleagues, doing this out of loyalty. They aren't many, but they're enough—for now."

"Loyalty's good," she says. "But I still want a full rundown of your estate's security."

I hesitate but relent. "Cameras at all entry points. Patrol routes both inside and around the grounds. Landmines on the eastern boundary."

Tessa's eyes widen. "Landmines? Jesus, Eve."

"They're remote-controlled," I clarify. "Strategically placed. And if anyone gets through the perimeter, there's more waiting for them inside."

She shakes her head, letting out a low whistle. "I don't even want to know how you got your hands on them."

"You're better off not knowing."

Tessa chuckles, standing and walking around the desk to stand in front of me. She's taller than I remember, or maybe it's just the boots. "You're so tense, Eve. You've always been wound tight, but now? It's like you've turned into one of those military-grade explosives. One wrong move and boom."

"Your charm is as subtle as ever," I deadpan, but there's a flicker of amusement I can't quite hide.

She grins, leaning against the edge of her desk. "Subtlety's boring. You know that."

"I need those officers by tonight," I remind her, steering the conversation back to the matter at hand.

"You'll have them," she promises, her tone softening. "I've got your back, Eve. Always have."

For a moment, the air between us shifts. Her flirtations fade, replaced by something heavier, something unspoken. Memories of nights spent together, of the brief connection we shared before I pushed her away, flicker in her eyes.

"Tess..." I begin, but she holds up a hand.

"No," she says, her voice steady. "You don't owe me an explanation. I get it. You had your reasons, and I respect them. But that doesn't mean I can't still look out for you. Even if it's just as a friend."

I nod, the weight of her words settling over me. "Thank you."

She waves me off, her grin returning. "Don't thank me yet. You still owe me dinner. And I'm not letting you back out."

I turn to leave, but her voice stops me at the door.

"Eve," she calls, and I glance over my shoulder. "Take care of yourself, alright? And those girls. They need you."

"I know," I say quietly, before walking out.

Behind me, I hear her mutter, "Still as complicated as ever, Lockhart."

The sound of her laughter follows me down the hall.

Sophia

The water wraps around my body like a lover, warm and teasing, its ripples licking against my skin in ways that make me wish it were hands instead. Above me, the stars wink through the glass ceiling, but I barely notice. My attention is locked on Iggy, slicing through the pool like she's chasing something—or being chased.

She's not graceful, not in the practiced way of someone who's spent hours perfecting their technique. Her strokes are wild, messy, raw. Her kicks send splashes cascading over the edge, soaking my arms as I lean back against the cool tile. But damn, she's fast. That kind of speed comes from instinct, from years of survival, from a life spent swimming in rivers and lakes where the water could swallow you whole if you weren't good enough. And she's more than good enough. She's… something else.

I watch her as she slows, coming toward me, her fiery red hair plastered to her neck and shoulders like a frame for her freckled face. The water clings to her pale skin, droplets sliding down her toned arms, her flat stomach, disappearing into the waistband of her bikini bottoms. Her hips move with every step closer, the water rippling around her tiny waist, and my gaze drifts lower before I can stop myself. She's got legs for days, thighs that look strong enough to crush me and soft enough to keep me coming back for more.

Her chest rises and falls, every breath making the curve of her small, perky breasts even more distracting. The thin fabric of her bikini top clings to her, wet and translucent, leaving little to the imagination. My mouth goes dry, and I hate myself for how badly I want to bite those perfect freckles on her collarbone, to trace the lines of her body with my tongue until I've tasted every inch of her.

"You're just going to sit there looking pretty all night?" she teases, stopping a few feet away. Her voice is breathless, her cheeks flushed—not just from exertion, I'd bet.

I shrug, smirking, trying to keep it together. "Someone's gotta appreciate the effort."

She takes another step closer, the water swirling around her hips. "Appreciate it, huh?" Her voice dips lower, playful but edged with something else. "Should I start charging you?"

I laugh, but it's weak. Hollow. Because she's right there, dripping wet, her skin glowing under the soft lights, and all I can think is how easy it would be to have her. Right here. Right now. I could pull her against me, feel the heat of her body under my hands, taste the salt of her skin as my lips find her neck. I could push her to the edge of the pool, slip my fingers under those tiny bikini bottoms, and feel just how wet she is for me.

But instead of reaching for her, my mind betrays me.

Instead of thinking about the beautiful girl in front of me, I'm thinking about Evelyn.

Evelyn, with her sharp edges and impossible abs, her long legs that I dream about having wrapped around my waist. Evelyn, whose smirk drives me insane, makes me want to grab her by the collar and kiss her until we're both out of breath— or slap her for how easily she gets under my skin. I see her in my head, the way her hands would feel on my body, firm, commanding, taking without asking. I imagine her voice, low and rough, telling me exactly what to do, how to move, how to take her apart piece by piece.

Why can't I want Iggy instead? Why can't I let this gorgeous, freckled, dripping-wet girl be the one I lose myself in? She's standing so close now, close enough to touch, her skin gleaming like it's been polished, her lips curling into a smile that could break hearts.

"You're zoning out," she says, snapping me back to the present. Her voice has a teasing lilt, but her eyes glint with something sharper. "Thinking about something naughty?"

I force a laugh, shaking my head as I smirk. "Always."

Her grin widens, and she takes another step, the space between us shrinking to almost nothing. "I knew it," she purrs, her voice soft and low, like she's trying to pull a confession out of me. "You're a little freak, aren't you?"

Her words make my stomach clench, my pulse racing. She's standing so close now that I can feel the heat radiating off her, the water pooling at her waist, her bare skin almost brushing mine. I could reach out, slide my hand down her toned stomach, push her back into the pool, and pin her there while I take my time making her fall apart.

But I can't. Because no matter how badly I want to, no matter how beautiful, how wild, how perfectly here Iggy is… Evelyn is still in my head. She's a ghost I can't exorcise, a storm I can't escape.

And it's killing me.

Iggy tilts her head, studying me, her freckled face lighting up with a teasing smirk that sends a shiver down my spine. "You're thinking about her again, aren't you?" she asks, her voice almost a whisper, but it cuts through me like a blade.

I force a laugh, trying to shrug off the weight of her words. "What? Who?"

Her grin widens. "Evelyn. You're thinking about how close you were to having her that night, aren't you?"

The air between us thickens, and my body betrays me—a flicker of heat crawling up my neck, a tightening in my chest. I try to look away, but Iggy steps closer, her green eyes sharp and knowing. Damn her for reading me so easily.

The water feels warmer than it should against my skin, but I'm still shivering. Maybe it's Iggy's words, or the way she leans in so close I can feel the heat of her breath on my ear.

"You are, aren't you?" she presses, her voice low and teasing, like she's just uncovered my deepest secret. "Bet you can still feel her hands on you. Bet you can't stop thinking about how she almost gave in, how close she was to breaking her own rules for you."

"But she didn't." My voice is quieter than I want it to be, almost breaking as I look away. I can feel Iggy's eyes on me, studying me like I'm a puzzle she's trying to solve. "That was my best chance. If she could resist that, then she can resist anything. I think… I think that was it."

"No," she says, shaking her head, her wet red hair plastered to her freckled cheeks. "I don't think so. I think she got a taste of you, Soph. Just enough to know what she's missing. Enough to drive her crazy. That moment? You sprawled out for her like dessert on a platter? It's playing in her head on repeat. She's going to break. Mark my words. And if she doesn't…" She giggles, flicking water at me with her fingers. "Well, you've always got me."

I laugh, but it's hollow. "No, trust me. If I can't have Eve, I'll be too wrecked to want anyone."

She tilts her head, curiosity flickering in her dark eyes. "So, it's that deep, huh? You really like her?"

"Yeah." I nod, and the words come out before I can stop them. "I really like her."

Her lips twist into a smirk. "You want to be her girlfriend, don't you?"

"Girlfriend? Lover? Shadow? Soul? Her heart?" I scoff, but the weight of my words lands heavy. "You don't get it, Iggy. She was everything to me growing up. She was my idol. The woman who made me realize there's no one-size-fits-all for how a woman should be. She could give you fifty push-ups in the morning and then slide into a bodycon dress at night, making every man in the room lose his mind—or in my case, leave a very green-eyed girl completely wrecked. She didn't conform. She was unapologetically herself, and I was obsessed."

Iggy lets out a low whistle, her grin widening. "Wow. That's a lot to unpack. But tell me, does this love of yours feel... real? Or do you think it's just lust?"

"It's both," I say, looking at her sharply. "Not that it's any of your business, Sherlock. And honestly, I can't think straight with the mafia after me, so forgive me if my feelings are a little scrambled."

She bursts into laughter, loud enough to echo off the glass ceiling. "God, you're funny," she says, wiping at her wet cheeks.

"And you're weird. But in the best way." I smile, the weight on my chest lifting slightly. "I'm glad you're here, Iggy. Emmy's amazing, but sometimes you need someone your own age, you know?"

"Exactly!" she says, her eyes lighting up. "What I wouldn't give to go to college with you after I finish school."

"Then do it!" I exclaim.

She shakes her head. "The colleges you're looking at? Too expensive. We can't afford that."

I lean closer. "We'll figure it out. You just need to decide, girl."

She shrugs, a wistful smile crossing her face. "Maybe. But enough about me. Let's get back to the spicy romance between the niece and the aunt!"

"Hey! Don't ruin something special!" I glare at her.

"Oh, I'm the one ruining it?" She rolls her eyes. "You literally call her Mommy sometimes."

I groan, covering my face. "I know. I'm so fucked up."

"And she's standing at the border of your little land of 'fucked up,' teasing you with one leg in and one leg out." She smirks, clearly amused. "Just grab her. Shake the tree until the apples, oranges, bras, and panties all fall off!"

Her laughter is so loud and infectious, I can't help but smirk, even as I shake my head. God, this girl is insane. But maybe, she's right.

Chapter Seven

Sophia

The morning air feels heavier than usual, like the estate is bracing for a storm. Emmy chatters over breakfast, but Eve is barely listening, her responses clipped and distant. Even the house staff, who usually handle her sternness with ease, seem to tread lightly around her today. Miriam looks downright offended when Eve snaps about the placement of a vase in the foyer.

She's not herself.

By the time lunch rolls around, she's asked me twice about gun practice, despite it being our designated off day. I've answered her both times, but her furrowed brow tells me she hasn't really heard me. Emmy tries to drag her into a discussion about the latest adventure she and Mr. Wonkers are planning, but Eve brushes her off, something she never does. That's when I decide to find out what the hell is going on.

I corner her in her study, where she's hunched over her laptop, fingers flying across the keyboard. She doesn't even look up when I knock on the open door.

"Did you lose a bet or something?" I ask, stepping in without waiting for her permission.

"What?" Her voice is sharp, tired.

"Did someone dare you to beat your own record for snapping at the most people in a single day?"

She sighs, not even glancing at me, her jaw tightening. "Not now, Sophia."

"Not now, not later. You know you can talk to me, right?" I lean against the doorframe, trying to keep my tone light. "I mean, I know I'm not a therapist, but I'm good at listening."

"Damn it, Sophia!" She slams her laptop shut, her glare pinning me to the spot. "Not everything is about you needing to fix something!"

I fall silent, startled by her outburst. For a moment, we just stare at each other, the tension thick between us.

She sighs again, softer this time, and gestures toward the chair opposite her desk. "Sit."

I hesitate but then cross the room and sink into the chair, folding my arms. "So? Spill."

Her gaze softens, almost imperceptibly, but the weight in her eyes tells me whatever this is, it's big.

Eve leans back in her chair, her hands rubbing her temples like she's fighting off the mother of all headaches. "He wants to come here," she mutters, almost to herself.

"Who?" I ask, leaning forward in my seat. "Who wants to come here?"

She looks at me, her piercing blue eyes heavier than usual.

"Grandpa Lockhart."

I blink, the name clicking in my head almost instantly. "Grandpa Lockhart? Your dad? Oh my God, I've always wanted to meet him!" The excitement bursts out before I can help it. "Dad used to tell me so many stories about him. About how he—"

"Yeah, well, those stories are ancient history," Eve cuts me off, her tone sharp. "Back when he had a semblance of sanity. Now? He's gone completely off the deep end."

I frown, the image of the stoic, commanding General Lockhart from Dad's stories clashing with whatever Eve's describing. "What do you mean? What's wrong with him?"

"We don't get along," she says, her voice clipped. She doesn't elaborate, but her lips press into a thin line, and her jaw sets in that way that says not to push her. "I don't want him here. But apparently, I don't have a choice. He's decided he wants to meet his granddaughters."

I can't hide the flicker of excitement in my chest. "Well… he should! I mean, he's Emmy's only blood relative left beside you. She deserves to spend time with him."

Eve lets out a bitter laugh. "You're assuming he'll be a warm and fuzzy grandfather. Trust me, the man is a nightmare. I'm not in the right frame of mind to deal with him."

"Then I'll handle him," I say quickly. "You don't have to worry about anything. I've always wanted to meet him, Eve. Please." My voice softens, and I meet her gaze, letting every ounce of sincerity I feel shine through. "Emmy needs this. I need this."

Her expression falters, and for a moment, she looks at me like I've just done something impossible—broken through her walls. She exhales heavily, her shoulders slumping. "Fine. But you're handling him. Don't come crying to me when he starts his crazy talk about weapons."

I grin. "How bad can it be?"

Eve arches a brow. "Bad. If he offers to 'help' with your shooting practice, say no. The man will hand you a bazooka and call handguns 'toys for pussies.' Don't say I didn't warn you."

I can't help but laugh, even as her words linger. There's a tension under her humor, a bitterness I don't fully understand. But for now, I'll take the win.

"I'll be the perfect granddaughter," I say, winking at her. "You won't even know he's here."

Eve shakes her head, a faint smirk tugging at her lips despite herself. "God help me."

∞∞∞

The heavy thud of boots against the polished marble floor sends a shiver down my spine. Emmy shifts closer to me, her small fingers clutching Mr. Wonkers like the stuffed bear might shield her from the storm approaching. I glance at her, trying to offer a reassuring smile, but the truth is, I feel as jittery as she looks.

And then, he appears.

Richard Lockhart.

The man is a walking storm cloud—tall, broad, and exuding a force that makes the grand hall feel too small to contain him. His silver hair is clipped military-short, his sharp nose and chiseled jawline giving him the appearance of someone carved out of granite. Those piercing blue eyes, identical to Eve's, sweep over the room like searchlights. He's dressed in a weathered leather bomber jacket, combat boots, and dark jeans, carrying a duffle bag that looks like it could hold explosives instead of clothes.

His gaze lands on us like a predator sizing up its prey. "So," he says, his voice low and commanding, "this is what the future of the Lockhart and Harlow bloodlines looks like."

I freeze. His tone isn't cruel, but it's far from warm. Emmy stiffens beside me, her grip on Mr. Wonkers tightening.

"I guess the taller one of you is James' stepdaughter?" he asks, his eyes narrowing.

I raise a tentative hand. "That's me."

He steps forward, and I swear the temperature in the room drops. "James talked about you," he says, his voice sharp enough to cut through steel. "Said you were sharp, though I see he forgot to mention you look like you'd blow away in a strong wind."

I blink, unsure how to respond. Before I can muster anything, his gaze shifts to Emmy. "And you must be Emily. A Lockhart through and through, eh? You've got the look, kid. Let's see if you've got the guts."

Emmy stares at him, wide-eyed, her lips quivering as if she's not sure whether to cry or run.

"Cat got your tongue?" he barks, his voice booming. Then, after a beat, he softens—just slightly. "Relax, kid. I don't bite. Much."

He throws his duffle bag to the floor with a heavy thud, the sound reverberating through the hall. Miriam, who's been standing silently to the side, looks like she's reconsidering her decision to escort him in. Even the guard lingers near the doorway, clearly wanting to bolt.

"Well?" Grandpa Lockhart demands, his arms crossing over his chest. "Are you two going to stand there gawking, or do I get a proper hello?"

I glance at Emmy, then back at him. My mouth opens, the word forming before I even think about it. "Hello, Grandpa."

The moment it slips out, I feel it. Wrong. Heavy. Like I've stepped into a space that isn't mine to claim. Calling him

Grandpa feels like claiming a seat at the Lockhart family table —one that comes with rules, expectations, and the weight of Evelyn. My stomach churns. If I call him Grandpa, what does that make me? What does that make Eve to me?

I falter, glancing at Emmy, who beams at him, clearly unbothered by the implications. But me? My mind is racing. "I mean... Mr. Lockhart," I correct myself, the words tumbling out awkwardly.

His eyes narrow, and the weight of his stare pins me in place. "Mr. Lockhart?" His voice drops, laced with disapproval. "You might be James' stepdaughter, but he spoke of you as his own. If you called him Dad, you can damn well call me Grandpa."

Emmy looks up at me, her lips parting as if to plead, but I hesitate. My tongue feels thick, the word caught in my throat. Grandpa. Saying it again feels like stepping deeper into a quicksand that ties me to Evelyn in ways I can't bear to think about right now.

But Richard Lockhart isn't the kind of man you argue with —not yet, at least. I swallow hard and push the word out. "Grandpa," I say, quieter this time, softer, though it still feels like a betrayal.

He nods, his expression unreadable as he steps forward. "That's better," he says, clapping a firm hand on my shoulder. It's meant to be reassuring, but it feels more like a brand, sealing me into something I'm not sure I can handle.

"Now," he says, turning to Emmy with a grin that's surprisingly warm. "Let me take a look at you. The spitting image of your dad."

Emmy giggles, the tension in her melting away instantly, but I stay frozen. My mind is still spinning, stuck on the word I just said and the weight it carries. Grandpa.

As he leans down to talk to Emmy, I catch my reflection in the polished marble floor. My green eyes look back at me, filled with the same questions that have been haunting me since I arrived here. What the hell am I doing?

Richard's sharp eyes scan the grand hall, narrowing slightly as he shifts his weight, his leather jacket creaking with the movement. "Where's Evelyn?" he asks, his voice a low rumble. "Too busy to greet her old man?"

I glance at Emmy, who's still beaming up at him, blissfully unaware of the sudden tension. "She's, uh, out on some important business," I offer, hoping to keep things light.

Richard's brows shoot up. "Important business?" he echoes, his tone thick with disbelief. "What could possibly be more important than her old man coming to her house after years?"

I open my mouth, then close it again. What do I even say to that? Honestly, I have no idea why Eve didn't clear her schedule for this. Maybe she's out hunting down the Mafia. Maybe she's just avoiding him. Either way, her absence feels like a landmine, and I'm tiptoeing around it. My internal monologue, however, is not nearly as composed: *Great, Sophia. Just lie to the retired general with the piercing death glare. That'll end well.*

I shift on my feet, forcing a smile. "I'm sure she'll be back soon. She's probably just—"

"Already got you running her errands, huh?" Richard interrupts, his lips curling into a smirk. "What are you, her little soldier? Taking orders, making excuses? She's trained you well."

My smile falters, but Emmy giggles, breaking the tension slightly. "I'm not a soldier," I say, trying to keep my voice steady. "And she doesn't give me orders."

Richard leans down slightly, his piercing blue eyes locking onto mine. "Don't let her win your trust, kid," he says, his tone dropping to something almost conspiratorial. "She'll break it when you least expect it."

The words hit me like a punch to the gut. My throat tightens, and I force myself to look away. *How does he know?* It's like he's reading my mind, pinpointing every fear I've ever had about Evelyn, and throwing it back at me.

I swallow hard, nodding without meeting his gaze. "I'll keep that in mind," I mutter, though the words feel hollow.

Richard straightens, his smirk returning like he's won some unspoken battle. "Good," he says, clapping a hand on my shoulder. "Now, where can a man get a drink around here?"

I manage a weak smile, but inside, my thoughts are spiraling. What did he mean? And why does it feel like his warning isn't just about Evelyn—it's about me?

The sound of my heels clicking against the polished floor echoes as I head toward the bar at the back of the hall. My steps falter when I hear Miriam's hurried approach behind me.

"Miss Sophia," she says, breathless. "You don't have to do this. The staff can handle it."

Before I can answer, Richard's sharp voice cuts through the room. "No, no! Don't make her soft like the rest of you. Let her make me a drink. Builds character." He glances at me, his piercing eyes narrowing. "You're not scared of a little hard work, are you?"

I barely suppress a grin, shrugging at Miriam, who looks like she might spontaneously combust. "What'll it be, Mr. Lockhart? Uh, Grandpa?" The word stumbles out awkwardly, and I'm pretty sure I hear him grunt in amusement.

"Whiskey. Neat. Double. None of that frou-frou nonsense," he barks.

I freeze. "Whiskey. Neat. Double," I repeat, more to myself than him, my mind racing. *What does neat even mean? Is it the opposite of messy? Do I need a towel?*

Miriam materializes beside me like an angel of mercy, whispering in my ear, "Neat means no ice, no mixers. I'll help you." She quickly grabs the bottle and glass and starts assembling the drink, all while keeping her voice low. "God knows Miss Lockhart was becoming difficult to handle, and now this? What's with the Lockharts?"

I stifle a laugh, whispering back, "I don't know, but if there's a survival guide, I'd pay good money for it."

Together, we finish the drink, and I carefully carry it over to the table, setting it in front of Richard. "Here you go, Grandpa. One 'character-building' drink."

He picks it up, giving me a nod of approval before turning his attention to Emmy. "Now, Little Lockhart," he says, his tone softening, "tell me about yourself. What do you like to do? Got any big dreams yet?"

Emmy beams, holding Mr. Wonkers tight. "I love coloring and painting! I have these glitter markers that make everything look like magic. And I want to make comics someday! Like the superhero ones, but with animals."

Richard's face lights up in a way that catches me off guard. "Comics, huh? That's something. You got any drawings to show me?"

Emmy nods eagerly. "I made one where Mr. Wonkers is a detective! He has a magnifying glass and a hat and solves mysteries like Sherlock Holmes. Do you want to see?"

Richard's lips twitch into something that might just be a smile. "Absolutely. Bring it here."

Watching them interact, I can't help but feel a strange warmth. Emmy's small, bright voice fills the hall as she talks about her adventures with Mr. Wonkers, while Richard listens intently, nodding and even chuckling at her stories. It's like he's an entirely different person with her, one whose sharp edges have softened.

Miriam catches my eye from the corner of the room, mouthing, "What the hell?"

I shrug, smiling as I sit across from them, sipping my own glass of water. Who would've thought the gruff, terrifying General Lockhart could turn into a softie in the presence of a tiny Lockhart and her wonky teddy bear? It's almost... wholesome.

The sound of Eve's boots echoes through the hall, and I swear the air shifts. My stomach knots as she steps into view, her sharp, commanding presence instantly filling the space. She stops near the sitting area, arms crossed, her expression unreadable.

Richard's gaze snaps to her, his blue eyes—so much like hers—narrowing. The tension is palpable, crackling between them like static electricity. Two soldiers, sizing each other up, neither willing to back down. I both love and hate it.

"Dad," Eve says, her voice clipped, betraying nothing.

Richard doesn't respond immediately. His eyes sweep over her, calculating, and finally, he asks, "Where were you?"

Eve's jaw tightens. "Taking care of some business."

He scoffs, leaning back in his chair, his drink forgotten. "You're an author. What business could you possibly have outside this house? Don't you sit in your study and write love stories all day?"

My breath catches, my fingers gripping the edge of my chair. So that's it—there's a crack in their armor. This isn't just about the past. There's something more, something raw, and it makes me anxious yet intrigued.

Eve's teeth clench, her voice barely masking her irritation. "Keeping these girls safe is my business. And for that, I need to go out on patrols."

Richard's eyes sharpen. "Oh, so you haven't forgotten how to be a soldier yet?"

Her response is quick, cutting, her tone like steel. "No. You won't let me."

The room goes deathly silent. Emmy, oblivious to the tension, tugs at Mr. Wonkers' ear, while I sit frozen, my heart pounding as I watch the silent war unfold.

Richard leans forward, resting his elbows on his knees. "Then why aren't you doing what a real soldier would? Why are you here, hiding behind a desk and calling it 'protection'?"

Eve's eyes blaze, but she doesn't respond, and the silence feels like it could break us all.

The tension between Eve and Richard is a tangible force in the room, the kind that makes my chest tighten. Their matching steel-blue eyes are locked in a silent battle, each refusing to give an inch. Emmy sits cross-legged on the couch, blissfully unaware, humming to herself as she tries to braid Mr. Wonkers' stubby arms.

"This estate is a beacon," Richard says, breaking the silence, his voice sharp and deliberate. "Visible from miles away, from the air, even from space if you squint hard enough. You call this safety, Evelyn?"

"It's secure," Eve counters, her tone clipped. "The estate is fortified. The perimeter is monitored 24/7. Moving them somewhere else is more risk than it's worth."

Richard scoffs. "You think cameras and walls are enough to keep them safe? You should know better. A safe house should be discreet, hidden, not a sprawling estate that screams privilege and power. This place is a goddamn invitation for trouble."

Eve takes a steadying breath, clearly holding herself back. "This isn't about appearances. This is about control. Here, I know every inch of the land, every weakness, and every strength. I can protect them here."

"You sound arrogant," Richard says, leaning forward, his voice dropping. "Arrogance gets people killed."

It's too much. "Enough!" I snap, my voice cutting through their argument like a whip. Both of their heads snap toward me, surprise flickering in their eyes. "This conversation doesn't need to happen in front of Emmy."

Richard's gaze narrows, his jaw tightening. "Don't tell me when I can discuss what," he says coldly.

But I don't back down. "I will, when it comes to my sister." I meet his glare head-on, my pulse racing but my voice steady. "Both of you might be soldiers or alphas or whatever you think you are, but when it comes to Emmy, no one is more alpha than me."

The room goes silent, the weight of my words hanging between us. From the corner of my eye, I catch Eve's lips twitch in the faintest of smiles, her gaze softening with pride. Richard's icy stare doesn't falter, but then, to my surprise, his stern expression melts into something else—a begrudging respect.

"Fair enough," he says finally, his voice softer. He rises from the chair with a heavy sigh, his towering frame seeming a little less intimidating now. "I'm tired. Show me to my room."

I nod, biting back a smile as the tension in the room eases. "Follow me, Mr. Lockhart."

As I lead him out of the great hall, I glance back to see Emmy still playing with Mr. Wonkers, but a hint of worry now etched on her face, and Eve standing tall, her eyes on me, brimming with something I haven't seen before—pride.

Eve

The mat feels harder underfoot today, or maybe that's just my patience wearing thin. Sophia stands in front of me, arms crossed over her chest, her face a picture of reluctant defiance. Her outfit doesn't help my focus—a fitted black tank top that clings to her like a second skin, paired with lilac leggings that highlight her every curve. Her hair is tied up in a messy ponytail, wisps framing her flushed face from our earlier warm-up. But there's no warmth in her expression now.

She huffs, shifting her weight to one leg. "Why are we doing this again?"

I tilt my head, trying to rein in my irritation. "Because," I say, emphasizing the word, "you need to know how to handle yourself in close combat. Guns aren't always an option."

"They are for me," she mutters, just loud enough for me to hear.

"Not if someone disarms you," I retort, stepping closer. "Now stop complaining and focus."

I demonstrate a takedown—quick, precise, efficient. "This one's basic. Just follow my movements."

She mimics me, half-heartedly. Her hands are limp, her stance is wrong, and her movements are as lackluster as her attitude. I correct her positioning, but she barely adjusts. My frustration mounts.

"Do it again," I snap. "Properly this time."

Sophia groans, rolling her eyes. "This is pointless, Eve."

"No, it's not," I counter, my tone sharp. "When someone grabs you, you'll thank me."

"For what?" she fires back. "Learning how to get slammed into the ground?"

I don't bother responding. Instead, I execute the takedown on her—carefully, but firmly enough to make a point. She lands with a soft thud, her ponytail splaying across the mat. She doesn't resist, doesn't try to counter. She just lays there, glaring up at me like I'm the enemy.

"See? This is exactly what I mean," I say, standing over her. "You're going to get yourself killed with that attitude."

She sits up, her cheeks flushed. "And you're going to kill me first with all this military boot camp crap."

I scoff. "This is a joke to you, isn't it? Until someone's got you tied to a chair, gagged, and staring down the barrel of a gun."

Her eyes flash. "Yeah? And when that happens, is your precious jiu-jitsu going to save me? No. It won't."

Her words hit harder than I expect, but I keep my face neutral. "I'm done arguing with people who doubt me."

"Oh, you mean your father?" she asks, her voice softer now, but her aim deliberate.

My stomach tightens. "This isn't about him."

She stands, brushing herself off. "Of course it is. You're pushing me because he's pushing you. You care about what he thinks of you, and you're doubling down to prove him wrong."

"That's not true," I say, but the words feel hollow.

She steps closer, her voice rising. "You're trying to turn me into something I'm not, Eve. I'm not you. I'm not a fighter. I'm nineteen. I have soft, feminine energy. I know how to pronounce Hermès and Givenchy perfectly. I'm not built for this."

Her words are like a slap, but I stay silent. She's not done.

"Ever since I got here," she continues, her voice trembling, "all you've done is criticize me, smirk at me, or... or look at me like you want something you'll never admit. Not once have you sat down with me, talked to me, hugged me. You're here physically, but emotionally? You're always somewhere else."

Her voice cracks on the last word, and something inside me shatters. The memories flood in, unbidden and unwelcome.

I'm seventeen again, sweat dripping down my face as I struggle to complete another set of push-ups in the rain. My arms are shaking, my stomach churning, but my father's voice is relentless. "Again," he barks. I puke, collapsing onto the wet ground, but he doesn't let up. "Weakness isn't an option, Evelyn. Get up."

The weight of it crushes me now, the years of pressure, the impossible standards, the cold, hard lessons in survival. I look at Sophia, her eyes wide and earnest, and I see myself.

"I..." The words stick in my throat. I take a step back, then another, and sit down hard on the mat, my legs folding beneath me. I bury my face in my hands, trying to breathe, trying to hold it together, but the dam has already cracked.

"Eve?" Sophia's voice is soft, hesitant. She kneels beside me, her hand hovering near my shoulder. "Are you okay?"

I shake my head, unable to speak. The tears come, hot and unrelenting, blurring my vision and soaking my palms.

"I didn't want to leave," I choke out finally, my voice barely above a whisper. "I didn't want to leave James, or you, or Emmy. But I had to."

Her hand rests on my shoulder now, grounding me. "What do you mean?"

"I was done," I say, lifting my head to meet her gaze. "I'd

retired. I was supposed to be free of all of it. But then... then I had to leave. I didn't have a choice."

Her expression softens, her green eyes glistening with unshed tears. "Why?"

"To protect you," I say, my voice breaking. "You don't understand. I couldn't stay. If I had, you'd be dead. James would be dead. I had to go undercover. I had to take that mission."

Her lips part, but no words come. She's searching my face, looking for answers, for something to make sense of the chaos I've just laid bare.

"I thought I could come back," I continue, my voice trembling. "I thought... but by the time I could, I had changed into someone else, someone I thought shouldn't be around a happy family like yours. I had come back broken. So, I stayed away."

Sophia doesn't hesitate this time. She wraps her arms around me, pulling me into a hug that feels like both a lifeline and an anchor. For a moment, I let myself fall into it, resting my head against her shoulder. Her touch is warm, steady, and it cuts through the storm inside me.

"You're here now," she whispers, her voice steady despite the emotion thick in it. "And that's what matters."

Her words are a balm, but they don't erase the guilt. I pull back slightly, meeting her gaze. "I'll never stop trying to make it up to you. To Emmy."

Her smile is small but genuine. "Then stop trying to turn me into a soldier and just be here. With me. For me."

I nod, swallowing hard. "I'll try."

"Good," she says, brushing a tear from my cheek. "Because that's all I need from you."

For the first time in what feels like forever, the weight on my chest lifts, just a little.

Her arms are still wrapped around me, firm but tender, and for a fleeting moment, I forget how to breathe. I'm Evelyn Lockhart, former soldier, trained to withstand pain, loss, and anything life throws at me. But here I am, crumbling into the embrace of a nineteen-year-old girl who should be the one demanding comfort—not giving it.

I pull back slightly, wiping my face with trembling hands. "This is all wrong," I whisper, my voice shaking. "You're the one who needs support. You're the one who should be falling apart in my arms, and here I am, breaking down in yours. What kind of protector am I?"

Sophia shakes her head, her green eyes blazing with an intensity that cuts straight through me. "Push-ups don't harden a heart, Eve. At least, I don't think so. Emotions are just emotions—they come and go when they want to. The love you have for someone can't be trained into being warm one moment and intense the next. Even soldiers are slaves to the whims of their hearts."

Her words hit me harder than any blow I've ever taken in combat. My lips part, but no sound escapes. I'm struck silent, watching her as she speaks with a conviction that shakes the very foundation of my being.

She leans closer, her hand brushing against mine. "Right now, you're not a hardened soldier or some beautiful Amazonian warrior," she says, her voice soft but firm. "You're Evelyn Lockhart. You loved your brother and your sister-in-law. You love your father, even if you can't stand him sometimes. You love Emmy, more than anything. And… maybe you love me too?"

The air between us thickens, charged with an unspoken truth I'm too afraid to admit, even to myself. I can't look away from her, her expression raw and open, her vulnerability cutting through my defenses like a blade.

"Sophia…" I start, but my voice falters.

"It's okay," she says, her lips curling into a small, knowing smile. "You don't have to say it. Just... let me be here for you. Just this once."

Her words, so simple yet so profound, undo me completely. I nod, swallowing the lump in my throat as I let her pull me back into her arms. This time, I don't resist. I let myself lean into her warmth, let myself feel the comfort I've denied for so long.

For the first time in years, I allow myself to simply be— no walls, no armor, no pretenses. Just Evelyn Lockhart, held together by the arms of the girl I swore to protect.

And for the first time, it feels like I might actually be whole again.

After a long moment, Sophia shifts slightly, resting her chin on my shoulder. "You know," she says, her voice light and teasing, "for someone who was just bitching and moaning a moment ago, I think I handled this like a pro."

I pull back, narrowing my eyes at her. "What?"

"I mean," she continues, a sly smile tugging at her lips, "you're the one who had a breakdown, and I was the calm, wise one with all the poetic wisdom. Who's the mommy now?"

My glare is immediate, but so is the corner of my mouth betraying me with the hint of a smile. "Sophia," I warn, my tone low.

"Admit it," she says, clearly relishing her moment of triumph. "You're impressed. You melted into me, Eve."

I take a deep breath, wiping the last remnants of vulnerability from my face. "Alright," I say, meeting her green eyes, still shining with an odd mix of triumph and tenderness. "I'll give you this—you handled that better than I expected. And you're right about some things. I've been too hard on you, Sophia."

Her grin widens, soft but victorious. "Finally. Progress."

I shake my head, smirking. "Don't get used to it. But I promise—no more endless training drills or relentless lectures for a while. And I'll spend more time with you, not as a trainer or bodyguard... but as a friend."

Her face lights up, and for a moment, I'm struck by how young she looks. The weight of everything—the mafia, the estate, her parents' deaths—it all seems to lift, replaced by pure joy.

"Promise?" she asks, her tone teasing, but there's something earnest in her gaze.

"Promise," I reply, holding her eyes so she knows I mean it.

Her hands clap together in excitement, and she beams. "Okay, great! So... let's watch a movie tonight."

I blink, caught off guard. "A movie? I thought you wanted to talk?"

Her grin turns mischievous, and she leans in closer, her voice dropping to a playful whisper. "We can talk after the movie. I'll pick it."

I roll my eyes but chuckle despite myself. "Fine. But if it's some romantic comedy or one of those artsy French films with subtitles—"

"You'll love it," she interrupts, bouncing to her feet with renewed energy. "Just wait."

I watch her practically skip out of the room, and for the first time in a long while, I feel something close to peace. Whatever she picks, I know it'll be worth it—if only because it's her.

Sophia

Emmy is tucked against my side, her tiny fingers gripping Mr. Wonkers like he's her personal knight in shining armor. Her wide blue eyes dart across the storybook, but her endless stream of questions makes me want to scream into the abyss.

"Why does the prince have to fight the dragon?" she asks, her head tilted up at me, curiosity dripping from every word. "Why can't they just... share the treasure?"

I inhale sharply, trying to keep my voice from snapping. "Because, Emmy, dragons don't share. They breathe fire and steal gold. That's kind of their whole thing."

"Maybe this dragon's nice," she counters, her tone absurdly serious for a nine-year-old. "What if it just wants a hug?"

I manage a strained smile. "Then I'm sure the prince and dragon will cuddle in the next chapter."

She giggles, her laughter soft and carefree, while my patience frays like an overused thread. My eyes flick to the clock.

Fifteen minutes.

Fifteen minutes until I'm in Eve's study, in her space, under her gaze. Maybe, if I'm lucky, on her lap again.

The thought derails me. The book blurs in my hands as my mind drifts. I can already see it—the low lighting in her study wrapping her in shadows, soft and seductive. She'd be sitting there, legs stretched out, one foot casually resting on the armrest of the couch, her body language screaming command. Those impossibly long legs of hers—toned, sculpted, a masterpiece in muscle and femininity—framed by leggings that hug every inch of her like they were made for her and her alone.

God, those leggings. I want to tear them apart with my teeth, let my tongue trail every inch of her skin beneath them, feel the strength of her thighs tightening around my head as I—

"What color is the dragon?" Emmy's voice cuts through the fantasy, and I blink, struggling to focus.

"What?" I ask, my voice sharper than I intended.

"Is the dragon green, or is it red?" she repeats, her pout deepening like the answer is critical.

"It's... probably dragon-colored, Emmy," I mutter, my voice clipped. "Scaly and terrifying. Use your imagination."

She giggles again, oblivious to the fact that I'm on the brink of madness. Fourteen minutes now. By now, Eve's probably lounging in her study, maybe still in those leggings and one of her loose tank tops that dips low enough to hint at the curve of her breasts. Maybe she hasn't changed at all. Maybe she's sitting there barefoot, her hair tied back, looking like sin incarnate with her piercing blue eyes and that maddening smirk that makes me want to either punch her or beg her to own my being.

"Can the prince and the dragon be best friends?" Emmy asks, her persistence relentless. "Like, maybe the prince lets the dragon sleep in the castle?"

"Sure, Emmy. The dragon can sleep wherever it damn well wants," I mutter, but my head is already spinning again.

What if tonight she doesn't just sit next to me? What if she leans in, her shoulder brushing mine, her hand casually resting on my knee? I imagine her fingers sliding higher, slow and deliberate, the heat of her touch burning through the thin fabric of my leggings. Would her lips curl into that cocky smirk, her voice low and commanding as she whispers in my ear, daring me to stop her?

No. She wouldn't stop there. She'd push me down onto the couch, pin me with her weight, her hands gripping my wrists as her mouth claims mine. I can already feel the scrape of her teeth on my neck, the way her fingers would tangle in my hair, pulling just hard enough to make me moan.

And when she's done teasing me? She'd slide her hand between my legs, pressing against the slick fabric, her voice a low growl as she tells me how wet I am for her. How filthy. How much I've been craving her.

"What's a chalice?" Emmy chirps, yanking me back to reality like a slap across the face.

"It's... a fancy cup," I say, my voice hollow, my knuckles white as I grip the storybook.

"Can the prince use the chalice to hold cookies for the dragon?" she asks, cheerful as ever.

"Sure, Emmy," I reply, my voice strained. "Cookies, cupcakes, a whole goddamn bakery. Whatever makes the dragon happy."

She beams up at me, snuggling closer, her warmth an innocent reminder of the lines I can't cross. Meanwhile, my mind is screaming for mercy. Just sleep, kid. Close your eyes before I lose my fucking mind.

Instead, she tilts her head, her expression thoughtful. "Do you think Auntie Eve likes cookies?"

The question hits like a punch, and I choke on my response. "I... I don't know. Why?"

"Because I think she's the kind of woman who likes cookies in secret but doesn't want anyone to know it," she says simply, her voice so innocent and sure it feels like a dagger to the chest.

My eyes dart to the clock again. Thirteen minutes. Thirteen

minutes until I'm face-to-face with the woman who already owns every filthy, desperate part of me.

And God help me, I know I'll leave that study even more wrecked than I already am.

∞∞∞

The hallway stretches out like a runway, every step of my heels echoing in the dimly lit space, a deliberate rhythm that matches the pounding of my heart. The polished wood reflects the glow of the wall sconces, but all I can see is the door at the end of the hall—Eve's study, her sanctuary, where tonight, I'll make her mine.

I've dressed for war.

The black dress isn't just revealing—it's scandalous, obscene, designed to destroy whatever flimsy excuses she's clinging to. The neckline plunges so low it's a miracle my breasts aren't spilling out entirely, the curve of them practically begging for her hands, her lips. The fabric is sheer enough that the outline of my taut nipples is visible, teasing through the thin, silky material. No bra, no padding—just bare skin pressed against a dress that feels like sin.

The hem is laughable, barely skimming the tops of my thighs, and the slit? It's cut so high that one wrong move could reveal everything. And I want her to see everything. I want her to lose her composure, her control, that icy restraint that she uses to keep me at arm's length. I paired it with heels so high they make my calves ache, arching my body just enough to add an extra sway to my hips with every step. The black thong I'm wearing is a concession—barely there, just a slip of lace that I could rip off in seconds if I wanted to.

I've done my makeup just right—my green eyes smolder

beneath perfectly winged eyeliner, dark enough to make them pop, sharp enough to cut through any excuse she might try to throw at me. My lips are painted a deep, wicked red, glossy and sinful, the kind of color that screams, *kiss me, ruin me, devour me*. My hair is loose, cascading in dark waves over my shoulders, brushing against the exposed skin of my chest and back where the dress dips scandalously low. Every inch of me is calculated, deliberate, a trap she won't escape.

I pause at the door to her study, my breaths shallow, uneven. My fingers trail down my side, smoothing the glossy fabric of my dress over my hips, making sure it clings just right. I tug at the neckline, letting it dip lower, exposing just a hint more of the swell of my breasts. A single bead of sweat slides down the back of my neck, and I brush it away with the back of my hand. Perfect. Everything is perfect.

She won't turn me away this time. She won't whisper, *Not yet*, or try to protect me from something we both know we want. Tonight, I'll show her exactly what she's been running from. Exactly what she's been craving.

I lift my hand, the dark polish on my nails catching the light as I hesitate for just a second. Then I knock, the sound loud and deliberate, echoing down the hallway like a warning. My heart pounds as I take a step back, adjusting the slit of my dress to make sure just enough of my bare thigh is visible. My chest rises and falls as I breathe, every inch of me screaming with anticipation.

And then I wait, trembling, knowing that when she opens the door, her world—and mine—will never be the same.

Eve

The words flow from my fingers like blood, dark and visceral, staining the pristine white of the document on my screen. My protagonist, Captain Naomi Cain, grips the cyclic stick of her helicopter, her knuckles white as she navigates a smoke-filled battlefield. Below her, chaos reigns—explosions ripple through the ground, bodies litter the dirt, and screams pierce the air like shrapnel.

Her co-pilot is shouting something, but Naomi can't hear him over the roaring blades and the deafening thud of her own heartbeat. Sweat drips down her temple as she zeroes in on the wounded soldiers below, waving frantically for extraction. The helicopter tilts dangerously, and I write her hands trembling as she struggles to maintain control. Another RPG whistles past, narrowly missing the tail rotor, and—

My chest tightens.

It's subtle at first, just a faint squeezing, like someone's hand gently pressing against my ribcage. But then it's more—an iron vice closing in, squeezing the breath from my lungs. I blink, trying to focus on the screen, but the words blur. The sounds of battle I've conjured on the page feel too real, too loud. The steady hum of my laptop fan morphs into the rotor's whine, and the faint tapping of the clock on the wall becomes the rhythmic percussion of gunfire.

Breathe, Evelyn. *Breathe.*

But I can't. My throat closes, my pulse pounds in my ears, and suddenly I'm not in my study anymore. I'm back there. The sandstorm rages around me, grit scraping against my skin as bullets snap past. A boy—just a boy—is screaming, his leg gone below the knee, his face contorted in agony. My hands are soaked with blood, trembling as I try to—

"Stop," I gasp, clutching my chest. My surroundings tilt, a nauseating swirl of reality and memory blending into a nightmare I can't escape. My breathing is shallow, erratic, and my vision tunnels until all I can see is that boy's face. His wide, terrified eyes. The blood.

The world tips sideways as I slump forward, my forehead hitting the desk. The wood is cool against my skin, grounding me for a split second before the darkness creeps in. My muscles go slack, my fingers twitching against the ink-streaked surface. Somewhere in the periphery of my fading consciousness, I hear a sound. A voice? No, a knock.

Sophia.

The knock grows louder, insistent, accompanied by a muffled voice calling my name. I try to respond, to pull myself upright, but my body refuses to obey. My heart hammers against my ribcage, and the edges of my vision darken. The study, the battlefield, the screams—they blur together into a cacophony of noise and chaos, dragging me under.

And then, there's nothing.

∞∞∞

The world comes back to me in fragments, sharp and jarring. My chest feels like it's caving in, my breaths shallow and uneven. The first thing I register is Sophia's voice, soft but urgent, cutting through the haze like a lifeline.

"Miriam, bring some water. Hurry," she says, the sweetness of her tone underlined by an edge of panic. It feels distant, like it's traveling through a tunnel, but it's there, grounding me.

I blink hard, the light of the room assaulting my senses, and groan as I try to sit up. My neck aches from the awkward position I've been slumped in, and my heart feels like it's trying to hammer its way out of my chest. A warm hand settles on my shoulder, firm and reassuring, and I force myself to turn toward it.

It's her.

Sophia stands there, her green eyes wide with concern, her lips parted like she's on the verge of saying something. And God, the way she looks… even in my disoriented state, she's breathtaking. The black dress she's wearing makes her look like a sexy, young goddess, the neckline plunging dangerously low, teasing every forbidden thought I've ever tried to bury. Her waves of dark hair tumble over her shoulders, framing her in the most delicate, yet sinful way.

"Wow," I whisper, my voice raspy and barely audible. My eyes roam her figure, unabashed, and I don't even try to stop myself.

Her cheeks flush, but she doesn't move her hand from my shoulder. "Eve, are you okay? You scared me!"

"You came prepared to beat me today," I manage, the corners of my mouth twitching in a faint smile. The words slip out before I can think better of it.

Sophia's eyes widen, panic flashing across her face. "Grandpa is here too," she says quickly, leaning in as if to warn me, her voice dropping to a whisper. "Careful."

The reminder sobers me faster than a bucket of ice water. I groan inwardly and try to sit up straighter, ignoring the warmth her hand leaves behind when she pulls it away.

Sophia steps back, brushing her hair behind her ear. "Miriam's bringing water," she says softly, glancing toward the doorway.

"Thanks," I mutter, my gaze lingering on her longer than it

should.

For a moment, the room is silent except for the sound of my uneven breathing. I can't tell if I'm more wrecked by the panic attack—or by her.

The rich, smoky scent of a cigar drifts through the room, curling lazily in the air as I finally notice him—Dad. He's lounged back in the corner of the study, his legs propped up on an ottoman like he owns the place. The leather of his bomber jacket gleams faintly in the low light, and his boots, dusted with mud, tap idly against the furniture. The picture of ease, as if this were his personal war room.

Between puffs of his cigar, he speaks, his voice low and gravelly, carrying that trademark Lockhart authority. "Had to break down your door. Don't ask me to reimburse you."

Sophia tenses beside me, but I can't help the smirk tugging at my lips. "I'm feeling better, Dad. Thanks," I say, sarcasm dripping off the words.

Dad doesn't flinch, doesn't even look at me directly. Instead, he inspects the glowing tip of his cigar like it's more interesting than the daughter he just rescued. "You should be. The way you were flopping around, I was about to ask for a medic."

Sophia's hand tightens on my shoulder, and I can feel her glaring at him. "I don't think now's the time to be descriptive with your words, Mr. Lockhart" she quips.

Dad turns his piercing blue eyes on her, arching a single brow. "That attitude of yours," he says, pointing the cigar in her direction, "reminds me of James. Smart-mouthed but sharp. You'd have made a hell of a soldier."

"She's a little busy keeping her sister safe," I cut in, my tone sharper than I intended.

Dad chuckles, a deep, rumbling sound. "Good thing too. Not everyone can handle it out there." His gaze shifts back to me, piercing and loaded.

The tension in the room thickens, but for once, I let it slide. I'm too drained to spar with him, and the warmth of Sophia's hand on my shoulder is grounding me in a way I don't want to admit.

I sit up straighter, ignoring the soreness in my neck from slumping over my desk. "You couldn't knock first? Or, I don't know, use one of the dozen guards patrolling the estate?" I direct my question at Dad.

"Your niece," he emphasizes the word with a pointed glance at Sophia, "rushed to my room. Told me she heard screaming. You scream now during these attacks? That's new."

I stiffen, my gaze darting to Sophia. She's leaning against my desk, her arms crossed, but her expression is unreadable. Then, almost imperceptibly, she mouths, *Let it go.*

God, she's impossible. Impossible to ignore, impossible to argue with when she's standing there looking like *that*.

My gaze locks on her, and it's like my brain short-circuits. The dress is absurd—black, tight, cut in ways that make me want to grab it, and tear it further, to rip it to shreds, and expose the deliciousness of her skin. The slit climbs so high up her thigh that it's barely a slit at all, revealing smooth, golden skin that seems to glow in the low light. My eyes follow the line of her leg, imagining what it would feel like under my hands, under my lips, my tongue. If she leaned just a little more to the side, I'd see everything. My mouth goes dry at the thought.

And those tits—propped up, soft, begging for my attention. The neckline dips low, showcasing a deep, juicy cleavage, bursting forth like water from a dam. I can see the faint imprint of her nipples, right next to where the dress barely hides it. If it hadn't been for my panic attack, I am sure those nipples would have been straining against my tongue instead of that damn dress. Her hair falls over her chest in loose waves, like it's trying to guard her breasts, hiding them like a dragon hoarding treasure. My fingers curl against the desk as I fight the urge to push that hair aside, to run my mouth along the curve of her neck, down her collarbone, and bury my face in that perfect valley.

What did you have in mind when you wore that tonight, Sophia? Whatever it was, I would've given it to you.

The thought slams into me with the force of a freight train, and I shift in my seat, trying to compose myself. I shouldn't be looking at her like this. I shouldn't be imagining kissing up the length of her thigh, following the path of that slit with my tongue until she's trembling. I shouldn't be picturing myself ripping that dress in two, tearing it apart just to give myself more room, more access. But I can't stop.

My chest tightens, my jaw clenches, and I force myself to look away, dragging my gaze back to Dad. His eyes are sharp, suspicious, and for a second, I wonder if he knows. If he can *see* how much I want her. How badly I need her. How close I am to losing every shred of control I have left.

Dad rises from his seat with a grunt, brushing a speck of ash from his jacket. "I'm heading back to my room," he mutters, puffing his cigar one last time before stubbing it out on the edge of the tray. As he makes his way toward the door, he pauses, turning back slightly. "And don't make me break any more doors for the rest of the night."

I smirk faintly, though I can't muster the energy for anything more. "I'm fine, Dad. Thanks for your help."

He huffs, clearly unimpressed. "You say that like I had a choice. Next time, keep your screams down, will you?" He strides out, his boots echoing through the hallway, leaving his words hanging in the room like a scolding.

Miriam steps forward hesitantly, hands folded neatly in front of her. "Miss Lockhart, do you need anything? Perhaps some tea or—"

I shake my head, cutting her off gently. "No, Miriam. You've done enough tonight. Go back to sleep."

She hesitates, her eyes darting toward Sophia before nodding reluctantly. "Very well. Goodnight, Miss Lockhart." The door clicks softly behind her, leaving me alone with Sophia in the dimly lit study.

Sophia leans against the desk, her fingers nervously caressing the edges as she studies me. There's a frown etched across her face, her green eyes filled with something between concern and frustration. Her silence speaks louder than any words.

I push myself up from the chair, testing my legs, but Sophia moves quickly, her arm brushing against mine as she steadies me. The warmth of her touch sends a jolt through me, but I wave her off. "I'm fine. It was just a panic attack, not a sniper. I haven't injured myself."

She doesn't step back, her eyes fixed on me like she's waiting for me to break again. It's unnerving. I stretch to shake off the stiffness, trying to reclaim some semblance of control.

A sharp laugh escapes before I can stop it. "I must look like a real mess. First, breaking down in jiu-jitsu, and now this. I've gone from ex-soldier to... whatever this is in less than a day."

Sophia doesn't laugh. Instead, she takes a step closer, her voice firm but soft. "You need to stop talking like you're some Greek goddess who can never be hurt."

I blink, caught off guard. "Excuse me?"

"You're not a goddess, Eve. You're human," she says, her voice steady but gentle. "A human who just happens to look like a Greek goddess, sure. But you can hurt, you can cry, you can fall apart. And that's okay."

Her fingers curl against the edge of the desk, her tension barely hidden. "It doesn't make you weak," she adds, softer now.

"It just makes you... you."

Sophia leans against the desk, her green eyes sharp, playful, daring me to look at her.

"You've got a talent for trouble, don't you?" I say, my voice tighter than I'd like.

Her smirk deepens. "What can I say? I've got a good tongue."

I laugh despite myself, low and rough. "Miriam's going to ask about that dress."

She shrugs, the movement making the neckline dip further. "Miriam? Nah. Iggy might, though. She'd love it."

"So...why are you dressed like you're heading to a nightclub?" I ask, stepping toward the bar and pouring myself a drink, anything to keep my hands busy.

She tilts her head, her dark curls brushing against bare shoulders, her smirk shifting into something wicked. "I like dressing up. And since I'm not hitting a club anytime soon, I figured I'd... improvise."

"To..." I gesture vaguely, swirling the whiskey in my glass before taking a slow sip. "...watch a movie with me? Dressed like *that*?"

She shrugs, the motion deliberate, making the already scandalous neckline of her dress dip even lower. More skin. More of her. My throat tightens as I catch a glimpse of her collarbone, her smooth, maddeningly perfect skin. "It's not my fault you're so easily distracted."

"Distracted isn't the word I'd use," I growl, taking a long sip of whiskey to steady myself.

"Oh? Then what is it?" she purrs, tilting her head, lips curling into a smirk. Her hair brushes her bare shoulders, teasing at her skin like it's guarding a treasure. Her eyes lock on mine, daring me to answer.

I clench the glass tighter, the burn of the whiskey no match for the fire licking up my spine. "You don't want me to say."

"Try me." She shifts, the slit parting further, her thighs begging to be touched. My chest tightens as I imagine my fingers gripping them, my mouth trailing up her skin, ripping the dress apart just to take more.

I set the glass down with more force than necessary, my hand trembling as I grip the edge of the bar. My pulse roars in my ears, but I turn back to her, finally letting my restraint crack.

"What that dress is doing to me?" I say, my voice low, rough, almost a growl. My eyes rake over her again, every curve, every inch of smooth, golden skin on display. "It's making me want to —"

A sharp, searing pain slices through my head, stealing the words from my throat. I stagger, gripping the wall as the room tilts, white-hot flashes sparking behind my eyes. My breath catches, and the whiskey glass wobbles on the bar.

"Eve!" Sophia's voice cuts through the haze, and she rushes to me, her hands warm on my arm as she steadies me. Her touch is grounding, but the pain pulses again, sharp and relentless. I squeeze my eyes shut, willing it to fade.

"You're not drinking," she murmurs, her voice soft but laced with concern. Her hand slides to my back, steadying me as I lean against the wall. Then, closer, softer, a whisper just for me: "You can tell me what you think of the dress later. Right now, you need to get into bed."

I nod, swallowing hard as the pain begins to ebb. The tension in my body shifts, the desire replaced by an overwhelming sense of exhaustion, of vulnerability I hate letting her see. But Sophia doesn't move away. Her hand remains on my back, firm, guiding, protective in a way that feels like a role reversal.

She begins to lead me toward the door, her touch light but

insistent. The silence stretches as my thoughts blur, but before we reach the hallway, I stop, turning toward her. My voice is quiet, hoarse, but deliberate.

"Sleep with me tonight," I say, the words spilling out before I can stop them. My hand brushes against her arm, grounding myself in her presence. "In my bed."

Her eyes widen slightly, just for a fraction of a second, before softening. A faint, unreadable smile tugs at the corner of her lips. "Let's get you to bed first."

∞∞∞

The room is still and vast, cloaked in dim light from the muted sconces. I stand motionless in the middle of it, my breath shallow, the weight of the day pressing on my chest. Around me, Sophia is a blur of movement, a flickering light darting from one task to the next, as if she's single-handedly trying to push the night's darkness away.

She crouches near the hearth, her slim hands expertly arranging the logs before striking a match. The fire catches, its orange glow spilling across her skin, and for a moment, I forget to breathe. Her hair falls in waves around her face, shadows playing over her cheekbones. She's focused, determined, entirely unaware of how captivating she looks in the golden light.

"Get into bed," she says over her shoulder, her voice soft but insistent. "You need to rest."

I don't move. My legs feel rooted to the ground, my gaze fixed on her as she rises and steps to the mantle. She lights the candles one by one, the flames blooming like tiny suns, their warm glow weaving a cocoon of safety around us. The way she moves —fluid, purposeful—makes my chest ache. She's nineteen, yet she carries herself like someone who's lived a hundred lifetimes, someone who understands how to create comfort out of chaos.

"Eve." Her voice pulls me from my trance. She turns, her brows knitting together when she sees me still standing. "What are you doing? Come on."

She takes my hand, her touch gentle but firm, and guides me to the bed. The sheets are cool as I sink down, and she hovers over me like she's protecting me from the very air itself. "Where's your nightdress?"

"To the left," I manage to murmur, nodding toward the grand cupboard. My voice is hoarse, and I hate how weak it sounds, especially when she looks at me like that—like she knows exactly what she's doing to me.

Sophia strides over, her hips swaying in a way that feels more deliberate than natural. My eyes follow her, drinking in the lines of her body, the way the fabric clings to every curve, teasing, taunting. She pulls open the cupboard with that quiet confidence that unravels me, returning with a satin slip. Dusty blue, soft, with lace so delicate it looks like sin. She sets it on the edge of the bed, then kneels in front of me.

Her green eyes meet mine, sharp and playful. "Arms up," she commands, her tone soft but with an edge that makes my stomach twist.

I comply, too stunned, too caught in the moment to argue. She peels away my jacket, her fingers lingering as if she has every right to touch me. Her hands slide to the waistband of my leggings, and when she tugs them down, the cool air brushes against my thighs, making my skin prickle. Her gaze doesn't waver, doesn't drop—not yet—but I see the way her lips twitch, as if she's holding something back.

She takes the slip and slides it over my head, the satin cascading down my body like water. Her hands smooth it over my skin, her palms skimming my hips, pressing lightly against my thighs before pulling away. The touch feels like a brand, burning through me, making my breath hitch.

"There," she whispers, her voice impossibly gentle as she tugs the blanket over me. "Now you look like someone who might actually sleep tonight."

I lie back, sinking into the softness of the bed, but I can't take my eyes off her. She moves to the center of the room, and the sight of her, back turned, fingers playing with the zipper of her dress, feels like a slap to the face. I want to look away. I *should* look away. But I can't.

She glances over her shoulder, her emerald eyes locking on mine, daring me to move. "Can you help?"

The air leaves my lungs. "Why wouldn't I?" My voice is low, rough, barely steady.

She walks back toward me, slow, deliberate. Every step makes my pulse hammer harder. She stops at the edge of the bed, standing over me, her gaze heavy, almost predatory. My hands tremble as I reach for the zipper, brushing the warm fabric that clings to her spine. I pull it down, agonizingly slow, my fingers brushing the bare skin beneath.

"What will you wear?" I ask, barely recognizing my own voice as I unbox the masterpiece before me.

"Nothing," she replies, the word falling from her lips like a taunt.

"You'll freeze to death."

She doesn't answer. She just waits, her breath soft and steady, as the dress slips off her shoulders. Gravity takes over, pulling the fabric down her body, revealing skin so smooth, so tight, it feels like a punishment just to look at it.

The dress pools at her feet, leaving her in nothing but lace. Emerald green panties hug her hips, while my fingers twitch to grab her waist, and sink my teeth into the juiciest part of her ass. My chest tightens as my gaze drinks her in—her slender waist, the curve of her hips, the way the lace clings to her thighs like it knows it doesn't belong there.

She turns, and the sight of her robs me of breath. Her tits are high and perfect, the lace doing nothing to hide the hardness of her nipples. Her stomach is flat, her navel a dip that my mouth aches to trace. The panties sit low, teasing, and I can see the faintest shadow beneath them—a promise, a threat, a gift I have no right to want but can't stop craving.

She tilts her head, her hair spilling over one shoulder, framing her body like a work of art. Her lips part slightly, her breathing steady but shallow, and her eyes—God, her eyes—watch me like she knows exactly what I'm thinking.

And she does. She knows I'm imagining tearing the lace from her body, using my teeth to rip it away so I can finally, *finally* feel her bare skin. She knows I'm picturing her in my lap, her thighs straddling me, her pussy pressing against me as I mark her neck, her collarbone, her tits with my mouth. She knows I'm dying to fuck her—hard, fast, with no hesitation, no excuses.

She steps closer, her bare thighs brushing against the bed. "Are you just going to look, Auntie?" she murmurs, her voice soft but wicked. "Or are you going to help me get warm?"

I swallow hard, my hands gripping the blanket so tightly my knuckles ache. She smiles, slow and teasing, like she knows I'm already hers.

And God help me, I think she's right.

Sophia doesn't wait for permission—she never does. The bed dips under her weight as she slides in beside me, her body radiating warmth like she's already decided she's mine. She shifts, her back pressing against my chest, her ass flush against my hips, and it takes everything I have not to let out a sound.

The satin sheets glide against her bare skin as she settles, one leg curling over mine, the lace of her panties brushing my thigh.

Her hair spills over my shoulder, the faint scent of her shampoo wrapping around me, intoxicating. I don't move, don't breathe, because if I do, I might lose control.

She shifts again, her back arching slightly, pressing her body closer, and I feel the faintest hitch of her breath. "Eve," she murmurs, her voice soft, teasing, deadly. "You're so stiff. Relax."

I grit my teeth, my hands clenching the edge of the blanket. "Sophia—"

"Shh." Her hand reaches behind her, finding my wrist, guiding it gently. She places it over her waist, her fingers curling over mine, holding it there. "Just hug me."

My chest tightens, and my head spins. I can feel every inch of her—the dip of her waist, the curve of her hip, the soft lace brushing against my fingertips. My hand twitches, desperate to move, to explore, to grip. But I hold back, barely.

"Sophia," I rasp, my voice raw, trembling. "You're making this—"

"Safe," she interrupts, her voice barely above a whisper. "I feel safe with you, Eve. Don't you want me to feel that?"

Her words cut through me like a blade, and my resolve cracks. Slowly, carefully, I tighten my arm around her waist, pulling her closer. My hand brushes against her stomach, soft and warm, and I feel the faintest shudder ripple through her.

Her body melts into mine, her back pressing against my breasts, her hips shifting ever so slightly. "See?" she whispers, her voice tinged with a satisfaction that makes my pulse race. "That's better."

Better? No. This is worse. This is torture. Every breath I take pulls me deeper into her—her scent, her heat, the way her body fits against mine like it was made to be there. My hand stays still, obedient, but my mind is a riot of filth. I want to slide my fingers lower, over the lace, under it. I want to grip her thigh, pull her leg higher, open her up to me.

Instead, I bury my face in her hair, my lips brushing against the shell of her ear as I breathe her in. Her heartbeat is steady, her breathing soft, and I wonder if she knows how close I am to breaking. If she feels the way my chest heaves against her back, the way my hips press against hers, the way my fingers tremble against her waist.

"You're so warm," she murmurs, her voice dripping with innocence that feels like a lie. "I like this."

I don't answer, can't answer. My throat is dry, my body taut, every nerve in me screaming to move, to touch, to take. But I can't. Not yet. So I lie there, holding her, hating myself for wanting more.

Her voice breaks the silence, soft but unwavering. "I forgive you," she murmurs, her fingers lightly brushing mine where they rest on her waist.

The words hit me like a blow. "What?" My voice cracks, rough and disbelieving.

She sighs, her chest rising and falling against my arm. "I forgive you for leaving. For abandoning me. I understand."

I tighten my grip on her waist instinctively, my head spinning. "How do you understand?" I rasp, my voice thick with disbelief.

She's silent for a moment, her fingers tracing idle patterns on my hand. Then, she speaks, her voice low, steady. "A lot must have been on the line for you to go back to a profession that still haunts you. That tortures you like this." She pauses, as if weighing her words. "Someday, when you're feeling better, I'll ask you why you had to go back to being a soldier. But for now, just know this—I forgive you."

I close my eyes, the tightness in my chest unbearable. She shifts slightly, her body pressing closer against me. Her warmth feels like a balm and a torment all at once.

"The one thread that was stopping me from completely loving you," she continues, her voice softer now, "has broken. Now, I'm all yours, if you'll have me. I'm yours to command, to protect, to own. I have no fear of anything now, because I know I have my Eve with me."

Her words make my breath hitch, my body tightening against hers. She turns then, her movements slow but deliberate, until she's facing me. Her green eyes meet mine, unflinching, full of something raw and dangerous.

Her hand brushes my cheek, her touch featherlight but devastating. "I just hope one day, you can break whatever chains are holding you back from taking me," she whispers, her voice trembling slightly. "Because I would give myself willingly to you, Evelyn Lockhart."

Her words leave me shattered, raw, and exposed. My voice is barely a whisper as I murmur, "I want you too. God, I hate that I do, but I want you."

Sophia's lips curve into a faint, wicked smile, her green eyes gleaming with something triumphant. "Don't hate yourself for it," she whispers, her tone sultry and soft. Her fingers trail down my arm, leaving a path of fire in their wake. "Let me be your babygirl. See?" She shifts again, her leg sliding over mine, her body pressing closer until her warmth is flush against me.

Her breath tickles my ear, and her voice drops lower, dripping with sin. "I can take care of you, be a woman for you. And when you want..." She shifts her hips, rolling them against me, her lace-covered heat pressing firmly against my thigh. "I can be your spoiled, horny little brat who just wants to rub her pussy all over you... like this."

I gasp, my body stiffening as she grinds against me, slow and deliberate. My hand tightens on her waist, but I can't bring myself to pull away. Her eyes never leave mine, daring me, taunting me, begging me to break.

"Sophia," I choke out, my voice thick with desperation and need.

She leans closer, her lips brushing against my ear as she whispers, "Do you feel that? That's all for you. Every inch of me is for you, Eve. Take me, claim me, ruin me. I don't care what it means, I don't care if it's wrong. Just... don't push me away."

Her words unravel me. My hand, trembling, finds her waist, my fingers digging into her soft skin as I try to pull myself back from the edge. But she moves again, grinding against me, her breath hot against my neck.

"You can't fight this forever," she whispers, her voice both a taunt and a promise. "We're inevitable."

"Sophia, we can't—" I try, my voice cracking, barely audible over the pounding of my own heart. "We need to think this through. This isn't—"

She doesn't let me finish. Her lips crash into mine with a force that knocks every word out of my head, every thought replaced by her—her heat, her desperation, her unrelenting need. It's not just a kiss; it's a conquest, wild and messy, her tongue demanding entry as her teeth nip at my bottom lip. My gasp gives her everything she needs, and she takes it, deepening the kiss until I can barely breathe.

Then she pulls back, her green eyes blazing with an intensity that pins me to the bed. Her chest heaves, her lips swollen from the force of the kiss. "Stop me if you want," she whispers, her voice trembling but defiant. "But I've had enough."

I can't speak, can't move. My hands grip the sheets like a lifeline, but it's no use—she's already claimed me. Her lips find mine again, harder, hungrier, her hands sliding up my arms, pinning me down as her body presses into mine. Her moan vibrates against my mouth, a low, primal sound that sends a fresh wave of heat pooling low in my stomach.

She tears her mouth away, trailing hot, open-mouthed kisses down my jaw, then to my neck. Her teeth scrape against my skin, her tongue soothing the sting before her lips latch on, sucking hard enough to leave a mark. A strangled moan escapes me, and her grip tightens on my shoulders as if she knows exactly what she's doing.

"You taste so good," she murmurs, her voice thick with lust as her lips trail lower. She pushes the straps of my nightdress off my shoulders, her fingers trembling but determined as she exposes more of me. The satin pools around my chest, barely covering me, and her breath hitches as she stares, her pupils blown wide.

"You're a fucking dream," she whispers, her lips brushing against the swell of my breasts. "You don't even know what you do to me, do you? How wet you make me? I'm soaked for you, Eve. You could slide two fingers in me right now, and they'd glide so easily." Her words make my breath hitch, my chest tightening as heat floods every nerve.

Her mouth presses to my skin, her kisses growing wetter, sloppier, as she works her way lower. My chest heaves, my breaths coming in short, ragged gasps as her tongue flicks over the curve of my breast.

"Sophia," I rasp, my voice breaking as her mouth closes over my nipple through the thin fabric, the heat of her tongue searing through the satin. She sucks lightly, her teeth grazing just enough to make my back arch, my body pressing into her.

Her hands slide lower, gripping my thighs, spreading them slightly as she adjusts her position. The satin nightdress shifts, sliding up to reveal more of my legs. Her lips leave my breasts, and she trails a hot, wet path down my stomach, her tongue flicking against my skin, her teeth grazing lightly. My hands fly to her shoulders, unsure if I'm trying to stop her or pull her closer.

She pauses at the edge of the nightdress, her breath hot against my bare thighs. There's no barrier, no lace, nothing to stop her now. Her lips hover just above my pussy, where I'm already aching for her, and her hands grip my hips, holding me firmly in place.

"I've dreamed of this," she murmurs, her voice low, almost reverent. "Dreamed of tasting you, of making you mine. Don't you want to see your Sophia's tongue on you? Don't you want to watch my pretty face between your legs, eating you like the filthy slut I am for you?"

Her green eyes meet mine, dark and wild, and I can't look away. She presses her lips to the inside of my thigh, slow and deliberate, her tongue trailing up, closer, until I'm trembling beneath her. Her moan is low and guttural, vibrating against my skin as she breathes, "You're mine, Eve. Every inch of you. All mine."

My head falls back against the pillow, my body arching, surrendering completely as her mouth moves higher. She's relentless, worshipping me with her lips, her tongue, her teeth, and I'm powerless to stop her.

With deliberate slowness, she angles herself further down, her face level with the apex of my thighs. I'm still lying on my side, and she positions herself the same way, her body curving with mine like we're two pieces of a puzzle fitting together. Her hands slide up my outer thigh, her touch firm and insistent as she grips the leg that's draped over the other. Gently, she lifts it, raising it just enough to expose me fully to her.

The motion leaves me bare, vulnerable in a way that should terrify me—but the look on her face ignites something primal. Her lips part, her breath warm against my skin as she takes me in, her pupils blown wide with lust. The intimacy of the position is undeniable—her body pressed so close to mine, her face nestled between my thighs, one leg draped over her shoulder as her hands hold me open for her.

Sophia lets out a soft, desperate moan as her mouth descends, her plush, pouty lips pressing a slow, lingering kiss against my center. The sensation is electric, her warmth, her wetness, her sheer reverence for the moment setting every nerve in my body on fire. She kisses me again, harder this time, her lips sliding over the most sensitive flesh of my pussy, as if she's savoring me.

My breath catches, a shudder wracking through me as my head falls back against the pillow. The sound that escapes my throat is guttural, raw, somewhere between a grunt and a growl, like an animal losing control. My hands clutch the sheets, my knuckles white as her mouth works me, her tongue flicking out to trace every contour, every ridge, exploring me with maddening precision.

Sophia moans again, her needy, desperate sounds vibrating against me, sending shockwaves through my body. "You're so perfect," she murmurs between kisses, her lips smacking softly against my flesh. Her words are muffled, almost drowned out by the wet, sinful sounds of her mouth devouring me. "You taste… God, Eve, you taste like heaven."

Her tongue slides against me, flat and firm, her pace unhurried but deliberate, like she wants to draw this out, to keep me on the edge as long as possible. My hips jerk involuntarily, pressing into her, seeking more, and she responds with a low, satisfied hum that sends another ripple of pleasure through me.

The combination of her lips, her tongue, her moans—each one more desperate than the last—pushes me closer to the brink. Her hands grip my thighs tighter, holding me in place as she loses herself in me, her mouth moving with a fervor that borders on worship.

"Fuck, baby," I gasp, my voice barely audible over the wet, obscene sounds filling the room. She doesn't answer. Instead, she sucks gently, her tongue swirling, her lips sealing around me in a way that makes my entire body tense. I let out another guttural sound, deeper this time, raw and unrestrained, as my hand flies to her hair, tangling in the dark curls, desperate for something to hold on to.

Her response is immediate—she moans against me, the vibrations shooting straight to my core as her pace quickens. Her lips slide over me again and again, her tongue teasing, exploring, tasting, while her nails dig into my thighs, grounding me in the moment.

I'm unraveling, every thought, every inhibition burning away under the relentless assault of her mouth. And the way she looks at me, even from this position, like I'm the only thing she's ever wanted—it's too much. Too much, and not enough.

My grip on her hair tightens until I hear her gasp softly, her lips parting as if she's waiting for my command. Sophia's eyes meet mine, glinting with challenge and submission all at once, and then she whispers it, soft and deliberate: "Auntie."

The word sends a bolt of electricity straight through me, my pulse pounding in my ears. I should pull back, stop this, but instead, I watch as her tongue flicks out, slow and deliberate, giving me a teasing, sinful lick that makes my thighs twitch. Then she says it again, softer, dripping with submission, her voice trembling with need: "Auntie."

I snap.

My body moves before my mind can catch up. My hand jerks her closer, forcing her face deeper between my thighs, my breath ragged and uneven as I growl, "You wanted this, didn't you? You've been begging for it, teasing me with every look, every word. Is this what you wanted, Sophia? To make me lose control?"

Her moan is muffled against me, vibrating against my skin, and I shudder violently. Her hands grip my hips, holding me steady as her lips press desperate, open-mouthed kisses to my thighs, each one wetter, sloppier, more frantic. Her breath is hot, her movements unrelenting, and every nerve in my body is on fire.

I shift, angling myself so I'm pressing her deeper into the mattress, my thighs framing her face, and her lips find me again. This time, her tongue slides against me, soft and slick, exploring me with a precision that makes my hips jerk forward. A guttural sound escapes me, low and primal, and I press down harder, grinding against her mouth.

"You've been torturing me," I growl, my voice raw, trembling with intensity. "All those filthy little words, the way you look at me, the way you walk around with your ass hanging out. Fuck... you make me fucking leak! Look where it's gotten you now—right here, tasting me like the filthy slut you are. You seduced me so good, girl. So good that I want to fuck your face until you can't feel it anymore. Ah, ah, aaah...fuck yes!"

Her response is a desperate whimper, her hands gripping my thighs tighter, her tongue moving faster, hungrier. She licks me like she's starved for it, her moans muffled but insistent as her nails dig into my skin. My grip in her hair tightens, guiding her, holding her exactly where I need her.

"Say it again," I command, my voice sharp, teetering on the edge of control. I pull back just enough to let her speak, every muscle in my body quaking with restraint.

"Auntie," she whispers again, her voice soft, trembling, her lips glistening with me. Her eyes flicker up to mine, pleading. "Please Auntie...fuck my face. Please! Cover my pretty little face with your juices!"

The sound of her begging, the sight of her flushed and desperate, undoes me completely. I shove her back into place, my thighs squeezing her head as I grind against her face, rough and unrelenting. Her tongue flicks and swirls, her moans growing louder, more frantic, and the wet, obscene sounds of her mouth working me fill the room. My pussy swallows her tongue whole and I still wish it was deeper.

"Good girl," I rasp, my voice shaking as I move faster, my body trembling with the force of my need. "Is this what you wanted? To make me lose control? To have me like this, using your mouth like it's mine?"

I grind harder, rougher, dragging myself over her lips, her tongue, her face, her breath coming in short, desperate bursts beneath me.

Her muffled cry sends another shockwave through me, and I can't stop myself. My hips jerk forward, pressing harder against her lips, her tongue sliding against me in a way that makes my vision blur. "Don't stop," I hiss, my voice a low growl. "Keep going. Show me how much you need this. Show me how filthy you are for me."

Her hands claw at my thighs, her fingers digging into my skin as she pulls me closer, holding me in place. I'm spiraling, every nerve on fire, my breaths coming in short, sharp bursts as I chase the release I've been holding back for too long. "You're mine," I snarl, my voice trembling with the weight of the moment. "Every inch of you is mine."

Sophia's moans grow louder, her tongue working faster, her desperation matching my own as I come apart, raw and unrestrained.

"Fuck me, *Mommy!*" she gasps out from between my thighs.

My body shudders, a wave of pleasure crashing over me, leaving me breathless, trembling, and completely undone.

And as I collapse back against the pillows, my grip loosening in her hair, she presses one final, soft kiss to my thigh. "Mommy," she whispers again, her voice soft but wicked, her lips curving into a satisfied smile.

A. GOSWAMI

I'm hers, and I don't even care anymore.

Chapter Eight

Sophia

The cockpit of the Cessna 172 hums like it's in on the joke, the controls in front of me steady while my brain? A complete circus. The headset clamps around my head like it's trying to hold my thoughts in place—not that it's succeeding. Dan Carter, my flying coach, has his hands folded like he's praying for patience, but I can tell by the vein pulsing in his temple that it's not working.

"Focus, Sophia," he barks, his voice slicing through my very vivid replay of Eve's hands sliding down my back. "You're drifting again. Keep this up, and you'll be landing us in a field of cows."

I glance at the horizon, pretending I wasn't imagining anything remotely inappropriate. "I'm fine," I say, trying to sound nonchalant. Totally believable, right?

Dan sighs, exasperated. "You're one of the best students I've had, but you're not a damn pilot yet. Flying in eight days doesn't mean you've got it all figured out. If you don't focus, you'll crash—and I don't mean the plane. Flying isn't about looking pretty in the cockpit."

Ouch. "Rude," I mutter, adjusting the yoke. "I'm more than just a pretty face, you know."

"Then prove it," he snaps. "Right now, you're flying like your brain's still on the ground. What's going on?"

What's going on? Oh, nothing much. Just the fact that last night, I was tangled in Eve's arms, her lips brushing against my skin in ways that should be illegal. Or the way she kissed me good morning, her voice so low and raspy it practically ruined me for the day. Or, you know, the casual game of footsie we played under the breakfast table while pretending everything was totally normal.

"Nothing," I say, my voice too high-pitched to be convincing. "I'm just... distracted."

Dan groans, scrubbing a hand over his face. "Harlow, distractions get you killed up here. You need to get your head out of whatever clouds you're stuck in."

The irony isn't lost on me. Clouds? Oh, I'm in clouds, all right. Big, fluffy, Eve-shaped clouds that have me replaying every moment from last night. The feel of her fingers tracing my spine, the way her lips curved when I called her *Mommy*—God, I'm a goner.

"Eyes on the instruments!" Dan snaps, and I jolt, gripping the yoke harder.

The instruments blur slightly as I refocus, but my thoughts? They're still 30,000 feet up with Eve. Because who needs to learn how to fly when you've already found the one thing that makes your heart soar?

Dan grumbles something under his breath about wasted time

and ulcers as he grips the controls, guiding the Cessna 172 down to the airstrip. The landing is smooth—because of course it is, Dan's a perfectionist, even when he's annoyed—but I'm too busy counting down the seconds until I can get out of this cockpit and back to my secret escapades with Eve.

"You can thank me later for ending this torture," Dan says as we taxi to a stop. He cuts the engine and turns to me, eyebrows raised. "Today was absolute shit, Harlow. Do better tomorrow, or you'll end up as roadkill for someone else's landing gear."

I give him a sheepish smile, unbuckling my harness. "Noted. Thanks, Dan."

He waves me off, muttering something about how I'm usually brilliant, and I practically leap out of the plane. My boots crunch on the gravel as I pull my leather jacket tighter around me against the chilly air. My eyes scan the lot for Eve's G-Wagon, hoping she's here so I can continue the dance we started last night. My stomach flips when I spot it parked near the edge of the airfield.

But then I notice who's standing outside of it—*Iggy*—dressed in a full-neck beige sweater emblazoned with the words *"Iggilicious is Bootylicious."* A laugh escapes me before I can stop it. Of course.

I reach the G-Wagon, and Iggy shoots me a smirk as I climb inside. "Where's Eve?" I ask, my brow furrowing. "Why didn't she come to pick me up?"

The bodyguard in the driver's seat starts the engine, and Iggy leans back, drumming her fingers on the window. "Try to at least hide your disappointment," she says sarcastically. "It's rude."

I roll my eyes. "Can you blame me after what happened last night?"

Iggy swivels toward me, her wide, twinkling eyes practically glowing with mischief, completely ignoring my remark. "Oh, you wanna know why your beloved Auntie Eve didn't pick you up?" she says, dragging out the suspense like a pro. "Let me enlighten you, dear Sophia. Her ex showed up this morning."

My stomach twists into a knot. "Her *ex*?" I whisper, my voice barely audible over the hum of the G-Wagon's engine. "In this town?"

"Yep," Iggy replies, popping the "p" with extra glee. "I can't believe I forgot to mention it before. And I'm *sure* Evelyn didn't bring it up, considering she likes to keep her past sealed tighter than Fort Knox. Her name's Tessa. She's the sheriff around here." Iggy pauses for effect, letting the bomb drop. "A *hot*, sexy policewoman with a long-ass ponytail and even longer legs. Like, legs that could rival Evelyn's."

My heart sinks, but I manage to keep my voice steady. "What does she look like?"

"Oh, glad you asked," Iggy says, practically vibrating with excitement. "Picture this—tan uniform, buttoned just low enough to tease but not enough to get written up. She wears her shirt two sizes too small, showing off her... assets." Iggy makes a deliberate gesture toward her chest. "She's basically what happens when you take a centerfold and slap a badge on her."

I blink, trying to process, but my brain refuses to cooperate. "And... they were together?"

"Oh, *very* together," Iggy says, grinning. "From what I hear, it was hot and heavy. Like 'I'll arrest you for public indecency if you keep looking at me like that' kind of heavy."

I sink deeper into my seat, staring out the window. "And now she's here?"

"Yup," Iggy says, popping her gum with a dramatic flair. "So buckle up, sweetheart. When we get back to the estate, you're in for a breakfast straight out of a soap opera."

∞∞∞

Tessa is all legs and laughter, her tanned, impossibly toned body perched way too close to Eve for my liking. I glare at her from across the long dining table, my fork stabbing aimlessly at the scrambled eggs on my plate. She's hot—I'll give her that. Her uniform clings a little too perfectly, the top buttons undone just enough to draw attention. When she laughs, it's a melodic trill, but it's what follows that grates on me most.

She touches Eve's hand.

What is this? A sheriff or a high school girl giggling away like that? I seethe internally, watching her with narrowed eyes. She's clearly staking her claim, and I don't miss the subtle glances she throws my way, as if to say, *Good luck, kid.*

"Why the long face, kid?" Tessa asks suddenly, her gaze shifting to me. The word *kid* lands like a slap, and I force a tight smile.

"I didn't do well at my flying lesson today," I say flatly, avoiding her smirking face to look at Eve instead.

"Why?" Eve's voice is calm, curious, and it makes my pulse race in a way I wish it wouldn't.

"Because I was distracted," I admit, letting my gaze linger on her longer than I should.

"By what?" Tessa leans forward, her perfectly plucked brows raised in mock interest.

I meet Eve's eyes and hold them. "By the memory of last night."

Eve's lips press together, a faint smirk threatening to break free. She quickly hides it behind her coffee cup.

Tessa frowns. "What happened last night?"

I tilt my head, feigning innocence. "Oh, just a very... intense physical activity. Lots of sweating. Left me sore this morning."

Eve chokes on her coffee, her eyes darting to mine, while Tessa looks between us, confused but intrigued. I savor the small victory, even as Eve glares at me over the rim of her cup.

I lean back in my chair, locking eyes with Tessa. She's too comfortable, too smug, and it's grating on every nerve. "So," I say, feigning politeness, "how did you and Aunt Eve become... friends?"

Tessa's grin widens as if she's been waiting for this question. She glances at Eve, who immediately stiffens. "Oh, that's a fun story," Tessa begins, leaning forward, resting her chin on her hand. "See, your aunt and I didn't exactly hit it off at first."

Eve groans, her fingers curling around her coffee mug. "Tessa—"

Tessa waves her off, eyes glinting with mischief. "So, Eve wanted to make some 'improvements' to the estate when she moved back—things like fencing off parts of the land and setting up private patrols. Problem was, some of that land skirted public territory, and I had to step in and say no. You can imagine how well that went."

I smirk, glancing at Eve, whose lips are pressed into a tight line. "I can imagine."

"She stormed into my office, all fire and fury, throwing words like 'rights' and 'security' around. I'm not ashamed to admit I enjoyed riling her up a little. There's nothing quite like seeing Evelyn Lockhart pissed off. She gets this vein in her neck—"

"Tessa," Eve warns, her voice low, her glare sharp enough to cut.

Tessa ignores her, grinning. "Anyway, one argument turned

into another, and before we knew it, we were grabbing drinks to 'discuss' things. And, well... one drink led to another."

My stomach tightens as Tessa leans back, smirking. "Your aunt is very persuasive when she wants to be. And let's just say she wasn't boring in how she negotiated. She's got this... commanding presence, you know? It's very hard to say no to her."

Eve pinches the bridge of her nose, muttering something under her breath.

"And after a while," Tessa continues, her grin turning downright wicked, "those negotiations stopped being about fences and patrols and started being about who could undo the other's shirt faster."

"Tessa." Eve's voice is sharp, her jaw tight as she shoots daggers across the table.

"What?" Tessa says innocently, looking between Eve and me. "She asked how we became friends. I'm just being honest. It was a rocky start, sure, but we found... common ground." Her tone drips with innuendo as she sips her coffee, her eyes never leaving mine.

I keep my expression neutral, but inside, I'm seething. Every smug word out of her mouth feels like a challenge, a reminder that she's had something with Eve that I haven't—yet. But the way Eve shifts uncomfortably in her seat, her eyes darting to me, tells me everything I need to know. Tessa may think she has the upper hand, but Eve's loyalty isn't with her anymore.

"Well," I say sweetly, leaning forward with a smirk, "it's nice to know Aunt Eve was... exploring all her options."

Eve shoots me a warning look, but I just grin, my eyes flicking to Tessa. Two can play this game.

Tessa's smirk falters for the briefest second, her sharp wit momentarily dulled. I lean forward, resting my chin on my hand in the same mocking way she did earlier. "It's better for a woman to taste all the dishes before she decides on the one she wants to eat for the rest of her life," I say, my voice sweet but laced with steel.

Tessa raises an eyebrow at me, clearly not expecting my response. "Care to explain...*kid?*" she parrots, her tone light but edged with curiosity.

I lean forward, resting my chin in my hand, a saccharine smile plastered on my face. "Oh, nothing, Sheriff. Just that tastes evolve, you know? It's like... trying out a menu at a fancy restaurant. Sometimes, you realize that the dish you've been raving about isn't quite what you want anymore."

Eve chokes on her coffee, quickly covering it with a cough. Her eyes dart between me and Tessa, and I can see the faintest flicker of amusement in them, though she tries to suppress it.

Tessa, however, isn't so easily brushed off. She narrows her eyes at me, her lips curving into a tight smirk. "Is that right? And what do you think Eve's... taste is now?"

I tilt my head, feigning innocence. "Oh, I wouldn't presume to know her tastes, Sheriff. But, you know, they do say it's better to explore all the options before settling down. Maybe she realized she wanted something a little... fresher. A little more exciting. Something that hasn't been sitting on the menu too long."

Tessa's smirk falters just a fraction, the tiniest crack in her composure. "Funny," she says, her voice cool. "Eve and I had plenty of excitement back in the day."

"Sure," I reply, letting the word hang in the air like a challenge. "But excitement doesn't always mean satisfaction, does it?"

Eve shifts in her seat, clearly uncomfortable but not intervening. Her eyes flicker to me, a silent warning that I gleefully ignore.

Tessa leans back, crossing her arms. "You're a bold one, I'll give you that. But bold doesn't always mean you know what you're talking about."

"Maybe not," I say, leaning back as well, my smile widening. "But if there's one thing I've learned, it's that people rarely forget their first taste of something... unforgettable. Wouldn't you agree, Aunt Eve?"

Eve's head snaps up, her eyes locking on mine. For a second, she looks like she's torn between scolding me and laughing.

She clears her throat, clearly trying to defuse the tension. "I think we're getting a little off-topic here."

"Oh, I don't think so," I say breezily, picking up my glass of water and taking a sip. "It's fascinating, really, hearing about the Sheriff's past adventures with you, Aunt Eve. But like I said, tastes change. And some dishes... well, they're just better left in the past."

Tessa's jaw tightens, but before she can retort, Eve steps in, her voice firm but calm. "All right, I think we've had enough reminiscing for one morning."

I grin, pleased with myself. Tessa shoots me a look, her expression a mix of confusion and annoyance. Eve's leg brushes against mine under the table—a fleeting touch, but enough to make my heart race. Victory is sweet.

Just as the tension at the table begins to bubble over, Emmy bounds into the room, her energy a sharp contrast to the lingering awkwardness. She's clutching Mr. Wonkers tightly, her curls bouncing as she slides into the seat beside me. Behind her, Miriam follows with a plate of toast and scrambled eggs, her face showing a mix of exhaustion and fondness.

"Good morning!" Emmy chirps, her voice bright and innocent, cutting through the weight of the adult conversation like a ray of sunshine.

Miriam sets the plate down in front of her and mutters, "Eat quickly, young lady, before you drag Mr. Wonkers into some mischief again."

Emmy giggles, picking up her fork. "Mr. Wonkers behaves, Miriam. It's me you have to watch out for."

Tessa pushes back her chair, standing with a casual grace that irritates me for no logical reason. She glances at Eve, her hand brushing her belt as if to remind everyone in the room she's still the Sheriff. "Eve," she says, her voice measured, "we need to talk about the estate's security. There are a few things I've noticed that need fixing."

Eve nods, her expression unreadable, but there's a subtle tension in her shoulders as she rises. "Let's step into the study."

Tessa turns her attention to me, her smirk firmly back in place. "Pardon me, kid, while Eve and this old dish talk grown-up stuff that'll keep you alive."

I meet her gaze evenly, my smile tight but polite. "Thank you for everything you're doing for us, Sheriff. It means a lot."

Her smirk flickers, almost imperceptibly, before she nods. "Sure thing."

I catch the way Eve looks at me as she adjusts the collar of her shirt—a flicker of something unreadable in her eyes before she glances away. Tessa heads out of the room, and Eve follows, her face carefully blank.

The moment they're gone, I let out a breath I didn't realize I was holding and turn my attention back to Emmy. Whatever Tessa has to discuss with Eve, I'm sure it's nothing I can't outshine in time.

Eve

The autumn sun casts a golden hue over the estate grounds, the crisp air carrying the faint scent of dried leaves and pine. I lean back on the picnic blanket, a sandwich half-eaten in my hand, my eyes locked on Sophia. She's lounging beside me, shades perched on her nose, her leather jacket discarded carelessly to reveal a white crop top and skinny jeans that cling to her little tushy like a sin.

A gust of wind tousles her dark waves, and she brushes a strand of hair from her face, her movements slow and unhurried, like she's completely at ease. My gaze flickers to Dad and Emmy in the distance, tossing a frisbee back and forth with an ease that makes me wonder when my father last smiled like that. Iggy's off in the woods, collecting berries or maybe just finding excuses to avoid Richard's booming laugh. The guards patrol lazily, the relaxed air of the afternoon making them seem less like soldiers and more like shadows blending into the trees.

I clear my throat, breaking the comfortable silence. "That was risky, what you did with Tessa."

Sophia doesn't even glance my way, her lips curling into a smirk as she takes a sip from her water bottle. "Risky? You mean calling out your ex who just so happens to be the sheriff of this quaint little town? The one who calls me a 'kid' every chance she gets? Yeah, super risky."

I tilt my head, smirking despite myself. "You *are* a kid."

Her head whips toward me, her eyes blazing behind the tinted shades. "Don't you dare."

I laugh, leaning back on my elbows. "I never thought the little flower I left behind years ago would grow into a wild rose, with thorns she uses when you piss her off."

Sophia scoffs, but I catch the slight tug of a smile at the corner of her mouth. "Yeah, well, this rose didn't know she had competition from a sheriff's badge."

"You have no competition, babygirl," I say, my voice low, and I watch as her smile slips through, unbidden.

Her head tilts slightly, her voice softening. "You know how that word makes me feel."

"That's why I say it."

"Thanks, *Mommy*," she retorts, her tone dripping with sass.

I chuckle, shaking my head. "You know how *that* word makes me feel." My hand moves instinctively, sliding under the back of her crop top, my fingers brushing the warm, smooth skin of her back. She shivers slightly under my touch but doesn't pull away. My thumb draws slow circles, tracing her spine, and I feel her breath hitch.

"I hate you," she murmurs, though her voice betrays nothing but amusement.

"No, you don't," I reply, my lips curling into a grin as I watch her relax against my touch. The autumn sun shines down on us, but the warmth radiating between us feels far more dangerous than the midday heat.

∞∞∞

The sun is still warm against my skin when a frantic shaking jolts me awake. I blink, disoriented, the lazy hum of the afternoon giving way to Sophia's voice, sharp and panicked.

"Eve, wake up! Emmy is missing. No one can find her. Emmy is missing, Eve!"

Her words slice through the haze of sleep, and I sit up abruptly, her worried face hovering inches from mine. Her green eyes are wide and brimming with fear, her hands gripping my shoulders like I'm the only thing keeping her tethered to the ground.

"What do you mean she's missing?" I demand, my voice rough, the weight of her panic already coiling in my chest.

"She and Richard went into the woods," she rushes, her words tumbling over each other. "He wanted to show her how to carve her name into a tree or something—God, I don't know! It's been over an hour, Eve, and the guards can't find them. They're not there!" Her voice cracks, and she's trembling now, her desperation wrapping around me like a vice.

I'm on my feet in seconds, the lingering sleep banished. "Slow down," I say, my voice steady but firm. "Which direction did they go?"

Sophia points toward the dense line of trees, her hand shaking. I follow her gaze and spot a guard lingering near the edge of the clearing. "You!" I bark, and he straightens instantly. "Follow me. Into the woods. Now."

Turning back to Sophia, I lower my voice, though it still holds an edge. "You stay here. Iggy, Miriam—take her inside."

Sophia shakes her head, her jaw set in that infuriatingly stubborn way of hers. "I'm not going inside."

"Damn it, Sophia, I don't have time for this!" I hiss, grabbing her arm. She resists, her heels digging into the ground as I half-drag her toward the manor steps. "Go inside, or else—Sophia!"

"Or else what? You'll hit me?" she snaps, her voice sharp, daring.

I stop, my breath coming in short bursts as frustration and fear bubble to the surface. "Fuck, why are you so stubborn?"

"Because she's my sister," she bites out, yanking her arm free. "And I'm not hiding in some house while you look for her!"

For a moment, our eyes lock, the tension between us crackling like a live wire.

Sophia glares at me, her jaw clenched, defiance radiating from every inch of her. I'm about to snap again when Iggy steps between us, her voice calm but firm. "We'll be in the hall, Sophia. You can look outside from the windows there—it's the same as being outside."

Sophia's gaze shifts to Iggy, her breathing sharp and uneven. I silently pray she'll listen. She glares at me one last time, then mutters, "Okay," her voice clipped. She spins on her heel, storming up the stairs and into the Great Hall, Iggy and Miriam trailing behind her like sentinels.

The moment the door shuts behind them, I take off, my boots pounding against the ground as I race toward the woods where the guard stands waiting. The chill of the autumn air cuts through me, but it's nothing compared to the cold knot of fear tightening in my chest.

"You have another gun?" I ask as I reach him, my voice sharp, my breaths already coming hard.

The guard nods, pulling a handgun from his holster and handing it to me. I check the chamber and safety with practiced ease as he grips his semi-automatic, his eyes scanning the trees.

"Who's already searching?" I ask, my tone brisk, no room for pleasantries.

"Sheriff's men," he replies, his voice low but steady.

"Aren't you one of Tessa's as well?" I ask.

"Yes, I decided not to be in uniform today."

"What's your name?" I ask, my eyes briefly darting to his mullet, and then back to his face.

"Logan."

I nod, and motion for the guard to follow as I crouch low, my eyes scanning the forest floor. The dense canopy overhead casts long shadows, but the faint impressions of small shoe prints stand out, leading deeper into the woods.

I follow the trail, my heart hammering as I notice a faint, uneven impression overlapping Emmy's footprints. *Dad's footprints.* My grip tightens on the gun as I motion for the guard to stay close.

"Stay sharp," I whisper, my voice barely audible over the rustling of the leaves. And then, without hesitation, I plunge deeper into the forest, following the trail with every nerve on edge.

The forest is unnervingly quiet as we move deeper into the trees. The sun, once casting long golden rays over the estate, is swallowed by thick, slate-gray clouds rolling in overhead. The wind shifts, cool and sharp, carrying with it the faint scent of rain. Each step feels heavier than the last, the crunch of dead leaves underfoot amplified by the oppressive silence.

"Stay close," I murmur to the guard, my voice low but firm. My eyes dart between the tracks on the forest floor—the small, uneven imprints of Emmy's boots, alongside Dad's larger, steadier ones. They weave between roots and moss, deeper into the woods, and my chest tightens with every step.

The guard grunts in acknowledgment, his semi-automatic held at the ready. His gaze mirrors my own—alert, scanning every shadow and rustle. The distant roll of thunder adds to the growing tension, a low growl that rumbles through the air like a predator waking.

A drop of rain hits my cheek, cold and sharp. Then another,

and another. Within moments, the drizzle becomes a steady, relentless patter, soaking through my clothes and slicking the ground beneath us. The tracks are clearer now, the damp earth capturing every detail—the deep press of Dad's boots, the lighter imprint of Emmy's sneakers. They're fresh. They can't be more than fifteen minutes ahead.

"Damn it," I hiss under my breath, quickening my pace. My boots slip slightly on the wet leaves, but I keep moving, my grip on the gun tightening. The rain drips from the brim of my cap, blurring my vision, but I don't dare slow down. Every second counts.

The trees grow denser, their branches clawing at the gray sky. Shadows pool between the trunks, the light dimming as if the forest itself is conspiring against us. My heart pounds, each beat a drum echoing in the stillness. The guard's breathing is steady beside me, but I can feel his tension, a taut wire ready to snap.

Then, cutting through the rhythmic patter of rain and the crunch of our boots, a sound shatters the quiet—a high, piercing scream.

"Noooo!"

The voice is Emmy's. Sharp. Desperate. The kind of scream that rips through you, primal and unrelenting.

"Shit!" I bolt forward, the world narrowing to the sound of her voice. Adrenaline floods my veins, sharpening every sense. The guard follows close behind, his boots slamming against the muddy ground.

The tracks grow erratic—Emmy's small prints veer off to the side, as if she stumbled or was dragged. Dad's heavier ones follow, deeper now, as though he was running or struggling. My pulse is a thunderous roar in my ears, louder than the storm breaking overhead.

"Emmy!" I shout, my voice cutting through the rain. "Dad!"

Another scream, this one shorter but filled with raw terror. It's close—too close. I raise my gun, scanning the darkened woods, every muscle in my body coiled like a spring.

And then, through the dense trees ahead, I see it—a flash of movement, a blur of red. Emmy's jacket.

"Go right!" I bark to the guard, motioning for him to flank as I push forward, my breath coming in sharp bursts. The rain intensifies, soaking my skin, but I don't care. All I can think about is Emmy—my little girl—alone and afraid in this godforsaken forest.

"Hold on, Emmy," I mutter under my breath, my voice a quiet plea as I press deeper into the gloom. Whatever's out there, whoever's out there, they'll have to go through me first.

The clearing opens before me, the rain slicing through the air like icy needles. Emmy stands in the center, her small frame shaking, her hands clutching her head. She's wailing, her voice raw and broken, cutting through the storm like a blade. Richard kneels in front of her, his face pale, whispering something I can't hear over the downpour.

"Emmy!" I shout, my voice razor-sharp. She doesn't look up, doesn't move—her cries grow louder, echoing off the trees. My pulse thunders as I raise my gun, scanning the perimeter. The sound of footsteps—rapid, deliberate—crackles through the underbrush. Leaves rustle. Shadows shift. Something—or someone—is out there.

"Run to me, Emmy!" I bark, the urgency in my voice cutting through her cries. "Get behind me now!" My gun snaps into position, trained on the moving bushes. My finger hovers over the trigger as the tension coils tight enough to snap.

The bushes part suddenly. Three figures emerge, breathing hard, their uniforms soaked. Tessa's men.

"We found her," one says, chest heaving.

"No shit, Sherlock," I mutter, lowering my weapon, the adrenaline still roaring in my veins.

I rush to Emmy's side, dropping to my knees. She collapses into my arms, trembling violently. "What's wrong, baby?" I ask, my voice softer now, desperate for an answer. "Why are you crying? What happened?"

Emmy's sobs come in sharp, uneven gasps as she burrows into my chest. Her tiny fingers clutch at my jacket like it's the only thing keeping her grounded.

"What's wrong, baby?" I repeat, brushing damp curls away from her tear-streaked face. "Tell me. Why are you crying?"

Her voice is muffled, broken by hiccupping sobs. "Mr... Mr. Wonkers."

"What?" I blink, thrown off. "What about Mr. Wonkers?"

"I lost him!" she wails, her words tumbling out in a rush. "He was in my backpack—I had him in there, I swear—but when we were walking, I must've dropped him! Grandpa and I looked everywhere, but he's gone! Mr. Wonkers is *gone!*"

Her backpack still hangs off her small shoulders, soaked through. I glance at Dad, who's still kneeling nearby, his face lined with worry and frustration. He meets my gaze but doesn't say anything, letting Emmy's cries fill the clearing.

"Wait," I say, trying to make sense of her words. "You're saying Mr. Wonkers was in your backpack the whole time?"

She nods, her face scrunching up as another sob escapes her. "Yes! But... but he's not anymore! I dropped him, and now I can't find him! We looked everywhere!" Her hands fist my jacket, her voice breaking. "He's gone, Aunt Eve. He's gone."

I glance at the trees around us, unease curling in my stomach. Something about this feels wrong. But I push the thought aside, cradling Emmy closer. "It's okay," I say softly, though my mind races. "We'll find him, baby. I promise."

Sophia

The rain taps against the window like it's trying to remind me it's still out there, still watching. The room is cloaked in shadows, save for the faint glow of the bedside lamp. Emmy is curled up under my blankets, her swollen cheeks streaked with dried tears. Her tiny hands clutch the corner of the comforter, like it's the only thing keeping her tethered to this world.

I run my fingers through her curls, hoping the motion will lull her to sleep. But her teary eyes stay fixed on mine, big and glassy and full of questions that I wish I had answers to.

"Why do I lose everyone I love?" she whispers, her voice cracking like something fragile and broken. "Was I naughty? Is that why God is punishing me?"

My heart shatters into pieces so sharp, they leave me bleeding inside. I force the lump in my throat down and cradle her face in my hands. "No, baby. You've done nothing wrong. None of this is your fault." I press a kiss to her temple. "I'm here. And you will never lose me."

Her lip quivers as she blinks up at me. "And Auntie Eve?"

My eyes dart to the shadowy corner of the room, where I feel her before I see her. Eve sits in the armchair, chin resting in her hands, her sharp blue gaze fixed on us. She doesn't say a word, doesn't move, just watches like a silent guardian.

I look back at Emmy and smile softly. "Auntie Eve is also never leaving you. And we will find Mr. Wonkers. I promise."

Emmy sniffles, her voice barely above a whisper. "You'll just buy me a new one and tell me it's him."

"No," I say firmly, tucking the blanket under her chin. "It'll be the same Mr. Wonkers. Some things can't be replaced, even if they look the same. We always know the difference. We always know when it's fake."

Emmy stares at me for a long moment, her lip wobbling. Then she nods, her eyelids fluttering shut.

"Go back to sleep, princess," I murmur, leaning down to kiss her forehead. "I'm here."

Her breathing evens out, her little body sinking into the bed. My gaze flicks back to the corner of the room where Eve sits, her shadowy silhouette a silent promise. A part of me wonders if she'll sit there all night, guarding us from the ghosts we can't see.

And, God help me, knowing she's there makes me feel safer than I ever want to admit.

Exhaustion finally claims Emmy. Her little breaths grow slow and steady, her tiny hands unclenching the blanket as she drifts off. I sit there a moment longer, brushing her curls back one last time, before carefully standing. My knees creak, stiff from being perched on the bed too long.

Eve's shadowy silhouette hasn't moved. She's still in the armchair, her elbows resting on her knees, her chin balanced on steepled fingers, like she's been carved from stone. Her eyes, though—they're alive, fixed on me, intense enough to make my pulse quicken.

"Are you gonna sit here all night?" I whisper, my voice low enough not to wake Emmy.

She shakes her head. "No. I need to talk to you about something."

I sigh, crossing my arms. "If this is about me losing my shit earlier tonight, I'm sorry. But I hope you understand—it wasn't personal."

"I know," she says simply. "This is about something else."

I raise an eyebrow, curiosity piqued. "What?"

"Not here." Her lips twitch into something almost playful. "Wanna have a drink?"

I can't help but smile. "Not bothered that I'm underage now?"

She stands, the motion slow and deliberate, her smirk darkening just enough to make my stomach flip. "Your age stopped bothering me a while ago."

Her words hit like a lightning strike, leaving me rooted in place. Before I can even process it, she walks over to Emmy, bending down to press a soft kiss to her temple. It's gentle, almost reverent, and something tightens in my chest.

Then, unexpectedly, she turns to me. Her movements are smooth, like a predator deciding its next move. She steps closer and leans down, her lips brushing against my temple, featherlight but scorching.

I shudder, heat rushing through me, my breath catching in my throat. My body betrays me, melting under her touch, even as my brain screams at me to stay in control.

"Come," she murmurs, her voice low and inviting. "Let's have a drink."

She pulls back, her smirk firmly in place, and I hate how much I want to follow her anywhere right now.

"Okay," I whisper, my voice unsteady. My legs feel like jelly as I trail behind her, Emmy's peaceful breaths the only sound left in the room.

The fire crackles in the hearth, throwing golden light across Eve's study. The room smells of leather and oak, of whiskey and rain-soaked earth, and it feels almost too intimate. I sit perched on one end of the maroon leather couch, my legs crossed, the hem of my skirt hitching up just below my knees. My beer bottle feels cool against my palm as I watch Eve take a slow sip of her whiskey.

She's sitting at the opposite end, her posture relaxed but her piercing gaze flicking to me now and then, like she's calculating something. The amber liquid swirls in her glass as she tilts it back, and I find myself wondering—not for the first time—why she allowed me a beer but won't let me try whiskey. The thought makes me smirk, and before I know it, my mind drifts to last night.

How is it I can't have a whiskey, but I'm allowed to suffocate between her thighs? The memory sends a flush up my neck, and I quickly take a sip of my beer, trying to hide the smile tugging at my lips.

Eve clears her throat, drawing my attention. Her expression is unreadable, but the weight in her eyes makes my stomach tighten. "Sophia," she starts, her voice low and steady, "I know things are tense right now, and I don't want to burden you with more. But there's something I need to ask you. It's important."

I set my beer down on the side table, straightening slightly. "Okay," I say cautiously. "What is it?"

She leans forward, resting her forearms on her knees, her whiskey dangling loosely in one hand. The firelight flickers across her sharp features, casting shadows that make her look even more intense. "I got an anonymous e-mail a few days back. I think it's from the Carmine mafia."

The words hit like a jolt, and my fingers twitch against the armrest. "What?"

She watches me closely, her blue eyes searching for something beneath the surface. "The email said you still have something of theirs. Something of value." She pauses, letting the words settle. "Do you have any idea what they could mean?"

I blink, the question throwing me off. "No," I say quickly, shaking my head. "Why would I have something that belongs to a criminal organization?"

Eve doesn't look convinced. She sets her glass down, her eyes narrowing slightly as she leans closer. "Think hard, Sophia. Did your dad ever give you something for safekeeping? Something he said was important?"

I hesitate, the question swirling in my head, but nothing clicks. "No," I reply honestly, my voice firm. "Dad was obsessive about keeping important things to himself. Mom didn't even know where her passport was most of the time."

Eve's jaw tightens, and for a moment, she just stares at me, her gaze heavy and unreadable. Then she leans back, running a hand through her hair, her frustration showing in the tight line of her mouth.

"All right," she says finally, her voice low. "But if anything comes to mind—anything at all—you tell me. Understand?"

I nod, but something in her tone keeps the tension thick between us. I glance at the fire, the light dancing across the room, but I can't shake the unease curling in my chest. What the hell could they possibly want from me?

Silence descends between us, thick and suffocating. The kind that wraps around your chest and makes every breath feel heavier. I take another sip of my beer, shifting to sit cross-legged on the couch. Why does it feel like the progress we made last night has come to a screeching halt? Like Eve has taken three steps back from where she was?

"You've been very quiet since you got back from the woods," I say, breaking the silence. My voice is steady, but there's an edge to it.

"Aren't I usually this quiet?" she replies, stretching her legs out onto the ottoman. The firelight dances over her long, toned legs, barely covered by her satin shorts.

"Usually," I admit, my gaze flickering back to her face. "But after last night... I wasn't expecting the usual from you."

She arches a brow, her expression unreadable. "What were you expecting from me, Soph?"

"I don't know. Anything but what I'm getting from you right now. It feels... weird. Last night, we were in each other's arms, and now here we are, perched on opposite ends of your couch like we're back to being..."

"Niece and aunt?" she offers, her tone dry but sharp.

"No," I say firmly, the word cutting through the air like a blade. "Protector and damsel in distress."

Her lips twitch into a smirk. "A damsel in distress who doesn't listen to her protector."

"So, you're still pissed off about this afternoon, huh?" I challenge, leaning forward slightly.

"You said some very foolish things, Soph," she counters, her voice calm but heavy with meaning.

"Yeah, because my sister was missing!"

"And I was the only one who could help!" she snaps, sitting up straighter now, her eyes blazing.

I frown, taken aback by the intensity of her response. "You really think we wouldn't make it a day without you, don't you?"

Her jaw tightens, but she doesn't back down. "No, you could. But it would be a hell of a lot tougher."

"You know what..." I gesture between us, my finger waving

back and forth. "This, right now, between us? This is tougher. Every time I think I've made progress with you, you shrink away."

Her gaze sharpens, her voice steady but defensive. "I'm not shrinking away. I'm being reasonable."

I laugh, the sound bitter. "Oh, I get it. Because having a nineteen-year-old girl eat you out two nights in a row would be unreasonable. But one night... that was fine, wasn't it?"

Her smirk vanishes, her expression hardening. The fire crackles loudly in the silence that follows, but I don't take my eyes off her. My words hang between us like smoke, heavy and unrelenting.

For a moment, she doesn't reply. Her gaze drops to her whiskey, her thumb running along the edge of the glass. "Sophia," she says finally, her voice low, measured, "you don't understand what you do to me. Last night..." She exhales sharply, shaking her head. "Last night was everything. But this —" she gestures vaguely between us, echoing my earlier motion —"it's not just about what I want. It can't be."

Her words sting, but there's something in her tone, in the way her eyes flicker with frustration and longing, that makes my chest tighten.

"Then stop pretending like it's not what you want," I whisper, my voice softer now. "Because you keep pulling away, but you never really let me go, do you?"

"No, I can't let you go," Eve says, her voice low and firm. She downs the rest of her whiskey in one smooth motion, her eyes fixed on the crackling flames in the fireplace. The flickering light dances across her face, but there's no warmth in her expression —only tension and something deeper, something raw.

"Then don't let me go. Make me yours in a way I can never leave," I say, my voice steady with authority.

"Not until you're safe," she replies, her gaze still locked on the fire.

"Why? What's that got to do with anything?" I press, leaning forward, refusing to let her hide behind half-answers.

"Because..."

"Because what, Eve?"

Her jaw tightens, and for a moment, I think she won't answer. Then she tears her eyes away from the fire, and when she looks at me, it feels like a punch to the chest. Her eyes are blazing, not with anger, but with fear and something heartbreakingly vulnerable.

"Because what if I let myself be yours," she says, her voice barely above a whisper, "and then..."

"And then what?" I push, my heart pounding in my chest.

"And then you're taken away from me."

Her words land like a thunderclap. I blink, caught off guard, and then—because I don't know how else to react—I laugh. It's shaky, nervous, but it spills out before I can stop it. "What? You're afraid I'll die the moment you start dating me?"

"Yes," she says, her voice steady and unflinching.

The laughter dies in my throat, leaving a heavy silence between us. Her words hang in the air, and the gravity of them pulls me in.

"Yes," she repeats, her tone quieter now, laced with pain. "Because it's happened before."

I stare at her, my chest tightening, my voice dropping to a whisper. "What happened, Eve?"

She doesn't look away this time. Her eyes stay locked on mine, the firelight reflecting in their depths, and I see it—the weight she's been carrying, the scars she doesn't talk about. The room feels impossibly small, and for the first time, I realize how terrified she is of losing me.

And damn it, my heart aches for her.

Eve stares into the fire, her shoulders stiff, her jaw tight, and I can see the battle waging behind her eyes. She grips her empty glass like it's the only thing keeping her grounded.

"It was years ago," she begins, her voice low and strained, like the words are being dragged out of her. "I was in training—advanced extraction techniques. There was this woman, Kate. She was..." Eve pauses, swallowing hard. "She was the best damn soldier I'd ever seen. Strong. Smart. Fearless. But more than that, she was... everything I didn't know I needed."

Her gaze drops to the floor, her hand trembling slightly. "We were paired together for every exercise, every drill. She had this way of making me better—pushing me to be sharper, faster, smarter. At first, I thought it was just admiration. Respect. But it wasn't."

I lean forward, the weight of her words pulling me in. "What was it?"

Eve's lips press into a thin line, and for a moment, I think she won't answer. But then, her voice softens, almost breaking. "It was love. And it scared the hell out of me."

She shakes her head, her fingers tightening around the glass. "We kept it a secret. We had to. No one could know—fraternizing in the field, especially in our unit, was unacceptable. But it didn't matter. We were all in. We confessed how we felt the night before our first real mission."

Her voice falters, and she looks at me, her blue eyes glossy. "We didn't even get a week, Sophia. Not one goddamn week."

"What happened?" I ask gently, moving closer to her.

Eve exhales sharply, like the memory is choking her. "The mission was an extraction—textbook. Get in, get the target, get out. But something went wrong. The intel was bad. There were more hostiles than we expected. We barely made it to the evac point, and when the chopper arrived..." She swallows hard, her voice dropping to a whisper. "Kate didn't make it out. She was pinned down, and I couldn't get to her."

Her hand trembles violently now, and I reach out, gently covering it with mine. She flinches but doesn't pull away.

"I begged the pilot to go back for her," Eve continues, her voice cracking. "I screamed, threatened, did everything I could, but the team leader said no. The risk was too high. And all I could do was sit there and watch."

Her free hand clenches into a fist, her knuckles white. "I saw her get dragged out by the bastards who'd ambushed us. I saw her screaming my name, Sophia. And there wasn't a damn thing I could do."

Tears slip down her cheeks, silent and unrelenting. "She died because of me. Because I left her. I've lived with that every day since."

"So, your first book, *Arrows Through the Heart,* was about Kate and you?"

"Yes," Eve forces the word out.

My chest tightens painfully, and I slide closer, taking both her hands in mine. "Eve..."

"She made me promise," Eve whispers, her eyes unfocused, staring into the past. "That if we ever got out of this life, we'd have a real chance. A real life. And I broke that promise before we even started."

I squeeze her hands, my voice soft but firm. "It wasn't your fault. You didn't leave her—you had no choice."

Eve shakes her head, her lips trembling. "I did have a choice. And I chose survival. I chose to live while she..." Her voice breaks, and she looks at me with such raw pain that it feels like the air's been sucked out of the room. "That's why I'm terrified, Sophia. Because if I let myself love you, and you're taken from me, I don't think I'll survive it again."

Tears sting my own eyes as I lean forward, pressing my forehead gently to hers. "You're not going to lose me, Eve. I'm here. And I'm not going anywhere."

Her breath shudders against mine, and for a moment, we sit there in silence, the fire crackling softly in the background.

Eve's breathing is uneven, her chest rising and falling in jagged rhythms against mine. Her hands are still trembling, caught between my own, as if the memories she's just unearthed are too much for her to carry alone. I don't say anything right away. Instead, I lean closer, closing the distance between us until I can feel the warmth of her against me.

"Come here," I murmur softly, wrapping my arms around her.

For a moment, she doesn't move, frozen in her grief and guilt. But then, slowly, her shoulders sag, and she lets me pull her in. Her head rests against my chest, and I cradle her there, running my fingers gently through her hair. She's always so strong, so composed, but right now, she feels fragile, like she's been holding herself together for far too long.

"No one is leaving anyone," I whisper, my voice steady even as my heart clenches. "Emmy, you, and I—we're going to live together. Happily. We'll figure this out. All of it."

Eve doesn't respond right away, but I feel her hands grip the back of my shirt, holding on tightly. Her breaths slowly even out, her body relaxing in my arms as though she's finally allowed herself to lean on someone.

The fire crackles softly behind us, filling the quiet with its gentle warmth. But at the back of my mind, the email from the mafia lurks like a shadow, whispering reminders of danger and uncertainty. I push the thought aside, focusing on the woman in my arms and the promise I've just made.

We'll face whatever's coming—together. No one is leaving anyone.

Chapter Nine

Eve

I wake to the muted crackle of dying embers in the fireplace, the room bathed in the dim gray of early dawn. The weight of a blanket draped over me feels unfamiliar—I don't remember covering myself before falling asleep. Sophia must have done it.

I glance toward the other end of the couch, expecting to see her curled up there, but it's empty. A faint pang tugs at my chest, sharp and unexpected. She must have left after I fell asleep, gone back to her room to be with Emmy. It makes sense. Emmy needs her right now. But still, the thought of not seeing her first thing stings more than it should.

My phone buzzes on the coffee table, cutting through the silence. The screen lights up with *Dad*. I exhale and rub my eyes before picking up.

"Evelyn," his voice is brisk, carrying its usual authority. "Can we talk?"

"Come to my study in an hour," I reply, keeping my tone neutral.

"Good," he says, then hangs up without another word.

I set the phone down, staring at it for a long moment. What could Dad want now? Whatever it is, it won't be simple. It never is.

∞∞∞

The coffee is strong, its warmth seeping into my hands as I stand on the balcony outside my study. The crisp autumn air bites at my skin, but I don't mind. It sharpens me, keeps me grounded. The Montana sky stretches out before me, a soft swirl of grays and golds, with the faintest promise of sunlight peeking through the clouds.

Below, the estate is alive with quiet motion. My guards, dressed in their usual black suits and ties, move in precise patterns, scanning every corner of the grounds. Tessa's deputies, in their tan uniforms, break up the monotony, their badges catching the weak light as they patrol the perimeter.

My eyes drift further down, to the grand staircase leading from the estate's front doors to the curved pathway below. Sophia, Emmy, and Iggy are there, riding bicycles around the gardens. Their puffer jackets and fur-lined boots make them look like winter postcards brought to life. Emmy's face is still clouded with sadness, but at least she's outside, pedaling along with quiet determination. Sophia glances back at her, smiling softly, and something in my chest tightens.

I sip my coffee, deciding that today, Sophia deserves a break —no gun drills, no flying lessons. Maybe we all need a break. I make a mental note to ask Miriam to prepare a grand dinner tonight. Something comforting. Maybe we'll even sit together in the Great Hall, watch a movie, and try to remember what it feels like to have fun.

My phone chimes. I glance at the screen. *Tessa:* "Today is Sunday. Don't forget our dinner. But you may forget to wear underwear, if you like ▢."

I sigh, slipping the phone into my pocket. Before I can dwell on her antics, the sound of footsteps in my study pulls me from my thoughts. I turn sharply, instantly on edge.

Dad stands in the center of the room, tall and broad, his presence as commanding as ever.

"Evelyn," he says, his voice calm but firm.

I set the coffee down on the railing and step inside. "Dad."

He's not one for pleasantries, and the look in his eyes tells me he's already halfway through his argument before I've even said a word.

"The estate isn't safe," he says, his tone cutting straight to the point.

I fold my arms, keeping my stance calm but firm. "We've been over this. The estate is as secure as it gets, Dad. No one's getting in without us knowing."

He scoffs, shaking his head. "You mean the same guards who couldn't even track my footprints with Emmy? The same ones who couldn't keep up until you arrived? They're in over their heads, Evelyn."

I grit my teeth, taking a deep breath to keep my voice level. "It won't happen again. I'll tighten security, bring in more patrols if I have to. There isn't another place in the country that's as fortified as this."

His laugh is bitter, cold. "There is, and you know it."

I pause, narrowing my eyes at him. "What are you talking

about?"

"You know exactly what I'm talking about," he says, his gaze piercing. "There's a place no terrorist, no insurgent, not even ISIS or Al Qaeda in their prime could touch. And you're damn well aware of it."

For a moment, I just stare at him, the air between us crackling with tension. "I'm never taking *his* help," I say, my voice low and steady. "If that's what you mean, I'd rather die."

"And let my grandkids die as well?"

My anger flares, and I step closer, my fists clenched. "When did you suddenly start caring so much for your grandkids? You didn't even call James when Emmy was born, if I remember."

His expression hardens, his steel-gray eyes locking onto mine. "And you abandoned them when they needed you the most."

"Because you—" my voice rises, trembling with anger. "You told me to go back for one last mission. A fucking mission that lasted five years, and put James and his family in danger. I did it for you, and now you're throwing it in my face?"

He doesn't flinch, his voice snapping like a whip. "You didn't do it for me! If you did, you'd still be in the army instead of living here like a recluse, writing your lesbian porn!"

The words hit like a slap, but I don't back down. My jaw tightens, my heart pounding as the fire inside me burns hotter.

"Writing this lesbian porn—which, by the way, isn't even porn, which you'd know if you ever bothered to read it—got us this estate," I snap, my voice rising. "It got you that damn cabin in the woods you love so much. The one you go to for your 'quiet time.' Being in the army wouldn't have given us anything except more trauma!"

Dad's jaw tightens, but I don't stop. The words are tumbling out now, years of buried frustration finally finding their way to the surface.

"You can't even watch a movie with gunfire without wincing in pain. I can't write a single war scene without my hands shaking so badly I can't hold a pen. I couldn't do it anymore, Dad. I couldn't live that life. And you—" my voice cracks slightly, but I press on. "You should have quit too. You should have spent time with your family. But you didn't. Doesn't mean I'll make the same mistake."

"I know," he says, his tone low but no less biting. "I know you won't. And I couldn't care less about you. But I do care about Emmy and Sophia."

His words feel like a slap, and I narrow my eyes at him. "Do you really care about Sophia? Or are you just saying her name because you have to? She's not your blood, and for a traditional man like you, that must mean something stupid, right?"

His hands ball into fists, his voice dropping to a growl. "She's part of the tribe."

"The tribe?" I echo, my anger flaring hotter.

"Yes," he snaps. "Us military men don't desert the tribe. I want to protect her and Emmy, and anyone who was part of my son's family. Because I lost him, Evelyn. I lost him and couldn't do a goddamn thing. But now, I can. And I don't like what you're doing."

"Let me guess," I say, folding my arms tightly across my chest. "You think I need to ask Jeremy for help."

"Yes!" he shouts, his voice booming. "Jeremy's facility is impenetrable. You know it. It's the safest place for them to be."

I scoff, taking a step closer to him. "Jeremy? The guy who got my girlfriend killed? The guy who wouldn't fly the chopper back to save her because he was too much of a coward?"

Dad's face darkens, his teeth gritting audibly. "He didn't want to jeopardize the lives of the entire team to save one woman. He was following protocol. He was being a good soldier, goddammit! And now, you should be too! Stop letting your ego get in the way. You weren't a good soldier then, and you're not a good soldier now. So let Jeremy and me help you. Let professionals take over!"

His voice cracks with fury, spit flying with every word.

For a moment, I just stare at him, my chest heaving as I bite back everything I want to scream at him.

"Leave, Dad," I say finally, my voice cold and steady. "Leave before I say something I'll regret."

He hesitates, his lips pressing into a thin line, but the fury in his eyes doesn't fade. Without another word, he storms out of the study, slamming the door behind him.

The silence he leaves behind feels louder than his shouting ever was.

∞∞∞

I stand in front of the ornate full-length mirror in my bedroom, adjusting the lapels of my sleek black blazer. The tailored fabric hugs my frame perfectly, the sharp cut exuding confidence I don't entirely feel tonight. My hands move to smooth the hem of my white blouse tucked neatly into bootcut trousers, the polished look complete yet unfamiliar.

The woman staring back at me isn't the soldier I've spent most of my life being. She's... softer. Feminine. Her blonde hair, styled into loose, flowing curves, frames her face in a way that feels foreign. Even my eyes look different, accentuated by mascara and the faintest touch of liner. There's a subtle shimmer to my cheeks, a delicate pink on my lips.

I take a step closer to the mirror, running my hand down the curve of my blazer. I look beautiful. But as Dad's voice echoes in my mind—*You weren't a good soldier then, and you're not one now*—I wonder if there ever really was a soldier in me at all.

The thought lingers, bitter and unshakable, when a knock at the door pulls me back to the present.

"Come in," I call, turning toward the doorway.

Sophia stands there, leaning casually against the frame, her fur boots peeking out from under her leggings. The oversized puffer jacket she's wearing makes her look impossibly cute, her cheeks pink from the chill outside.

Her green eyes sweep over me, wide with surprise, and a smirk tugs at her lips. "Well, well," she teases, her voice light but dripping with sass. "I've never seen you so dressed up. Who's the lucky woman?"

I roll my eyes, a faint smirk breaking through my composure. "Not what you think, Soph."

"Sure, sure," she says, stepping into the room, her gaze lingering on my tailored blazer. "You've got the whole 'power lesbian' vibe down tonight. What's the occasion?"

I cross my arms, looking her over. "Shouldn't you be with Emmy?"

Her smirk deepens as she flops onto the edge of my bed, clearly not planning on leaving until she gets answers. "Emmy's with Miriam. You're stuck with me, Auntie Eve. So... spill."

Her gaze is playful, but there's a hint of genuine curiosity in her eyes. I sigh, grabbing my clutch from the dresser and sparing one last glance at the mirror.

"It's just dinner," I say, stepping up to her, closing the space between us.

"With?" she asks, raising an eyebrow, her voice sharp with curiosity.

"Tessa," I reply simply.

Her smile vanishes instantly, her lips pressing into a tight line. "Why?"

"Because I promised her dinner in exchange for some security enhancements around the estate."

Her arms cross over her chest, and her tone grows curt. "She blackmailed you for three guards?"

"It's not just three guards," I explain, catching the flicker of jealousy in her eyes. "More patrols on the roads, upgraded cameras, and some other enhancements. It's just a dinner, Soph."

Her jaw tightens, and her green eyes flash with insecurity. "But why does she want this dinner?"

I shrug. "I don't know."

Her voice hardens. "Oh, you know. You just don't want to admit it in front of me. She wants to get back with you. She wants to fuck you again."

I exhale sharply, stepping away to the balcony door. "Yeah, maybe she does," I admit, throwing the words casually over my shoulder. "But her wanting it doesn't mean anything. And for the record, I don't get fucked—I *do* the fucking."

I push the door open, letting the cool night air rush in. The wind brushes against my face as I pull a cigar from the box on the table and light it.

Sophia stands abruptly, following me in a flurry of indignation. "Why do you need to look so sexy, then? Especially with that cigar? I've never even seen you with one before."

"You haven't," I say, taking a slow drag and blowing the smoke out into the night. "Doesn't mean I don't enjoy one every now and then."

She narrows her eyes, stepping closer. "I hope you don't have the same policy with women. Enjoying one while I don't see it."

I laugh, leaning back against the balcony railing, watching her with amusement as she glares at me, fire practically shooting from her eyes. "You look cute when you're jealous."

"I look cute all the time," she snaps, her voice dripping with sass. "That's not the point. The point is, are you going to cheat on me tonight or not?"

"Cheat on you?" I raise an eyebrow, smirking. "Are we exclusive?"

She huffs, her cheeks flushed with a mix of anger and embarrassment. "Do you see me dressing sexy and meeting other women for dinner?"

"No," I admit, tilting my head, "but I see how close you are with Iggy. I know she likes you. And I also know you humped her leg at a raunchy sleepover. But I don't keep an eye on you."

"That's your problem," she says, stepping closer, her eyes locked on mine. "I'm the possessive type. Plus, I give you permission to hump Iggy's leg, as long as I am watching. She's keen on a threesome, ya know?""

I chuckle, taking another slow drag from the cigar, letting the smoke curl lazily between us. "Noted."

Sophia steps closer, her green eyes dark and smoldering, like she's daring me to stop her. Without a word, her hands slip into the back pockets of my pants, fingers pressing firmly against me. It's not just a touch—it's possession, and damn if it doesn't send heat pooling low in my stomach.

"I also know you got into it with Richard this morning," she murmurs, her voice low and sultry, as her fingers knead me through the fabric.

My breath catches for a beat, but I keep my face neutral. "How?"

She leans in, her lips brushing against my ear, her breath warm and teasing. "I was eavesdropping."

I narrow my eyes, trying to sound unaffected. "I don't like you eavesdropping, Soph."

Her grin widens, wicked and unapologetic. Her hands grip me tighter, pulling me closer. "Why? You only like me when I drop my panties for you?"

My pulse spikes, my composure cracking under the weight of her words. "Sophia..." I growl, low and rough. "What did you hear?"

Her smile softens, her hands still exploring, slow and deliberate. "That the General is crazy," she whispers, her voice dipping into something tender. "And that he doesn't deserve a daughter like you."

Her words hit me harder than I expect. Before I can respond, she pulls her hands free, sliding them around my waist, her palms flat against me, her touch warm and searing. Her body presses flush against mine, and I feel every curve, every line, against me.

"Tell him," she says, her voice soft yet commanding, her lips brushing against my cheek, "that I'll follow you to the ends of the earth. That I'll follow you anywhere, even if it means death. Tell him you're the only soldier who makes me feel safe. The rest of them can go to hell—including whoever the hell Jeremy is."

Her words ripple through me, pulling something loose inside, but I manage a small, shaky smirk. "You're putting a lot of pressure on me to prove myself."

"No," she murmurs, shaking her head as her grip tightens on my waist, her lips hovering just above mine. "I'm only telling you the truth."

Then her voice drops lower, sultry and dark. "Now, go tell Tessa to keep her hands off my woman, or I'll show her who the real sheriff of this estate is."

Before I can say anything, she closes the distance in a rush, her lips crashing into mine, wild and unrelenting. Her hands slide under my blazer, gripping my back with a need so fierce it leaves me breathless.

Her kiss is a claim—hot and demanding, her tongue sliding against mine with a rhythm that makes my knees weak. I press back, one hand tangling in her hair as the other trails down to grip her waist. She moans softly, the sound vibrating against my lips, spurring me on.

Her hands travel lower, finding the curve of my hips, her nails biting just enough to leave a lingering burn. My body responds instantly, arching into her, craving more, needing more. She pulls me impossibly closer, her lips never relenting, her kiss deep and intoxicating.

When she finally breaks away, her breath warm against my lips, she whispers, "Mine." Her green eyes are heavy-lidded and filled with fire, and all I can do is stare at her, my chest heaving, my resolve shattered.

I let myself fall. Into her fire. Into her claim. Into her.

∞∞∞

The drive into town is quiet, the low hum of Tessa's car filling the space between us. Outside, the Montana night is an endless stretch of darkness, broken only by the headlights carving a path ahead. The faint scent of her perfume lingers in the air—sharp and sweet—but it doesn't settle the unease crawling beneath my skin.

We pull up to a small, intimate restaurant glowing softly against the darkened street, warm light spilling through frosted windows. Tessa steps out first, moving with the deliberate grace of someone who's used to being watched. I follow, taking in the scene as she rounds the car to hand her keys to the valet.

Her outfit is impeccable—high-waisted leather pants that sculpt her figure, a deep-red blouse that clings in all the right places, its neckline skimming the edge of propriety. A tailored black blazer hangs open, adding an edge of authority, and her sleek black ponytail swings like a blade with every step. It's polished, deliberate, and meant to draw attention.

She looks good. I'll give her that. But that's as far as it goes.

Because in my head, I'm still on the balcony. Sophia's lips on mine. Her hands pulling me close like she couldn't get enough. The memory burns, unshakable, searing through everything else.

"Eve." Tessa's voice cuts through the fog, a hint of laughter in it. She's holding the door open, one brow arched. "You coming?"

I slip my hands into my pockets and smirk faintly. "Depends. Is the food worth the company?"

She chuckles, but I barely hear her as I follow her inside. My thoughts are already elsewhere. Back where they shouldn't be. Back where Sophia left them.

∞∞∞

The clink of glasses echoes softly as the waiter pours the wine, the deep red catching the candlelight. I swirl the glass in my hand, letting the aroma linger for a moment before taking a slow sip. Across the table, Tessa watches me, her lips curved into a knowing smirk as she leans back in her chair.

"You dressed for a date," she says, her tone teasing, "although you promised this wasn't going to be one."

I lower the glass, meeting her gaze with a small, amused

smile. "I hadn't dressed up in a while. Thought I'd give it a try and see if I've still got it."

Tessa bites her lip, her dark eyes flicking over me in a way I don't miss. "You've definitely still got it."

I raise an eyebrow, my lips twitching into a half-smile. "Care to elaborate?"

"You've still got the body—no one had any doubts about that," she says, her voice low and deliberate. "But you've also not lost the confidence. You can still intimidate."

I chuckle softly, leaning back. "I don't think even I can intimidate Sheriff Tessa Reynolds."

"You can, and you do sometimes," she replies, her smirk still in place, though her eyes glint with something less playful. "Although... your niece was trying her best to intimidate me that day, too. Runs in the family, I guess."

I shrug, letting a faint smile touch my lips. "She's a firecracker."

"Yeah," Tessa says, her gaze sharp, lingering too long as she swirls her wine. "A hot firecracker. She must have been very sought after by the boys."

I pause briefly, then shrug again, feigning nonchalance. "Maybe. I don't really know much about her love life."

"You should," Tessa replies smoothly, her tone almost casual, though something in it pricks at me. "You're basically her mother now."

My frown is immediate, sharp and unfiltered. I set my glass down, leveling her with a look. "Why do I need to be her mother? Why does anyone need to be her mother? I'm just Evelyn for her. Someone who really cares for her, without putting any labels on it."

Tessa takes another sip of her wine, her smirk tempered by

something sharper now—something that cuts. "But there is a label, Eve. You are her aunt, and she is your niece."

I stiffen, the words digging in deeper than they should. "She's not my blood," I reply, too forcefully, the edge in my voice making her eyebrows rise slightly in surprise.

"Yeah, I know," she says, her tone cooler now. "But... for society, she's your niece, and you're her aunt. That's how they see it."

I narrow my eyes at her, my hand tightening around the stem of my glass. "Why are you so interested in what she is to me, Tess?"

She shrugs, leaning back in her chair, but the casual act doesn't quite land. "I'm just curious. Suddenly, the sexy, mysterious recluse—the soldier-turned-author—has two nieces and a retired general living with her. Your quiet life's been thrown into chaos, and yet you seem to be enjoying it."

I study her, my gaze steady. "I have," I admit, my voice even. "I love them."

"But you always said you didn't want kids," she pushes, her eyes sharp as they hold mine. "One of them is nine, Eve. That's a kid who needs looking after. Are you sure you're up for it?"

I pause, feeling the weight of the question settle over me like stones. "I don't know," I reply honestly, my voice low. "But I'll try to do what's best for them."

The waiter appears then, breaking the moment as he sets down our plates. Tessa thanks him with a polite smile, but as soon as he's gone, she leans forward slightly, her voice dropping. "My offer still stands, Eve."

I look up at her, frowning. "What offer?"

"Marry me," she says softly, almost like it's a casual suggestion, though the intensity in her eyes says otherwise. "I'll leave my job. Just as I had left my husband for you. I raised two little sisters on my own, remember? I can look after the girls too. You wouldn't have to do it alone."

I exhale slowly, the weight of her words heavy in the air between us. "Kids and marriage weren't the only things that broke us up, Tess," I say, my voice careful, measured, "And I had never asked you to leave your husband for me. You did it on your own and told me later."

She doesn't miss a beat. "I did, because you told me you didn't like sneaking around with a married woman! And I know, kids and marriage weren't the only things that broke us up. It was your PTSD as well." Her voice is steady, but there's a flicker of something—hurt, maybe—in her eyes. "You said no woman would want to live with a walking time bomb. And I said, I'm a policewoman. I can handle bombs."

I close my eyes briefly, letting the words hit me like they always do. "It's too late now, Tessa."

"I don't think it is," she says simply, picking up her fork and knife and starting on her food. "You're changing, Eve. You're doing things you told me you never could. You just needed the right girls—or girl."

I freeze, my fork halfway to my mouth. "What do you mean?" My voice is calm, but there's a thread of warning beneath it.

Tessa doesn't look up, cutting into her food with deliberate care. "I see the way Sophia looks at you," she says, her voice light but cutting. "And I hear the way you talk about her."

The air between us thickens, tension crackling like a live wire. I lower my fork, my pulse quickening. "What are you implying, Tess?"

Finally, she looks up, her dark eyes meeting mine with unflinching certainty. "Don't make me say it, soldier."

I glare at her, but it's not enough to hide the flicker of something else—guilt, fear, maybe anger—simmering beneath the surface.

"How dare you?" My voice cuts through the low hum of the restaurant, sharp enough to make Tessa's smirk twitch.

She raises an eyebrow, utterly unfazed. "I haven't even said it yet, and look how worked up you are," she murmurs, her tone mockingly soft. "And I'm just one woman, Eve. A friend. Imagine what others will say. You don't want that kind of chaos in your life, baby."

She reaches across the table, her fingers brushing against my hand. I pull back immediately, but she doesn't stop. Her voice drops lower, dripping with condescension and something dangerously close to pity. "I get it," she continues, her eyes narrowing. "She's hot. She's forbidden. She's the only thing that could infuse some life into this tortured body of yours, and I'm happy for you." She pauses, her smirk curling like smoke. "But it will end. She'll leave for college, and you'll be left here. Alone. With me."

I grip the edge of the table, my knuckles whitening, as her words seep in like poison. "Tessa—"

"What does she do in bed, huh?" Tessa presses on, ignoring the warning in my voice. "Tell me. I can do that. I can *be* that." She leans forward, her smile turning manic, desperate. "I'll raid her closet, wear her clothes, slap on a pair of green contacts. Hell, I'll even call you 'Mommy' if you want."

"Tessa, stop," I bite out, my tone low and hard, but my stomach coils with disgust.

Her eyes gleam as if she's winning some sick game. "What?" she taunts. "This coming from a woman lusting after her stepniece? Don't look so righteous, Evelyn."

"You're crossing a line," I snap, my voice icy, but my anger feels like a wildfire spreading beneath my skin.

Tessa just laughs softly, shaking her head as if I'm the one being unreasonable. "Oh, come on. I'm on your side here, baby," she coos, her voice sugar-sweet but hollow. "I'll help you with this... kink of yours."

My jaw tightens, but she doesn't stop.

"I'll even let you have fun on the side," she continues, her voice turning conspiratorial. "When she comes home for the holidays. You can sneak off, get it out of your system. I won't ask questions. Just marry me, Evelyn." She leans back, picking up her glass and swirling the wine lazily, her eyes locking onto mine. "I'll do it all for you."

I stare at her, the words slamming into me like a punch to the gut. My pulse thunders in my ears as the sheer audacity of what she's saying sinks in.

"Tessa," I say slowly, my voice dangerously calm, though the rage burns hot beneath it. "You don't understand a damn thing."

Her smirk falters for the first time, and I let the silence stretch between us like a knife.

"Don't you ever talk about her like that again." My voice is low, cutting, final. "And don't you *ever* assume you know me."

I stand abruptly, my chair scraping against the floor, and toss a few bills on the table. I don't wait for her response. I can feel her stunned silence trailing me as I stride for the exit, the cold night air a bitter relief against the fire raging inside me.

Outside, I pull out my phone, my thumb hovering over Sophia's name. I don't call. I don't text. But as I stand there, staring at the screen, all I can think about is her—her hands on me, her kiss, her fire.

And Tessa's words echo like a curse in my mind. *She'll leave for college, and you'll be left here. Alone.*

But that's not today. And I'll be damned if I let anyone—*anyone*—make me feel ashamed of how I feel.

Sophia

The window seat is cold beneath me, my legs tucked close as I peer through the glass at the estate grounds. Outside, the world is cloaked in darkness, the faint glow of moonlight catching on the mist hovering over the treetops. I've been sitting here for over an hour, my phone next to me, screen glaring back with my unanswered texts.

Where are you?
When will you be back?

Nothing. Not even a little gray "seen" checkmark.

I scowl at the phone like it personally betrayed me. Dangerous thoughts crawl in the back of my mind, twisting and looping like a never-ending reel of *what-ifs*. What if Tessa—outrageous, smug, slutty Tessa—was seducing Eve right now? Like maybe she "accidentally" spilled wine on her blouse and pulled a *Whoops, Eve, I guess I'll just take this off*. Or maybe she threw a silk scarf on the bed and purred something about tying Eve up, because, of course, Tessa would have silk scarves. And Eve—stoic, brooding, guarded Eve—was just sitting there, letting it happen.

"Stop it, you lunatic," I mutter to myself, glaring at the window like it's going to give me answers. I stare at my phone again, thumb hovering over the call button. I want to call her, demand to know where she is and what she's doing. But I don't want to seem too controlling or immature.

Except… screw it. I *am* immature. I'm nineteen years old and if I want to throw a tantrum because the woman I love is out with someone else, then so be it.

I sigh, pressing my forehead against the cool glass, my eyelids drooping slightly. A wave of exhaustion hits me, unexpected and heavy. I need coffee. I don't want to fall asleep, not tonight. I want to be awake when Eve gets back. I need to know she's back.

I slip off the window bed, grabbing my phone before stepping quietly into the hallway. The house is dark, the sconces on the walls casting weak, flickering light. I notice how *quiet* everything is—eerily so. The guards aren't pacing their usual spots, and for a moment, I pause, frowning.

Weird.

But I shake it off. Maybe I'm just too tired. My boots barely make a sound as I descend the staircase, my hand trailing along the banister for balance. The house feels larger at night, like it's holding its breath.

Reaching the kitchen, I flick on the small lamp over the stove and start making coffee. I keep my movements slow, methodical, but my thoughts race back to Eve. *Is Tessa making her coffee right now? Naked?* The mental image is ridiculous, but it gnaws at me anyway. I shake my head violently, pouring the steaming liquid into a mug. "Get a grip, Sophia."

As soon as I take a sip of my coffee, the faint glow of the kitchen's ambient lighting flickers and dies, plunging the room into darkness. I freeze, the mug hovering near my lips, my heartbeat quickening as I strain to hear beyond the sudden silence. Any second now, the backup generators should hum to life—but they don't. Seconds stretch into what feels like an eternity, the oppressive darkness thick with unease. A chill creeps up my spine as an unsettling thought takes root: what if this isn't just a routine power outage?

I step back into the Great Hall, coffee in hand, my eyes adjusting to the darkness. For a moment, everything feels still. Too still. My gaze sweeps across the cavernous room until it catches on something—something strange—in the middle of the long dining table.

I squint, stepping closer. A silhouette. Small. Furry. My heart stutters.

"A cat?" I whisper aloud, taking another step. But no... something's wrong. The color of the fur isn't right. It's not brown or black. It's *pink*.

My stomach drops. Pink fur.

No. No, no, no.

My steps falter as I inch closer, my breathing ragged and shallow. The outline starts to sharpen. The ears. The tiny body. The limp head—

The clouds outside shift, and moonlight spills into the room, illuminating the table.

And I see it.

Mr. Wonkers.

The stuffed bunny's body sits upright, placed carefully in the center of the table. The severed head lies next to it, lopsided, the white fabric stained dark with blood. *Real blood*. The kind that pools, thick and sticky, into small splatters across the polished wood.

The mug slips from my hand, shattering on the marble floor. The sound snaps something inside me. My chest tightens, air refusing to fill my lungs.

"No..." The word is a choked whisper, barely audible.

The room spins. My hands fly to my mouth as panic claws up my throat. My ears ring, muffling everything except the wild thud of my heartbeat.

And then I scream.

The sound rips out of me, loud and raw, echoing through the empty hall as I stare at the horrific scene.

They beheaded Mr.Wonkers.

And I know, in the pit of my stomach, that this is only the beginning.

(End Of Book One)

Sophia and Eve's story continues in ***"The Ways She Owns My Heart"***

Paperback readers can order the next part on Amazon. Just search for ***"The Ways She Owns My Heart"***

The Ways She Owns My Heart

Sophia and Eve's story takes a dangerous turn, as a beheaded Mr. Wonkers signals the beggining of the end. Will Eve succeed in keeping Sophia safe, while opening herself up to being more than just her protector?

Find out by downloading part two, "The Ways She Owns My Heart" by clicking here, or searching for the book on Amazon!

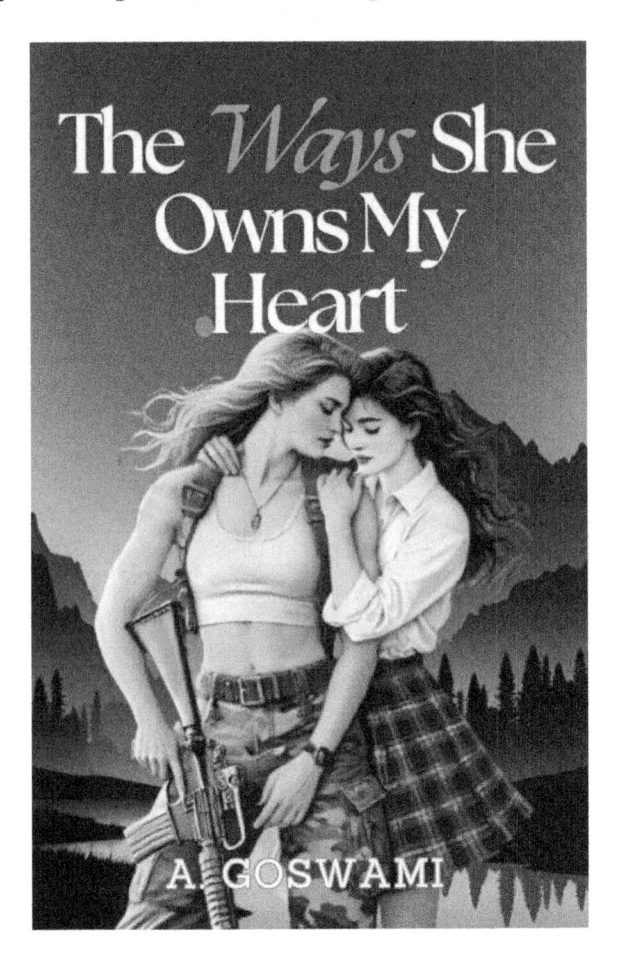

THE WAYS SHE MAKES ME SIN

Printed in Great Britain
by Amazon